TO PROTECT
THEIR CHILD

SHERYL LYNN

D0039267

HARLEQUIN®

TORONTO • NEW YORK • LONDON
AMSTERDAM • PARIS • SYDNEY • HAMBURG
STOCKHOLM • ATHENS • TOKYO • MILAN • MADRID
PRAGUE • WARSAW • BUDAPEST • AUCKLAND

ISBN 0-373-22608-X

TO PROTECT THEIR CHILD

"I thought you didn't like McClintock."

"Changed my mind," Ric said.

"Must have. From what I hear, you looked at just about every property for sale in the valley."

"It's interesting."

Elaine made a musing noise. "I've also heard you and Deputy Tate Raleigh are best buddies now. Tight as ticks." Her smile faded and those big brown eyes turned hard. "What are you up to, Ric? Why are you looking for dirt on my father?"

Couldn't get any more blunt than that. "What makes you think that's what I'm doing?"

"Oh, come on! You never liked Daddy." She stabbed a stiff finger in the direction of his chest. "Now I find you with my daughter. Just what exactly did you say to her? What are you trying to pull?"

Our daughter, Ric wanted to say, but didn't...

Dear Harlequin Intrigue Reader,

We have another outstanding title selection this month chock-full of great romantic suspense, starting with the next installment in our TOP SECRET BABIES promotion. In *The Hunt for Hawke's Daughter* (#605) by Jean Barrett, Devlin Hawke had never expected to see Karen Ramey once she'd left his bed—let alone have her tell him his secret child had been kidnapped by a madman. Whether a blessing or a curse, Devlin was dead set on reclaiming his child—and his woman....

To further turn up the heat, three of your favorite authors take you down to the steamy bayou with *three* of the sexiest bad boys you'll ever meet: Tyler, Nick and Jules—in *one value-packed volume!* A bond of blood tied them to each other since youth, but as men, their boyhood vow is tested. Find out all about *Bayou Blood Brothers* (#606) with Ruth Glick—writing as Rebecca York—Metsy Hingle and Joanna Wayne.

Amanda Stevens concludes our ON THE EDGE promotion with *Nighttime Guardian* (#607), a chilling tale of mystery and monsters set in the simmering South. To round out the month, Sheryl Lynn launches a new series with *To Protect Their Child* (#608). Welcome to McCLINTOCK COUNTRY, a Rocky Mountain town where everyone has a secret and love is for keeps.

More action and excitement you'll be hard-pressed to find. So pick up all four books and keep the midnight oil burning....

Sincerely,

Denise O'Sullivan
Associate Senior Editor
Harlequin Intrigue

ABOUT THE AUTHOR

Sheryl Lynn lives in a pine forest atop a hill in Colorado. When not writing, she amuses herself by embarrassing her two teenagers, walking her dogs in a nearby park and feeding peanuts to the dozens of Steller's jays, scrub jays, blue jays and squirrels who live in her backyard. Her best ideas come from the newspapers, although she admits that a lot of what she reads is way too weird for fiction.

Books by Sheryl Lynn

Don't miss any of our special offers. Write to us at the following address for information on our newest releases.

Harlequin Reader Service
U.S.: 3010 Walden Ave., P.O. Box 1325, Buffalo, NY 14269
Canadian: P.O. Box 609, Fort Erie, Ont. L2A 5X3

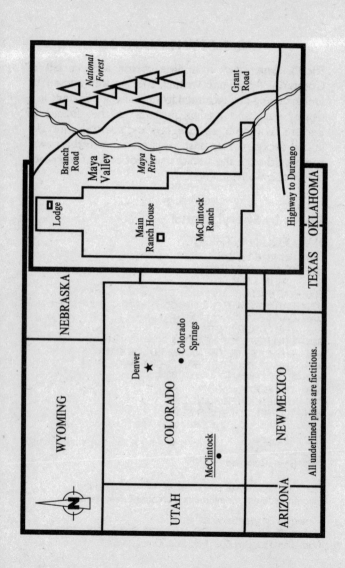

WYOMING

NEBRASKA

UTAH

COLORADO

Denver ★

• Colorado Springs

McClintock
•

National
Forest

Branch
Road

Lodge □

Maya Valley

Maya River

Main
Ranch House □

McClintock Ranch

Grant Road

Highway to Durango

ARIZONA

NEW MEXICO

TEXAS   OKLAHOMA

All underlined places are fictitious.

N

CAST OF CHARACTERS

Ric Buchanan—A wounded warrior who's returned to the town that made him an outcast and to the woman he's never stopped loving.

Elaine Greene—Not even wealth and power can help her resolve her torn loyalties or save her from a past that threatens her future.

Bobby Greene—Elaine's husband is an honorable man who committed a dishonorable act that might have gotten him murdered.

Jodi Greene—The apple of her parents' eyes—all three of them.

Tom Greene—He'll prove his son was murdered, even if it means his life.

Sheriff King McClintock—He declared Bobby's death an accident, and nobody better say anything different, especially Ric Buchanan.

Del Crowder—Did Elaine's father's death come from committing a murder or trying to prevent one?

Axton Cross—Del's business partner has a shady past.

Linda Pallo—Del's fiercely loyal office manager knows where all the skeletons are buried.

Tate Raleigh—A lawman willing to risk his livelihood in order to find the truth.

For Denise O'Sullivan, an editor with vision,
a charming laugh and faith enough for both of us.
Thanks for helping me pull this project together.

Chapter One

Ric Buchanan struggled with the door of the Track Shack Bar and Grill. Brake lights flared on his uncle's pickup truck. From behind the wheel, the old man watched Ric. Ric waved to show he was fine, and his uncle needn't worry. He pulled the door open. He wished he could ease his own nervousness. He wasn't ready to face his hometown, not yet.

But Bobby Greene needed to talk to him, urgent, face-to-face. Bobby was a natural born worrier, but this sounded unusually serious. Curiosity had drawn Ric out of hiding.

He balanced on his crutches, made certain the door wouldn't knock him down and then hobbled inside. A rush of familiar aromas—beer, spicy roasted chilies, lemon wax—brought a smile and memories. Old Junior Haversham with his barking laugh, endless advice and willingness to help out a kid struggling with math homework. Consuela Ortiz, who made the best green chile stew in the world. McClintock, Colorado had its faults, but the Track Shack wasn't one of them.

The man standing at the end of the bar caused Ric's smile to fade. Sheriff King McClintock rested a glossy boot on the brass foot rail. His big belly strained his tan uniform shirt. He had broad, square shoulders and bowed horseman's legs. A gun belt and holster were as polished as his boots.

For a moment, Ric felt fifteen years old again, cowering before the stern-faced sheriff who considered this town, the entire valley, his personal domain. A booming voice of authority who did not tolerate shenanigans, especially from a drunk's brat with a wild reputation.

The sheriff turned his head. He sported a snowy handlebar mustache, and his hair was thinning. He looked as tough as ever. He swept Ric with a hard, suspicious gaze. Then his leathery cheeks creased in a grin.

"Well, well, look what the cat drug in."

Ric stood as tall as the crutches and his aching back allowed. Rule number one in his life: Never suck up to anyone, for any reason. If a person disliked him, too bad. He didn't need approval. That included big-mouthed law officers. "Sheriff."

"I heard rumors you were visiting your uncle. Hoo-wee! Did you get the number of the truck that hit you?"

There were few people in the bar; all of them hushed, watching. Ric's neck prickled, and his scalp tightened. Until the incident that nearly killed him, he hadn't been aware of how very vain he'd been about his muscular physique. Between physical therapy, weight training and sheer determination, he was growing stronger every day, but it was slow going. He spotted Bobby seated at a corner table. His friend was staring, too, his mouth agape.

He maneuvered the crutches for a turn. He hated the damned, clumsy things.

The sheriff settled a dark brown cowboy hat on his head and slid his arms into a nylon windbreaker. He nodded to the man tending the bar. "Square away that paperwork, Tate. See you tomorrow." He stepped in front of Ric, blocking his progress.

A year ago, Ric could have twisted the despotic sheriff into a pretzel and enjoyed doing it. At the moment, he had to take whatever the man wanted to dish out. He made a point of staring down his nose, emphasizing the difference between his six feet three inches and the sheriff's five feet five. "Can I help you?" he asked coolly.

Soft strains of country music trickled from a radio in the kitchen. Nothing and nobody else made a sound. The whole place seemed to be holding its breath.

"Will you be staying long?" the sheriff asked. A polite enough question, but dislike shone in his eyes.

"Long as I need to."

"Just so you remember, boy, this is a nice quiet town. We don't like trouble here. Bad elements aren't welcome."

"I'll remember not to jaywalk."

The sheriff gave up all pretense at friendliness. "Straight and narrow, boy. Then we'll get along fine." He strutted through the door. It banged shut behind him.

Ric thought a few choice words, then shoved irritation away. King might belong to the oldest, richest family in the Maya Valley, but he was still just a little man in a little town. Ric didn't intend to hang around McClintock long enough to seriously cross swords with his old nemesis. He crutched across the speckled linoleum to Bobby's table.

Bobby rose. He'd been a skinny kid, and he'd grown into a lean man as tough and springy as rawhide rope. "Damn, old son. What happened to you?" He sounded like that skinny kid again.

Ric eased onto a chair and settled the crutches against the wall. His back seized, as if saying, "Hey, here I am!" He reached for the bottle of pain killers he carried in his coat pocket, then stopped himself. It had taken Herculean effort to wean himself off narcotics. He didn't need an over-the-counter analgesic monkey on his back. He clasped Bobby's hand, which felt like sandpaper from all the calluses.

A few days ago, he'd called his boyhood friend, the same way he always did when he visited his hometown. As usual, Bobby had filled him in on the doings of his wife and daughter, his parents and his in-laws. Ric hadn't bothered mentioning his injuries or that the army had medically discharged him.

"I see King is still a sixty-pound ego in a ten-pound sack," Ric said.

Bobby looked abashed. King was his uncle by marriage. "You probably won't believe it, but he's not such a bad guy. He's got a good heart under all that crust."

"You're right, I don't believe it. So, what's up with you? What's urgent?"

Bobby gave himself a shake. "Want some pie?" Before Ric could answer, Bobby called an order for pie and coffee to the man behind the bar.

"What happened to you?" Bobby asked.

Ric didn't like talking about it. "Don't worry about me. I'm on the mend."

"Were you shot?"

Bobby was sounding like Ric's uncle, mixing concern with irritation over Ric's reticence. "My Humvee hit a mine. Killed my driver and busted my back."

"Da-ahm," Bobby breathed.

"The army medically retired me." He squashed the bitterness. He'd joined the army when he was eighteen years old, and it had been his life. He'd have stayed in thirty years if the powers-that-be had allowed it. But no sense going back over that, again.

"So what are you going to do now?"

He'd asked himself that question a million times. The

skills he'd learned in the army didn't have much value in civilian life. "Not sure."

Bobby's mouth and brow twisted in a grimace Ric recognized as worry. Bobby had always been a worrier, and much too serious. "Are you going to stay in McClintock?"

Ric looked significantly at the crutches. The army had been his life; he didn't know how to be a civilian anymore. "For a while." He looked over his shoulder at the door and chuckled. Seeing Ric must have stripped the color right out of King McClintock's day. "Hey, this is home. Where they have to take me in."

"Your uncle never said you were hurt."

"Didn't tell him. No sense him driving eight hours up to Denver just to watch physical therapists torture me."

Bobby cocked an eyebrow. Before he could comment, the man from the bar brought coffee and pie. He plunked heavy earthenware dishes on the table. A real bear, Ric surmised, sizing up the beefy, sloping shoulders and corded forearms. Some big men were just bulky, but this one had the bone and muscle that promised immense strength. His face was hard cut, too, so it wasn't fat building that wall beneath his white cotton shirt.

"Here's your coffee, Bobby. How you doing?"

He had an accent. New York? McClintock really had changed.

"Tate Raleigh," Bobby said, "This here's Ric Buchanan. Walt's nephew."

"Get outta here! You must be the war hero the old man's always bragging on. Army grunt, right? Me, I'm former Marine. *Hoo ahh!*"

Grunt? "Airborne ranger," Ric said darkly.

"A snake-eater! That's almost as good as a Marine. *Hoo ahh* squared." He thrust out a big hand.

Tate's hand nearly swallowed Ric's. He had to push down the resentment over his lack of strength. Before the accident he could have taken this big jarhead, or made a darned good effort anyway. Consuela yelled from the kitchen. Grinning, Tate ambled away. Ric noted the cat-footed walk, quick and silent. Definitely not the type to get on the bad side of.

"New Yorker?" he asked.

"Don't hold it against him." Bobby chuckled. "He's a good old boy, even if he does talk funny. He was a cop back east and works part-time for King now. Mostly he hangs out here. Junior Haversham decided he didn't want to run the Track Shack full-time anymore, so Tate bought half interest."

Ric winced at the idea of Junior giving up the bar—to a New Yorker no less! At least Consuela Ortiz continued to command the kitchen. From the sound of it, Tate's size and boss status didn't intimidate Consuela in the least. Ric dug into the pie. The peaches retained their firmness and perfume, and the crust flaked delicately. He almost purred.

The two ate in silence. Used to be silence didn't bother Ric. Neither he nor Bobby were big talkers; they'd spent many hours with fishing lines dangling in the Maya River, never saying a word. Right now, the silence led to thinking and thinking led to Elaine and how Bobby had stolen her away. Some nasty part of him hoped Bobby was about to say Elaine was divorcing him. And with Bobby out of the way...? He disgusted himself.

"What's up?" he asked.

Bobby worked his tongue against his teeth and fiddled with a spoon. He eyeballed the crutches as if judging their weight. "So you're really out of the army. For good."

Ric sensed something more than worry in his friend's

voice. Were he poetic, he'd call it torment. "We already covered that."

"I screwed up, old son."

Ric tried to laugh off the doom and gloom. "Who hasn't?"

Bobby's squeezed his eyes shut. *"Bad."*

"Spill it," Ric urged.

Bobby's Adam's apple bobbed. In the light offered by a grimy window and neon beer signs, he looked tired and drawn. "I stumbled across some information. Pretty shabby stuff."

"How shabby?"

Waving a hand and shaking his head, Bobby said, "That part's...personal. It's got nothing to do with you. But I can't keep it to myself, and I'm pretty sure when it comes out, something else is going to come out, too. There's going to be trouble."

"I'm not following."

"You need to hear it from me. You were my best friend, and I did you poorly. I'm ashamed of myself."

Ric glanced at other diners, but no one appeared to be paying attention to him and Bobby. "Are you talking about Elaine? I got over her years ago, man." Only partly a lie. He'd accepted it. He didn't like it, but there wasn't a thing he could do about it.

"Not Elaine. Jodi." He gulped. "She's your daughter."

Pain flared in his back, and he realized he was trying to rise from the chair. He forced his back muscles to relax, then breathed deeply until the fire died to a dull ache. "Jodi, your little Jodi, is *my* kid?" He managed to keep his voice down. Barely.

He thought back, trying to remember the details. He'd received Elaine's Dear John letter after he'd deployed overseas. He'd received Bobby's announcement of Joanna

Denise Greene's birth…when? All he clearly remembered was tearing up the letter and flushing it down a latrine, then getting sloppy drunk. He hadn't returned to McClintock for almost four years after that.

Bobby licked his lips and took a sip from his coffee cup. His hands shook. "Elaine was pregnant when we got married. Don't blame her! God, don't do that. She was only eighteen, scared. And you were gone and no telling when you could get back. I talked her into marrying me. I always loved her. She wanted to tell you, but I thought…I thought…"

"This is real cool, Robert," Ric said icily. When he'd heard about the marriage, he'd wanted to beat the stuffing out of his friend. Bobby was lucky Ric didn't have even a kitten's strength, because that old impulse was back in full force. "Why are you telling me now?"

"You need to know," Bobby muttered. "I didn't think you'd get so mad."

"Hell, yes, I'm mad! Fine, you got Laney. Better man wins and all that. But now you're saying you stole my kid, too? You backstabbing son of a bitch!" He'd have started shouting—eager listeners be damned—but Bobby looked near tears. Disgusted, Ric yanked out his wallet and dug out enough money to cover the bill and tip. He flung it on the table. "My treat. *Again.*"

He grabbed his crutches.

"Ric, wait. You don't understand."

He nearly fell getting to his feet. A hammer-and-sickle team began marching drills on his spine. That didn't hurt nearly as much as the betrayal. "I understand I want to take your head off with this crutch."

"Ric—"

"Go to hell."

He made his clumsy way to the bar where he asked to

borrow the telephone. Tate gave him a hard once-over, then did the same to Bobby. Ric felt every eye in the place squarely on him, but no longer cared. Tate handed him a cordless phone.

"Ric," Bobby said. "Let's talk. Please."

Paused in the midst of punching in the number to his uncle's wood shop, Ric turned his head slowly. He glared into Bobby's eyes. "I think you've mistaken me for a much bigger man. Like I mistook you for someone with integrity."

Bobby looked as if he had more to say. Then he whipped a baseball cap from his back pocket and settled it on his head. He strode out of the bar. Ric watched him go, unable to decide which was worse, the pain in his back or the pain in his heart.

ELAINE GREENE ate supper with her mother and her daughter. On one side, Jodi talked excitedly about the upcoming Halloween party at the McClintock elementary school. As a sixth grader and class president, Jodi was head of the haunted house committee. Her classmates were in for a real treat with Jodi's wild imagination running the show. On the other side of the table, Lillian Crowder complained about her husband.

In the middle, Elaine attempted to give both the attention they craved. "More chicken, baby?" she asked her daughter.

"—so Joey Taylor wants to use tapioca pudding for the bowl of guts. How stupid is that? I told him we gotta use sausage casings and he says—"

"Mama? More chicken?"

"—he doesn't fool me for one second. I know why he went up to the lodge, and it's not so he can work on business! He's up there drinking. He thinks I don't know about his bourbon stash. Do you know what his cholesterol count is? His medication won't do any good if he drinks.'' Lillian pointed with a fork. ''Jodi, baby, eat some more chicken. You're skinny as a rail, child. What's this about a bowl of guts?''

Elaine sighed, wishing Bobby were home for supper. He had a calming influence on Jodi and Lillian. Around her, however, their natural exuberance ran wild. Sometimes being in the same room with both of them plumb wore her out.

Jodi leaped away from the table and ran down the hallway to fetch her Halloween costume to show her grandmother.

Lillian leaned in close and lowered her voice. ''Do you know why I'm really mad? Axton!''

A few weeks ago Lillian had been crowing with delight that her husband and Axton Cross had signed the paperwork making them full partners in Crowder Realty. From Lillian's point of view, it meant her husband could relax and spend more time at home. Elaine raised her eyebrows. ''I thought you liked Axton.''

''I do—I did...I don't know!'' She sighed. ''You know he's got his eye on the riverfront. He wants to chop it up into ranchettes and build mini-mansions for city folks.''

''That's the price of living in such pretty country, Mama. Can't stop people from wanting to live here.''

''I know for a fact that Axton has been talking to King. That section along the river belongs to him, you know.''

That made her laugh. ''Oh come on, Mama! Uncle King would no more sell off any portion of the ranch than you would.''

''I don't know about that. He's been sheriff going on twenty-five years now. He's getting bored, making noises about dabbling in politics. Running for office takes real money. Way things are, if he wants to sell there isn't a thing I can do to stop it.''

Right, Elaine thought with amusement. Nothing on McClintock Ranch happened without Lillian McClintock Crowder's full approval.

Jodi returned, nearly hidden by a froth of bright orange taffeta. ''It's gonna be a pumpkin, Grandma. I'm making it myself.'' She tossed an impish grin at her mother. ''With a little help from Mommy.'' She struggled with the bulky outfit, mindful of pins while stretching it out for display.

The telephone rang. Hoping it was Bobby saying he was on his way home, Elaine rose from the table.

''If that's Bobby,'' Lillian said, ''remind him that the vet is coming first thing in the morning to check out Big Red. I need every hand to help me with that ornery critter.''

''I like Big Red,'' Jodi said. ''I feed him apples, and he just loves me!''

Jodi was fearless around animals. Big Red, however, was a thousand pounds of full-blooded shorthorn who liked nothing better than hurting men and horses. He'd turn a skinny eleven-year-old into oatmeal mush. ''I better not ever catch you getting in the pen with that bull, young lady.'' Elaine emphasized the words with a glare while she picked up the phone. ''Hello.''

''Elaine? It's Uncle King, honey. Is your mama over there at your house?''

''Sure. She's sitting right—''

''Hold on. Just sit tight and keep her there. I'll be over in a minute.''

Only then did she catch the strange, tight quality of his voice. Her nape prickled and gooseflesh covered her arms. ''Is everything okay?''

''I'll be there in one minute.'' He hung up, leaving her

with a dead line and dread in her heart. She forced a smile. "Jodi? Don't you still have some homework to do?"

"Just reading, Mommy."

"You go on to your room and do it."

"But—"

"I'll clean the kitchen, okay?"

The little girl didn't need any more incentive than that. She gathered her costume and scampered away.

Lillian drew her head warily aside. "What's going on, honey? Who was that?"

Swallowing hard, Elaine turned her gaze out the window over the sink. The big ranch house where she'd grown up was less than a hundred yards away, sitting big and sprawling and silent in the dark autumn night. King had asked for Mama, which meant whatever made him sound so worried had to do with Daddy.

Daddy with his bad habits and high cholesterol and angina attacks. She swallowed hard again. "That was Uncle King. He's coming over. He wants you here."

Lillian leaped to her feet. "Delbert...?" she whispered.

Elaine reached for her mother. When lights swept the side of the house, preceding the sheriff's cruiser pulling into the driveway, the two women walked outside into the crisp night to meet him. Elaine shivered but barely noticed the cold. Her parents had been married thirty-five years. They'd be lost without each other.

She, herself, would be lost without her father.

King emerged from the car. His normally square shoulders sagged, and he lurched as if asleep. "There's been an accident," he said, his voice raw.

Lillian straightened her spine and lifted her chin. "Is it Delbert...where...what happened? Where is he?"

King herded them into the house. His eyes were red-rimmed and swollen. He made them both sit before he would speak. "They were up at the lodge. Looks like a gun discharged by accident. Del tried...I know he tried...his heart must have give out. He called for help, but—"

"Who is *they?* What are you talking about?" Elaine demanded to know. Bloody splotches stained the front of King's uniform shirt.

"They're gone, honey. Bobby and Del. Both of them...we tried, but there was nothing anybody could do. We lost them and now they're gone."

"ELAINE, HONEY, why don't you sit down?" Alice Darby tapped the kitchen table. Her normally sweet face was stiff with concern.

No! Sitting down meant relaxing. Relaxing meant thinking. If she began to think for even one moment, she'd go out of her mind. Elaine kept scrubbing the stovetop. The smell of cleanser burned her nose. She avoided looking at Alice. Her friend had accompanied her to the funeral home yesterday and today, to arrange for the double funeral and service. Though it was nearly midnight, Alice refused to leave Elaine alone.

"You need some sleep," Alice said. "You're going to end up sick."

"I can't...I just can't." She slapped a wet rag over the stovetop. She concentrated on her task, her temples throbbing.

"Take one of those pills the doctor gave you."

Drug-induced oblivion tempted her. Escape the pain, escape the horror. She couldn't, not yet. Lillian had collapsed; the doctor was keeping her sedated and monitoring her blood pressure. Elaine's brother and sister had raced home from college and now prowled like lost puppies through the big ranch house. Bobby's parents seemed to have aged twenty years overnight. It was up to Elaine to make sure her father and her husband were buried properly.

"At least eat something," Alice said.

"I'll throw up." A sob rose in her throat, and she choked it down.

"You don't have to be this strong, Laney."

Oh, but she did. Somebody had to be strong.

She flung the rag into the sink and moved restlessly into the laundry room off the kitchen. She began sorting dirty clothes into piles. Bobby's boxer shorts, T-shirts, socks, shirts and jeans. Each item she touched made her dizzy and sick with the reminder that he was never coming home again. She went through the pockets of Bobby's work shirts and jeans. The last time she'd seen him, he had dropped Jodi off from school and changed his dirty clothes before he went out again.

He'd been distracted, worried. He was always worrying. About pregnant cows, horses with sore feet, hired hands, how Jodi was doing in school, and, if everything were okay, he worried that he was missing something. Caught up in his thoughts, he hadn't even kissed her goodbye.

She hadn't told him she loved him. The last thing she'd told him, the last thing he'd heard from her mouth, was, "Don't get caught up yakking with those old coots at the feed store."

She should have told him she loved him. Now it was too late.

He'd been a tidy man but had a quirky habit of filling his pockets with junk. For years she'd been nagging him to please clean his pockets before he put clothes in the hamper. He kept forgetting.

She pulled a folded receipt from the feed store from a shirt pocket. A blue jay feather, striped glossy blue and black, came out of another pocket: a gift for his daughter. Tears burned her eyes. Packs of gum, a drill bit, more receipts. A sheet of paper folded into a tight square. More tears as she recognized the logo for Crowder Realty. Her father had pads of this paper made up by the hundreds, passing them out like candy around the valley—as if anyone could forget that he would gladly handle all real estate needs.

The message was typewritten. Uneven printing and faded letters distracted her. Everybody used computers these days. Who even owned a typewriter? She imagined some elderly rancher pounding away on an ancient manual keyboard in an attempt to make his missive look business-like.

She blinked away tears.

Maybe some folks ought to mind their own business! Especially folks in glass houses! Ric Buchanan is back in town. How would he like knowing what you really did to him? You don't know what you think you know, so you better just keep your big mouth shut! You go blabbing, and I'll do some blabbing myself.

The tea kettle began to whistle. Startled, Elaine crunched the note in her fist.

"I'm forcing some soup down your throat," Alice said, one hand inside an open cupboard. "You will not throw up."

"Sure." With fumbling fingers, she folded the note back into a little square then shoved it into her pocket.

Ric Buchanan? Blabbing?

It finally occurred to her to wonder why her husband had been at her father's lodge. Daddy had never invited

Bobby up to the lodge for a visit or to join a hunting party. Nor had he ever asked Bobby to run supplies or make repairs on the place. The lodge was Del Crowder's private domain.

It had been a horrible, terrible, unthinkable accident. Her father had accidentally shot Bobby, then died of a heart attack while trying to save him. Her father wasn't a murderer, and Bobby hadn't died because he blabbed.

"Elaine?"

Her friend's voice seemed to come from far, far away. A gray curtain teased the edges of Elaine's vision, coming closer, widening, closing again. Hands clutched her arms. Her knees buckled. Blessed oblivion finally found her.

Chapter Two

"Did you do it, Daddy?" Elaine whispered through clenched teeth. She pawed through a file cabinet drawer. "Show me you didn't murder Bobby."

Uncle King called it an accidental weapon discharge. Elaine couldn't get her mind around it. Daddy had been an absolute fanatic about firearms safety. She couldn't count how many times she'd heard "always assume it's loaded" while she was growing up.

She looked wildly around her father's home office. Despite Del's being enamored of computers, constantly upgrading his systems and glomming onto every new gadget that came on the market, a paper-free environment remained a pipe dream. The office contained thirty-plus years of paperwork. And this mess accounted for only the papers he kept at home. She hadn't been to the realty office in town yet.

She hadn't found a typewriter. Could not remember if her father owned a typewriter. She lifted her gaze to the ceiling. The attic was stuffed full of belongings accumulated by five generations of McClintocks.

She slammed the drawer shut and sat back on her heels. Her heart fluttered painfully. She refused to believe her father was a killer. He'd been aggressive, had an awful temper and could be self-righteous to a fault, but not a murderer, never that.

She couldn't explain away the threatening note. She couldn't ignore that Bobby was dead because of a bullet fired from Daddy's gun.

Questions were making her insane. She didn't want to search her parents' home for a typewriter. She didn't want proof that Daddy was a cold-blooded killer. She was terrified someone else might stumble over something incriminating.

She pulled open another drawer and began rifling through contracts and receipts.

Rumbling startled her. She slammed the drawer shut just as her sister slid open the office doors. Marlee's eyes narrowed suspiciously. With a six-year age difference, the sisters had never been close, but Marlee had always been too intuitive for her own good. Elaine felt as if she'd been caught stealing from a collection plate.

"You have a visitor, Laney," Marlee said.

Visitors had been streaming through her mother's house ever since the funeral. The entire valley was in mourning. Folks expressed their sorrow by filling the ranch kitchen with flowers, baked goods and covered dishes. Love and kindness expressed in small ways and large bolstered Elaine, gave her strength. At the same time she felt horrible. Everyone who knew Bobby had loved him. Her father, being a non-native, wasn't as well liked, but even his detractors respected him. She couldn't bear it if his legacy were clouded by suspicions of murder.

She cast a guilty look at the file cabinet. "I don't feel up to a visitor right now."

"You can't hide in here forever." Marlee pushed the doors all the way open and stepped aside. "What are you doing anyway? Look at the mess you're making. Mama will have a fit when she sees."

What if Daddy is a killer? she wanted to scream. Instead, she forced her expression into what she hoped was a picture of calm. "I'm helping. Some of these papers are thirty years old. You know Daddy. He saved everything."

Marlee made a skeptical noise. She whispered something Elaine didn't catch. A man, leaning heavily on crutches, hobbled into the office. Marlee graced Elaine with an enigmatic smile then left, her boots tapping crisply on the hardwood floor.

Elaine bumped a window sill, and realized she'd been backing away, seeking escape. She gave herself a shake, meaning to stop staring, but she couldn't help it. It *was* Ric. Oh, but he looked awful! His complexion was sallow, and his cheekbones jutted like blades over gaunt cheeks. His coat sleeves rode up, revealing bony wrists and hands. What caught her attention and roused her sympathy was his hair. No longer a crisp crewcut with a golden sheen outlining a noble head, it hung untidily over his ears, dull brown in color.

"Ric?"

Ric Buchanan is back in town...how would he like knowing what you really did to him?

"Hey, Laney." He glanced over his shoulder. "If you really don't want visitors, I can come some other time."

She noticed the way he shifted his legs. "Please, have a seat." She hurried to a leather chair and turned it toward him. "What happened to you?" As soon as she asked, she was embarrassed. She sounded like a schoolteacher chastising a tardy child.

He eased onto the chair and blew a long relieved-sounding breath. When he lifted his head, his eyes caught and held her. Beautiful eyes, exotically slanted, of a rich, dark blue, like sapphires in moonlight. His eyes hadn't changed. They had the same gleam of intelligence and watchful intensity. Nor, it seemed, had their affect on her lessened.

She turned abruptly. Her gaze fell on the photographs covering her father's desk. As the only grandchild of Del and Lillian Crowder, Jodi had been photographed more often than a movie star. Jodi laughing on a swing set; Jodi riding a horse; Jodi looking prim in a school photo. Jodi with golden hair and slightly slanted eyes the color of dark blue denim.

Ric had seen Jodi only a few times years ago when she was very young. When Ric had come home on leave, Bobby went to town to visit with him. She and Bobby had shared a tacit agreement to not parade their daughter before Ric.

Elaine perched on the edge of the desk, blocking his view of the photographs. "When did you get into town?"

"About a week ago. I was at the funeral. How are you doing?"

Terrible! Frantic! Overwrought. Falling apart. Going out of her mind. "I'm hanging in there. Were you in a car accident?" Her cheeks warmed. It wasn't her place to pry.

"Something like that. I'm so sorry about Bobby and your dad. I don't know what to say."

"I don't know what to say either. I keep listening for Bobby's truck. Expecting him to walk through the door. None of this seems quite real."

"I saw Bobby the day...I'm glad I got to see him."

The day he died, she filled in. She craved knowing what Bobby had said to Ric. Maybe someone else had threatened Bobby. Perhaps Ric would tell her Bobby had gone to Daddy for help. But if he claimed Daddy had threatened Bobby, she didn't know what she'd do.

"Bobby always liked it when you came home for a visit. He kept all the letters and cards you wrote." She bit her lower lip to keep from blurting that Jodi had collected all the postcards Ric had mailed from exotic locales. No need to bring the child into the conversation. "So, uh, how long are you staying? Where are you going from here?"

He scratched the back of his head and pulled a face. "I don't know where I'm going. I'm out of the army."

"What? Why?" She was genuinely shocked. She also worried. The last place she wanted Ric Buchanan was in McClintock, Colorado, where keeping him and Jodi apart might prove difficult. Where separating past from present could prove impossible. Ric's presence added to the swirling confusion in her overwrought brain.

He tapped a crutch. "Medically retired."

"Oh, Ric, I'm so sorry. Walt never said a word."

"I didn't tell him. Not until I got home. No sense worrying him."

Sadness tightened her throat. Walt Buchanan was the only family Ric had. She couldn't imagine being sick or hurt and not having family swarming around, offering comfort. "You always were the lone wolf. Never needing anyone."

He averted his gaze. "Let's not talk about me. I just wanted to see how you're doing. Offer my condolences. Walt brought some home-baked bread for your mother. She looks pretty shell-shocked. So do you."

He didn't know the half of it. She'd managed to get through the funeral; how, exactly, she wasn't sure. During the eulogy for her father, she'd been braced for someone to leap to his feet and denounce Del Crowder as a murderer. Now she waited for Uncle King to make an official ruling about the deaths. If the sheriff's department found evidence of foul play, then Mama would be devastated worse than she was now.

Ever since she'd read that horrible note, it felt as if a massive weight held by a slender thread were hanging over her head. A weight that would destroy her entire family.

"I miss Bobby so much. I just can't believe he's gone."

"Mommy?"

Elaine lurched off the desk, knocking over a pile of papers and sending them scattering across the burgundy rug. Her daughter stood in the doorway. With her shoulders hunched and her face down, Jodi was a picture of woe.

Ric stared at the girl. Elaine feared that he might see the resemblance to himself.

"I want to go home, Mommy." She sounded like a cranky three-year-old instead of the self-assured eleven-year-old that she was. Her whine grated Elaine's ears; Jodi never whined.

"Not now, baby. I promised Grandma we'd stay for a few days."

"I want to go home."

Elaine flashed an apologetic smile at Ric then hurried to her daughter's side. She urged the girl down the hall, out of Ric's view. She smoothed golden hair off Jodi's face and tucked it behind her ears. "Grandma needs us right now. We need her, too. Family should stick together."

"My tummy hurts."

Jodi never complained either. Especially not in this whiny way. Elaine enfolded her in a hug. "Go on in the kitchen, baby. Greta made some soup. Mr. Walt is visiting. You can say hi to him."

"I want to go home."

Racked with despair, Elaine swayed, rocking her child,

and herself. Jodi's adoration of Bobby had been unwavering—the epitome of a Daddy's girl. As terrible as Elaine's own grief felt, she imagined it must be a hundred times worse for Jodi. "Okay, baby, we'll sleep at home tonight. You have to eat something first. Okay?"

Jodi nodded against Elaine's shoulder. She headed down the hallway, then stopped and turned around. "Maybe we should stay with Grandma. She needs us."

Elaine pinched the bridge of her nose, shutting off tears before they began. "You eat, then we'll decide."

Nodding, the girl slouched away.

"Poor kid," Ric murmured when Elaine returned. "I feel so bad for her. Bobby always talked like they were real close."

"She worshipped him." Jodi had worshipped her grandfather, too. He'd never tired of her endless questions. He'd never lost his patience or temper with her. He puffed with pride whenever Jodi claimed that when she grew up, she was going to be Grandpa's partner at Crowder Realty.

Ric whistled softly, snagging her attention—she'd zoned out again. He balanced on the crutches. "Time to go. Call me if you need anything."

What she needed was the truth. Ugly questions lodged like huge black worms beneath her diaphragm, gnawing at her insides. Yet, that Ric said nothing meant he knew nothing. He'd hated her father, and with good cause. If he knew the awful thing Bobby had caught her father doing, there was no better revenge than for Ric to tell everyone about it. Her secret was safe, for now.

"I mean it, Elaine, call. I'm staying with Walt."

She couldn't look at him. The love they once shared was over and done with, ancient history. The only thing that could come out of any dealings with Ric was irreparable harm to Jodi.

"Sure," she said, ambiguously. Avoiding a person in a small town was almost as difficult as keeping a secret. Elaine had no choice except to do both.

RIC STOPPED in the foyer, arrested by an oil portrait of Del Crowder hanging on the wall. Murderer, he thought, as he studied the noble face with its *I'm-superior-to-thou* expression.

Elaine knew. When her sister said Elaine had been hiding away in Del's office, and then Elaine looked like a kid caught with a hand in the cookie jar, Ric guessed she was searching for evidence. He wondered what Bobby had told her.

The shooting appeared to be an accident. Bobby had been shot through the heart with the gun Del carried in his car. Paramedics who'd been at the lodge claimed Del was covered with Bobby's blood, as if he'd been administering CPR when the heart attack hit. Despite Del's efforts, Bobby had been dead when he hit the floor. A tragic accident.

Ric believed it was a tragedy, but in no way accidental. Elaine knew it, too.

He didn't consider himself cowardly. He had a chest full of medals, including a Silver Star, proclaiming his bravery and valor. But he'd rather charge a machine-gun nest than confront Elaine with what Bobby had told him.

"Ric?" Walt asked. "You coming?"

The housekeeper held the front door open. Clammy-cold air seeped inside.

He shifted his attention to the opposing wall. A painting showed Lillian McClintock Crowder smiling down from the back of a palomino horse. Dark hair shining, brown eyes bright and lively, her mouth quirked as if she were about to burst into laughter. In the portrait she was about the age Elaine was now. Mother and daughter looked so much alike that Elaine could have posed for the painting.

"Always the lone wolf," Elaine had said. "Never needing anyone."

Not true. He'd needed her. Seeing her again had driven a hard truth home. For all she'd done to him by marrying his best friend and denying him his child, he'd cut off his own head before hurting her.

He swung the crutches forward, placing them carefully on the rose marble floor. He followed his uncle out of the big ranch house. There was nothing he could do here. Nothing anyone could do except grieve and go on.

Del Crowder was dead and buried. Justice was done.

"WHERE'S THE JUSTICE?" Tom Greene's cry accompanied a blast of frigid December wind and snow. Wind rattled the light fixtures in the wood shop and stirred up sawdust.

Ric put down the sanding block he'd been using on a cabinet door. After weeks of lazing around his uncle's house, the need to relieve boredom grew greater than the need to avoid pitying stares and whispers of speculation. Walt had endured one day of Ric's loafing, then put him to work. It felt good being useful again, even if he was slow and clumsy. He loved the smell of cut lumber and loved even more bringing out the beauty of fine wood through sanding, varnishing and waxing.

Bobby's father stood rigidly right inside the door. He clutched a crumpled issue of the *Bugle,* the town's weekly newspaper. Melting snow dripped from Tom's hat.

Ric had accompanied Walt on a few visits with the Greenes. While Walt and Tom talked, Ric would sit in Gwen's kitchen, watching her cook or work needlepoint, as if by chopping, stirring, kneading or compulsively pushing a needle through cloth she could somehow ease the pain of losing her only child. He loved Gwen; she'd always been kind, motherly to a motherless boy. He loved Tom, too, though the man had never been easy to like. Hard, taciturn and serious, he'd had little patience for boyish antics. He'd taught Bobby and Ric how to be horsemen, tend livestock and work like men. On the rare occasions he told a boy, "Good job," it was the highest of compliments.

Tom seemed to be disintegrating. Under fluorescent lighting, a patch of whiskers he'd missed shaving glittered like glass. He had the sunken, bruised eyes of an insomniac. He looked eighty years old and perhaps a little mad.

Walt shut off the planer-jointer, pulled off his goggles and swiped sawdust off his hands. "Hey, buddy, what's the matter with you?"

Tom rattled the newspaper. "Did you see this? Did you see?"

Walt took the paper, read the article Tom pointed out, then without a word handed it to Ric.

Double Tragedy, the front page headline read. After a nine-week investigation, the sheriff had made his ruling about the shooting at the lodge on McClintock Ranch. The death of Robert James Greene was ruled accidental; Delbert George Crowder had died of a massive heart attack. King McClintock was quoted: "An unfortunate fact of life is, when firearms are present, accidents are always a possibility." Case closed.

Lies, Ric thought, incredulous, but wondering why he should be surprised. King McClintock had been Del Crowder's brother-in-law.

"King is covering up murder!" Tom plopped onto a stool. He slumped over, his hands dangling between his knees. "Ain't no way in hell that shooting was accidental. Walt, you know it wasn't an accident."

Walt pushed the snowy hair off his brow, hemmed and hawed, pulled his beard, then shrugged. "That old Del could be a slick-talking aggravating man, but I can't see him killing anyone on purpose. Especially Bobby. He loved that boy."

"You know how Del was about guns," Tom insisted. "Hell's bells, he's been a hunter all his life. Had all them trophies, the competition medals. You ever see him act careless with a firearm? And why was Bobby up to the lodge anyway? Lillian kept my boy hopping so much with ranch business, he didn't have no time to run up to the woods to jaw-jack at Del's hidey-hole."

"Have you talked to King?" Walt asked.

"Struttin' banty rooster," Tom growled. "Says there ain't sign one of foul play, but he didn't even look. No sir! He locked up the lodge and filled out a bunch of papers—" he pointed a shaky finger at the newspaper, "—and that's it. I talked to the boys who ran the ambulance up there. They say King didn't take pictures and wasn't nobody taking fingerprints or nothing. Says they did their business, then King hustled them out like they was hoodlums at a school dance. He wouldn't even let his own deputies go inside for a look-see. He's covering up cold-blooded murder."

Ric's jaw tightened so much his teeth ground. Bobby hadn't said what the problem was, or even if it had to do with Del. What Ric did know was that Bobby must have confessed about Jodi because he meant to confront his father-in-law.

He lacked the heart to tell Tom what he knew. It would mean revealing that his grandchild, the only grandchild Tom and Gwen would ever have, wasn't his. He couldn't do it.

"I can't let this ride," Tom said. "What am I going to do?"

"There is nothing to do," Ric said, earning a harsh look that threatened to burn holes in his head. As a kid, a look like that would have sent him running triple-time to do whatever he was told. Right now it made him sad. "Even if it is murder, what's the point of pushing it? You can't send Del to prison."

"Bobby deserves justice. Folks gotta know the truth."

"Folks like Jodi?"

That shut Tom's mouth.

"I agree with you, I think Del's fully capable of murder. But pushing this will hurt people. It sure won't bring Bobby back."

"How am I supposed to face my boy in Heaven if there's no justice?" On that plaintive note, Tom stormed out of the shop.

Walt grabbed a coat off a peg and went after his friend.

Guilt rose up fresh and sore within Ric. Bobby had been a good man, decent and generous. Before Elaine had come between them, they'd been closer than brothers. Bobby did deserve justice. But at what cost? So Lillian's husband could be branded a killer? So folks could whisper when Elaine and Jodi passed by?

Walt soon returned. "I'm worried about that man. Going to end up having a heart attack." He swiped snow out of his hair and beard.

"You know that day I went to see Bobby?"

Walt nodded. "You was in a state. I figured you had a spat."

Ric smiled ruefully. One of Walt's most sterling qualities was that he never gossiped or pried. He minded his own business, and didn't pass judgment. "He told me he had a problem. That he found out something 'shabby.'"

"About Del?"

"He didn't name names. Or give any details." His throat felt thick and funny, but he had to get it off his chest. "He did say some information was going to come out and I needed to hear it from him first. I'm Jodi's biological father."

Walt ambled to the jointer and picked up the piece of oak he was planing. He eyeballed the edges. "Ironic ain't it, how history repeats."

Ric winced at the rebuke, gentle as it was. His mother, Walt's sister, had been an alcoholic who went off with any man willing to buy her booze. Ric didn't know who his father was; he doubted if his mother had known. He thought he'd been careful with Elaine, but he'd been twenty years old and relatively inexperienced; she'd been eighteen with no experience at all.

"I never knew. Never suspected. I don't know what to do now."

"About Del being up to no good? Or Jodi Greene?"

"Either one."

"I did my best growing you into a man. Army did even more. Reckon you can figure out what needs doing." He settled goggles on his face, and flipped the switch on the jointer. Its high-pitched whine drowned out further conversation.

ELAINE PARKED at the curb in front of Crowder Realty. Up and down Main Street, Christmas lights twinkled amongst plastic garlands strung around light poles. Windows sported canned snow snowflakes and paintings of Santa Claus and decorated trees. The orange tide of seasonal hunters had departed the valley. Tourists in ski togs replaced them. They crowded into gift shops and boutiques in search of local crafts. Happy people, their faces pink with cold and their arms laden with purchases, strolled the sidewalks.

Coming into town was hard for Elaine. Even though Uncle King had ruled the shooting accidental, there were people—Bobby's father especially—who accused the sheriff's department of covering up murder. Elaine tried not to hear the rumors and whispers. It was impossible, just as it was impossible to not hear the suspicions plaguing her mind.

She'd searched her parents' home top to bottom. She'd found an ancient adding machine, an old Victrola and a pump-action vacuum cleaner, but no typewriter. Out of sheer relief she would have given the note to Uncle King and insisted he find out who typed it, except she'd found an earring in her father's car. A piece of junk jewelry she was positive did not belong to her mother. Perhaps she could dismiss it as belonging to one of the many real estate clients who'd ridden in Daddy's car, but she'd remembered something odd Bobby had said a few days before he died. He'd said he wouldn't haul trash from the realty anymore because Bardie Hoff had caught him and accused him of cutting into his livelihood. When she spoke to the trashman, and apologized for Bobby, Bardie had denied any knowledge of the incident. It was as if Bobby had witnessed something so awful at the realty that he felt compelled to lie about it.

Elaine refused to believe her father had been stupid enough to cheat on her mother. Nobody played Lillian McClintock Crowder for a fool and escaped with hide intact. If he were cheating and had been caught...

Daddy was dead; he couldn't defend himself. The people who were hurt the most by suspicions and rumors were her mother and Jodi.

"Mommy?"

Elaine startled. She sat as if braced for a crash. Her gloved hands clutched the steering wheel so tightly her fingers were aching.

"Are you okay, Mommy?" Jodi asked.

She had no choice except to be okay. "I was just admiring how pretty the street is."

"Looks junky," the girl muttered. She stared at the bridle on her lap. "Like this dumb old bridle. It's junk."

"We can get it fixed. I promise." She left the Jeep and stepped over slushy puddles. She gathered a pile of wrapped gifts from the back seat. Presents for Axton Cross, Linda the office manager, Kay the receptionist, and the agents who sold real estate. Usually Del and Lillian hosted a huge Christmas party, inviting all the people who worked for them. There would be no parties this season. Maybe there never would be again.

Barely able to see around the boxes, she picked her careful way to the sidewalk. Jodi slung the bridle over her shoulder and took a few packages from Elaine's arms.

She paused at the door, struck by a rise of panic. She hadn't been inside the realty office since her father died. She'd found nothing incriminating among Del's papers in his home office. She didn't know what she'd do if she walked into the realty and there was evidence right there, out in the open for all the world to see.

It was absurd. An attorney was handling the probate of Del's will. If Del had been doing something illegal, it would have been discovered by now.

Unless Bobby caught Del cheating on Mama and—

"Elaine!"

Her heart gave an unpleasant jitter. Across the street, Ric Buchanan waved to her. He looked right and left, then stepped off the sidewalk. He used a cane instead of crutches. She couldn't help checking him with an anxious eye. He'd looked so awful the day he visited her mother's house.

Despite a heavy limp, he appeared much improved. His face sported healthy color, and his tawny hair shone like beaten gold beneath the winter sun. A down coat concealed his body, but he seemed to have gained some weight. He no longer looked fragile.

He smiled. She felt the power of it thrumming deep in her belly. With the unexpected pleasure came guilt. He'd left several messages on her answering machine, all of them polite and concerned. She hadn't returned his calls.

"Hello, ladies," he said, smiling at Jodi. "Remember me, kiddo?"

Frowning thoughtfully, Jodi peered up at him. Elaine shifted uneasily. Jodi had Ric's coloring, from the honey-gold blond hair to the dark blue eyes. Her eyebrows winged the way his did, too, straight and dramatic, lending her face exotic expressiveness. Years ago, Elaine had convinced herself that Ric was the wrong man for her, that he was no family man and he wouldn't have married her anyway. She'd been a summer fling for a handsome soldier before he shipped out overseas.

"Yeah," Jodi said, her smile a ghost of what it used to be. "You're Mr. Ric. How come you limp?"

"Jodi!"

"That's okay," he said with a chuckle. "I had an accident."

Jodi wrinkled her nose. "That's sad."

"Afraid so. So what are you ladies up to? Looks like you're playing Santa."

"What kind of accident, Mr. Ric?"

"Jodi, please don't be nosy," Elaine said, her cheeks warming.

"Well, now," Ric said to the child, "that's a story better told over hot chocolate and Uncle Walt's oatmeal cookies. Maybe your mom will let me steal you away some afternoon and I can tell you about it.''

Jodi nodded eagerly. "Can I, Mommy? Today?"

"We have errands to run. We need to get the bridle fixed."

The girl turned gloomy again. "Yeah."

"What's the matter with the bridle?" Ric asked.

"Oh," Jodi replied with a groan. She shrugged the bridle off her shoulder and held it out to him. "I mail-ordered it special for Grandma. See, it's got her initials. Only the buckle on the throatlatch is busted."

Ric took the bridle. "I see."

"It's too late to send it back. I'm hoping Mr. Paul over at the hardware store can fix it."

He jerked a thumb over his shoulder. "Uncle Walt has boxes full of buckles and whatnots. I bet he can make it better than new. Only thing he's doing right now is looking at cookie recipes."

"Can I ask him, Mommy? Please?"

Elaine looked across the street. Faded lettering on a concrete block building announced Buchanan Fine Carpentry. Walt Buchanan had owned the wood shop for longer than Elaine had been alive. Before he joined the army, Ric had worked after school and on weekends for his uncle. Back then folks called him Betsy's brat, speaking with a superior sneer. Even when she was a child, Elaine had thought it unfair how people looked down on him. As if no one noticed, or cared, how polite he was or how hard he worked. All they noticed was that his mother was a drunk and his father was unknown.

She'd been barely older than Jodi was now when she developed a crush on Ric. She'd wheeled her bicycle to the shop to see if Walt could repair it. Walt hadn't been there. Ric fixed the bike. He'd called her sweetie. A nice boy being nice to a little kid, but she'd been thunderstruck.

Melancholy rose in her throat. "Sure, go ahead. But if he's busy, don't bug him."

Jodi thrust the gift-wrapped boxes at Ric, then took off at a run, the bridle jouncing and her blond braids flapping against her shoulders.

"She's sure a pretty little thing. Going to be tall, looks like."

Elaine didn't want to discuss her daughter with Ric. "I better go. My feet are getting cold."

He pointed his chin at the realty door. "Going inside?" With packages balanced on his arm, he hobbled to the door and opened it for her. Christmas carols drifted from the office.

"Thank you." She shifted her grip on the gifts and waited until he piled the others on top of them.

"I'm always at the shop. Drop in for a visit."

Head down, she mumbled, "Sure," but knew she wouldn't. She couldn't. She bustled inside, not even daring to breathe until the door shut behind her.

RIC GLOWERED at the door. Who did she think she was treating him like a pariah? If Elaine expected him to grovel and beg for her precious attention, she better prepare for a long, long wait. The anger surprised him and made him feel vaguely ashamed. Elaine seemed wispy, somehow, as if she hadn't merely lost a few pounds but was fading like mist off a river. He'd meant to tell her that he knew about Jodi. Her wounded forest creature eyes had stopped him. Only a Class A creep would get angry at a woman whose husband had died less than three months ago.

She needed time. He'd give it to her—call it a Christmas gift.

He limped across the street, entered the wood shop and a blast of hot air made his cold cheeks sting.

Jodi Greene leaned her elbows on a work bench, watching Walt rivet a new buckle onto the bridle. His daughter. He still couldn't quite get his thoughts around the knowledge that Jodi was his child, his blood. Strange hunger gnawed him, revealing an emptiness he'd never known was there.

After Elaine there had been other women: dates, flings, even a few affairs that threatened to turn serious. None of them had made him hunger for family, the way he hungered now.

If the only woman he'd ever loved was lost to him, at least he could still know his child.

"Was I right?" he called, shrugging out of his coat.

Jodi beamed, her elfin face alight with her smile. The resemblance to his mother staggered him.

"He's fixing it good, Mr. Ric. Grandma's gonna love it!" She rested one foot on the toe and it waggled back and forth in time with "Jingle Bell Rock" blaring from the radio.

"I'm sure she will. So what did you ask Santa for Christmas?"

Her narrow face darkened, and the glow died in her eyes. Her foot stopped dancing. "Santa's for little kids."

Walt skewed his face in mock dismay. As he did every winter, he allowed his beard to grow, giving him a more than passing resemblance to jolly old Saint Nick. He relished playing Santa Claus at the elementary school and at the lodge party. "Now, now, honey-pie. It's a time of joy and goodwill. Not for being glum. Wishes come true at Christmas, you know."

She shook her head. "Not mine. All the wishing in the world won't ever bring my daddy back."

Wanna bet? Ric thought. Over the girl's head he met his uncle's gaze. Walt quirked an eyebrow, his smile challenging.

A challenge Ric accepted. No more fatherless children in the Buchanan family. He couldn't replace Bobby, he hadn't the slightest idea how to care for a child or how be a father, but he was here for his daughter anyway.

Chapter Three

The first thing Ric noticed when he entered the Track Shack was a fancy arrangement of daisies in a teddy bear-shaped pot, proudly displayed on the bar. Banners of red foil hearts strung along the walls and red cloths on the tables drove home the fact that Junior Haversham no longer ran the place. Junior wouldn't have decorated for Valentine's Day if Cupid himself held a gun to his head.

Whistling, Tate Raleigh pushed through the batwing doors leading to the kitchen. He carried a stack of beer glass racks. The racks were full, but Tate handled them as if they weighed no more than Styrofoam.

"Ranger!" he called. "Good to see you again. Consuela was starting to think you didn't like her cooking."

Ric took a seat on a stool. He inhaled the savory aroma of stewed pork, caramelized onions and roasted chilies; his stomach growled. "Been busy. Uncle Walt's put me to work." He pointed his chin at the flower arrangement. "Which one of your employees has an admirer?"

Tate passed a hand over the side of his glossy black hair. "I do. Alice Darby sent it."

Ric had met the willowy blond schoolteacher; she was Elaine's best friend. Though Elaine remained cool and dis-

tant, Alice always had a warm smile for him. He laughed.
"Yeah, right."

"Honest," Tate insisted. "We went dancing. Might
even go out again." He whistled admiringly. "They didn't
make teachers like that when I was kid. So what can I get
you?"

Ric ordered stew and coffee. He pulled off his coat. It
hadn't snowed since January, but it was bitterly cold outside. Wind rattled the windows and howled against the
roof vents. Yet, after long stints in the Middle East, Central
America and Texas, he appreciated the cold weather. It
was a whole lot easier to warm up than to cool down.

While waiting for Tate, he studied the empty dining
room. The lunch crowd had left, and the afternoon coffee
drinkers hadn't arrived. Good timing. When Tate set the
food in front of him, Ric asked, "So how do you like
working for the sheriff?"

"I like it fine." Glassware rattled while Tate unloaded
the racks. "I patrol three days a week. Make a few emergency calls. Easy street. The sheriff warned me about you,
by the way."

No doubt.

"Said you were a juvenile delinquent. You burned down
a barn."

Dumbfounded, Ric stared at the big man. Then he got
it and laughed. "Yeah, only it was a toolshed. I was ten
years old, trying to smoke a cigar a kid filched from his
dad. The other boys ran off. I wouldn't have got caught if
I hadn't tried to put out the fire. A real master criminal."

Tate *tsk-tsk'd*. Then he laughed. "Small town, gotta love
it. Back in my old neighborhood, kids rob liquor stores
when they aren't shooting each other."

Ric used a hand-pressed tortilla to dig into the stew. He
could eat Consuela's green chile three times a day, every

day. Its heat blasted his sinuses while the spicy, earthy flavor filled his mouth. He swallowed, wondering how to approach Tate with his questions. He finally decided straight out was best. "What's your opinion of the sheriff's ruling on Bobby's death?"

Tate kept stacking glassware on shelves. "Got a good reason for asking?"

"Probably not," Ric said honestly.

"Does Tom Greene have something to do with it?"

"Maybe."

Tate poured himself a cup of coffee and leaned his elbows on the bar. "I really liked Bobby. Good guy. I like his old man, too. Might say he meets all my expectations about the Wild West. Decent, plain spoken, lots of common sense." He waggled his eyebrows. "Stubborn."

That described Tom Greene perfectly. "Has Tom been talking to you?"

Tate stirred enough cream into his coffee to turn it pale tan, then dumped in sugar. "He's not one bit satisfied with the ruling. I don't blame him. I'm not satisfied either."

Ric's gut tightened. Getting involved in a mystery went against the grain. He made a point of minding his own business and never pushing his nose into places it didn't belong. Especially in McClintock, where as a kid he'd been treated as an outcast. He still felt unsure about his place in the community. If he weren't careful, he could end up run out of town, quite possibly tarred and feathered as a bonus. Bobby deserved justice, though, and Tom deserved the truth.

"Why aren't you satisfied?" Ric didn't know if Tate would answer, but no harm in asking.

"Once a murder police, always a murder police."

"You were a homicide detective?"

"Six years, New York's finest. I was good, too, don't

mind saying. I answered the call up to the lodge that night. Got there right behind the ambulance. I had time to shoot one roll of film and process Del's weapon before the sheriff hustled me out.''

Ric's prickling turned into an itch. "He didn't let you examine the bodies?"

"It sounds more suspicious than it is. In twenty-five years the sheriff has seen plenty of homicides, but only three were murders." He snorted. "I've done more than that in a single day. There he walked in on family members and freaked out. He panicked."

"So he is covering up murder."

Tate gave him a hard look. "I didn't say that. I've known my share of bent cops. Sheriff McClintock isn't one of them. He's too rich to be bought and too concerned about that whole McClintock legacy thing to get caught up in scandal."

"Did he talk to people? Check to see if Del had a motive for murder?"

"Barely. And he ordered me flat out not to stir up trouble." He lowered his voice to a menacing rumble. "If you don't think it's not driving me freakin' crazy, think again. Tom's been talking to everybody, then telling me what he learns, but my hands are tied. The sheriff doesn't like what Tom is doing one little bit."

"I imagine so." Ric ate a few bites of stew. He liked Tate and felt him trustworthy. "Remember that day I met you?"

"You and Bobby had a fight. Same day he died."

That almost sounded like a warning. Ric pushed ahead anyway. "Bobby told me he'd run across some shabby information. No names, no details, but he was troubled. He acted like it was a big deal. Maybe it was motive for murder."

"So what were you fighting about?"

Ric grinned wryly. He walked a fine line between seeking justice for his best friend and shattering his daughter's life. "Bobby pulled something on me a few years back. He confessed so I wouldn't hear about it from another source." He held up a hand, stopping Tate's questions. "I won't hurt innocent parties by going into it." He paused, considering how much he knew as a fact, which was precious little. He didn't like placing blame where it didn't belong, but then again, what other conclusion was there? "I think Bobby caught Del doing something. I don't know what, don't even have a clue. But I'm pretty sure Del threatened Bobby, trying to keep him quiet. Bobby wasn't the sort to back down from a bully. It might be the reason Del shot him."

"Tom hasn't turned up anything illegal, immoral or unethical in Del's background." Again the low voice and shifty glances toward the kitchen. "I haven't either."

The implication was clear. Tate was defying direct orders, jeopardizing his position with the sheriff's department in a search for the truth.

"What about the realty office?" Ric asked. "Tom says no one will talk to him. Not even Linda Pallo, and she's known him all his life."

"His people skills aren't real…polished. I've had a few chats with the receptionist, Kay Taylor. Nice lady. I can't get a whiff of anything fishy." Tate drew back, his dark eyes thoughtful over the rim of his coffee mug. "Must be getting kind of crowded there in your uncle's house. There are a lot of nice properties for sale in the area."

Tate could not possibly mean for Ric to go undercover in the realty office. A sly grin said that was exactly what he meant.

"This valley is the prettiest country I've ever seen,"

Ric said. He laughed out loud. "Wouldn't King Mc-
Clintock love it if I became a homeowner in *his* town?"

"Just don't burn down any barns, boy," Tate said, in a
fair imitation of the sheriff's pompous drawl, "and we'll
get along just fine."

"WALT. RIC. I'm so glad you could come out today."
Lillian Crowder invited Ric and his uncle into her home.
Both men removed their hats and took pains to wipe mud
off their feet before entering her spotless kitchen.

Walt clasped Lillian's tiny hands in his callused paws.
"You're looking real fine, Miz Lillian."

Amused, Ric cocked an eyebrow. They'd come to the
ranch about a carpentry job, but beforehand Walt had
changed into a clean, pressed shirt and clean blue jeans,
shaved his face and slicked back his hair. Now the old
man looked a bit starry-eyed. Must be spring, Ric thought.

"You are looking well, Mrs. Crowder," Ric said. He
meant it sincerely. She was in her fifties, but still a beautiful woman. Looking at her made it easy to imagine what
Elaine would look like in twenty years.

"Oh, drop the formality and call me Lillian." She stood
on tiptoes and brushed his cheek with an airy kiss. "How
is your back doing, hon? I see you aren't using a cane
anymore."

Unlike her husband had, Lillian Crowder didn't put on
airs. Her great-great grandfather had discovered a gold
mine, made millions of dollars, and created an empire. She
was so warm and earthy, it was easy to forget she worked
a ranch that comprised half the Maya Valley. She served
them coffee, chitchatted about a May snowstorm that had
skiers ecstatic but fruit growers in a panic, then asked Ric
about the property he'd recently purchased.

Caught off guard by her question, he stiffened. He'd

spent a lot of time in Crowder Realty talking to Kay Taylor, Linda Pallo, and Axton Cross. Ric hadn't sniffed anything remotely fishy. If Del had been engaged in monkey business, then none of his employees had known about it.

Lillian's smile eased his discomfort.

"I bought ten acres up north of town. Right up against national forest. It has a good well and electrical hookups. I'm going to build a house."

"Good for you," she said, sounding as if she truly meant it. "So, let's talk about my renovation project. I know you aren't a general contractor, Walt, but I trust you more than anyone else. You know who does good plumbing and electrical work. I need the bunkhouse completely done over. The kitchen in there dates back to the Forties, and it can use another bathroom. When the seasonal workers come in, they probably feel like they're living in a tent city." She turned a large sheet of paper covered with sketches so Walt could see it. "This is pretty much what I want."

"Building something nice for you is a dream come true for me, Miz Lillian," Walt said. She fluttered her eyelashes at him. He actually blushed.

"Grandma! I'm home from school." The back door slammed and Jodi skipped into the kitchen. She dropped a backpack on the floor.

Ric's heart warmed at the sight of her. Jodi was smart, funny, curious and charming. Every glimpse he'd had of her over the past few months fueled his hunger to know her better. Elaine, however, was making a point of avoiding him. He never got the chance to really talk to the girl.

Jodi smiled at him and Walt, and went straight to the refrigerator. "Mommy's not home from the store yet." She pulled two carrots from the fridge. "I didn't see the farrier's truck. Has he been here?"

"I'm sorry," Lillian said. "He had engine trouble. He can't make it until tomorrow."

"Poor Rocky! He's all alone in the barn." She explained to Ric and Walt, "My horse threw a shoe, but he has to have corrective shoes, so Mr. Jordan has to do it. Rocky's real sad about being penned up. Want to see him, Mr. Ric? He's champion material, right, Grandma?"

Ric's entire body tingled at the opportunity. He would have accepted her offer if she wanted to show him a mud puddle. "I'd love to see your horse."

"Mr. Ric is here on business."

"You and I can handle it, Miz Lillian," Walt said. "He's just my gofer anyway."

"What's a gofer?" Jodi asked.

"I go for more wood, go for nails, go for coffee," Ric said.

Jodi giggled as if the joke weren't older than the Rocky Mountains.

Ric exchanged a look with his uncle. They hadn't talked about Jodi's paternity, but it was there between them. Walt nodded ever so slightly. Ric followed the child outdoors.

"School is almost over, isn't it?" he asked.

"Another week. I'm gonna be a seventh grader next year. I'm kind of nervous 'cause some of those eighth graders are real big and mean. I'm gonna miss Miss Darby, too. She's the best teacher I ever had in my whole life." She jumped over a puddle, her braids flying.

Ric guessed that she was as tall or maybe taller than her mother. Not that it was much of a stretch. Elaine was barely five feet two.

Paddocks with white painted fencing corralled quarter horses enjoying the greenery that had sprung up after the last snow. Far in the distance, fat red-and-white cattle grazed the rolling hills. A good place for a kid to grow up.

"Course, I can see Miss Darby when I want to. Her and Mommy are good friends. But I like her best as a teacher. She never yells at kids. Some teachers do, you know." The barn door stood open, and she walked inside.

He followed her down the aisle between stalls. All were empty save one which held a buckskin quarter horse gelding with a neat, pretty head and expressive eyes. Jodi rattled off his pedigree. She assured Ric that she and Rocky would take some ribbons at the county fair and in the rodeo, too, where they'd compete in barrel racing. Ric stroked the horse's face. Rocky contentedly munched the carrots.

"I've been thinking about getting a horse," Ric said. He hadn't actually, but now that he said it, the idea held appeal. It also gave him and Jodi something to talk about.

She gave him a once-over. "You know how to ride?"

"I used to work Papa Tom's cattle with your dad. My riding and roping skills are rusty, but they'll come back. It'll have to be a very special horse, though."

"How come?"

"I have a bad back. So it'll have to be soft-footed and easygoing."

"Maybe you ought to get one of those fancy five-gaited horses. Do you know Mr. Gorshen? He's got a pair of foxtrotters. Says a baby could ride them without falling off."

"I don't think I want to pay that much. You seem to know quite a bit about horses. Maybe you can attend some stock auctions with me."

"Daddy called me a natural," she said, her boyish chest puffing with pride. "Said my eye's as good as Grandma's. And she knows more about horses than anybody in the whole world.'' She climbed on the slatted stall door and planted a noisy kiss on Rocky's nose. The horse snorted, blasting them both with grassy breath. Jodi stood straight on the stall door, looking Ric in the eyes. ''You're real tall.''

''I work on it. A little bird told me your birthday is coming up.''

She laughed, a silvery sound that caused the gelding's ears to prick forward. ''I'm gonna have a slumber party. I'll be twelve. That's almost grown-up.''

''Jodi?''

The girl jumped off the stall door. ''In here, Mommy!''

A frisson of pure anticipation rippled down Ric's spine. Such eagerness annoyed the devil out of him. By refusing to return his calls and acting barely civil whenever they happened to meet, Elaine had made it clear she wasn't interested in being friends. Fine by him. He didn't need her anymore than she needed him. Still, his heart lurched whenever he saw her.

''I've got groceries to unload. You have homework and chores.'' Elaine took a few steps into the barn, then stopped, staring at Ric.

Ric pulled off his hat and combed his hair with his fingers. He ran a finger around his shirt collar. ''Good afternoon,'' he said.

She looked a lot better than the last time he'd actually talked to her. Her cheeks had lost the hollow look and her step had a bounce. She caught her daughter in a one-armed hug. Jodi was at least an inch taller than her mother.

''What are you two up to?'' Elaine asked.

''Mr. Ric's going to buy a horse. He asked me to help him find a good one. He's got a bad back, so we have to find a horse with a real easy gait.''

''Is that so?''

"Seems a shame," Ric said, "to have property without a horse mowing the lawn."

Jodi laughed. "We can go to stock auctions, Mommy. I can help him find the perfect horse."

"I'm sure you can. Right now, you have things to do. I'm sure Ric does as well. Go get those groceries out of the car."

"Did you remember the cupcake papers?"

"Yes, I remembered. And the sprinkles and the food coloring. So scoot!" To Ric she explained, "End of the year party at school. The social event of the season."

He ruffled Jodi's hair. "Good seeing you again, kiddo. We'll talk horses later."

"Okay." After a final pat on Rocky's nose, she skipped out of the barn.

"Great kid," he said. He meant it, but it was oddly discomfiting to admit. If he'd married Elaine and raised Jodi, she'd have grown up as a transient. She'd have been stuck in base housing on army posts, growing up nearly fatherless, while Ric deployed on assignments that took him far from home for nine months a year. An army brat without roots and fleeting friendships and a new school to attend every year or so. Bobby might have betrayed Ric, but he'd done Jodi a good turn.

She reached over the stall door to pet Rocky. "I heard about you buying land."

Her voice held a dangerous note, one he couldn't quite put a finger on, but it alerted him anyway. "Ten acres."

"Funny. I thought you didn't like McClintock."

"Changed my mind."

"Must have. From what I hear, you looked at just about every property for sale in the valley. You're also very interested in the business end of real estate."

He'd been careful in the questions he'd asked and in

how he engaged Del's former employees and partner in conversations. Not careful enough, apparently. "It is interesting. I never knew there were so many ways to finance a sale. How much paperwork is involved."

She made a musing noise. "I've also heard you and Deputy Tate Raleigh are best buddies now. Tight as ticks." Her smile faded and those big brown eyes turned hard. "What are you up to, Ric? Why are you looking for dirt on my father?"

Couldn't get any more blunt than that. "What makes you think that's what I'm doing?"

"Oh, come on! You never liked Daddy. Plus, it's no secret how close you are to the Greenes. Tom has been turning over every rock in this valley looking for some way to prove Bobby was murdered." She stabbed a stiff finger in the direction of his chest. "Now I find you with my daughter. Just what exactly did you say to her? What are you trying to pull?"

Our daughter, he wanted to say. If he did, and she denied it, then what? She might cut him off cold from all contact with the girl. He could demand a DNA test, go to court, maybe win partial custody or at least visitation rights. Then mean-spirited kids could teach Jodi what the word *bastard* meant. She'd be the brunt of catcalls, nasty jokes and bullying. Tom and Gwen Greene would lose their only grandchild.

He wanted to know his child. He wanted, if not to be her father, to at least be her friend. He could tell by the way Jodi latched onto him that she needed a man in her life. Putting Elaine on the defensive was not the way to go about it.

Having her mad at him wasn't productive either.

"I'll be honest with you," he said. "I don't believe the shooting was accidental."

She folded her arms and lifted her chin. Now she was definitely angry.

Ric sighed. "Bobby was my best friend since kindergarten. I hate what happened to him. I really hate that King didn't investigate the shooting. There are a lot of unanswered questions. Bobby deserves better."

"Daddy was not a criminal. And Uncle King did so investigate."

He'd heard complaints about Del's bordering on ruthless business practices, but not a hint about anything underhanded. "I agree Del wasn't a criminal."

That gave her a start. She backed a step, eyeing him sideways. "I don't appreciate your snooping."

"I'm not trying to hurt you." He wanted to touch her hair and trace a finger over the curve of her cheek. He jammed his hands in his pockets. "That's the last thing in the world I want. But can you blame me for needing to know what really happened? Don't you want to know? Aren't you curious?"

She scuffed the layer of sawdust on the floor. "It was an accident. Nothing more. I wish everyone would just accept it."

He couldn't resist the poignant plea. "I wasn't pumping Jodi for information, if that's what worries you. I would never do that."

She searched his face.

"We were talking about horses. I'd really like to take her with me to a stock auction."

"I don't think that's such a good idea."

He struggled with impatience. He was the wounded party, not her. He didn't appreciate her acting as if he were up to no good. "Hey, you don't want me ending up with a mule or a camel or something. You can come along, too. I remember how much you love auctions." He chuckled.

"I happen to know there's a real competitive streak under that dainty exterior."

She covered her mouth as if hiding a smile. "I am not competitive."

"Huh. Let me see. Who was it insisting on competing in the barrel races after she sprained her ankle?"

"I refuse to discuss this, Cedric Buchanan."

He tapped his chin. "And there were about two hundred jars of pickled peppers you made before you had an entry good enough for the county fair."

"Stop."

"Who said," his voice rose in a warbling falsetto, "Walt Buchanan does not make better biscuits than I do, and I'll prove it!"

She laughed and flung up her hands. "All right! You win."

Better a tiny victory than none at all. "Then come to the auction with me. I need expert help."

"I'll consider it." She glanced at her wristwatch. "I have things to do. I'm sure you do as well." She turned for the door.

Ric fell into step beside her. It would be so easy to slip an arm around her shoulders. Smell her hair and see if her sweet scent still drove him wild with desire. Only an idiot would try it.

She headed toward home, a dollhouse version of the big ranch manor. Filled with longing, he watched the gentle sway of her hips and the way her sable hair caught sunlight.

At one point in his life, he'd tried his best to hate her. Then he'd tried to forget her. He'd failed miserably at both endeavors. Now he called himself twenty-seven kinds of fool for wanting so much for her to want him.

Chapter Four

The Maya Valley Cemetery covered a hill south of McClintock. Aspen groves and mountain ash lined the graveyard. Beneath a half-moon shining in the early morning sky, the trees stood like ghostly sentinels.

Ric drove his pickup truck slowly through the cemetery. He could hardly believe it was October already, a full year since he'd returned to McClintock, a full year since Bobby's death.

He had plans to come out this afternoon with Tom and Gwen, to visit on this sad anniversary. He wanted some time alone with his friend. The McClintock family mausoleum dominated the highest hill. Made of Colorado marble in a Grecian temple design, it glowed by moonlight. Marble monuments marked other family plots, some dating back to the 1880s.

Recollecting old ghost stories that used to circulate among the kids, and probably still did, made him smile. One story claimed this was once a sacred burial ground for Ute Indians. On full-moon nights, Ute warriors who'd died in battle and maidens who'd killed themselves because of lost loves could, supposedly, be seen dancing among the graves.

A creepy-crawly sensation tickled his back and arms.

He heard a rustling, and his gut lurched. He chuckled at his own foolishness. Elk and mule deer found the grassy grounds irresistible, and this was the time of day for them to be out in force.

He carried a wreath he'd woven from woodbine and black-eyed Susans up the hill to the Greene family plot. Stars were so bright the sky seemed alive, and the air was so cold it crackled against his face. Bobby's grave was easy to find by moonlight. Weathering hadn't yet stripped the shine from the brass marker.

He lowered himself to his knees. Chrysanthemums were scattered over the grave. He picked one up and pressed it to his nose. It was soft and fresh. Bony fingers tip-tapped down his spine. He tried to laugh off the rise of superstitious nervousness. Bobby had a lot of friends. Ric probably wasn't the only one desiring private communion. He rested the wreath against the marker.

"I sure do miss you," he said. "I wish we hadn't fought the last time we saw each other. I feel bad about it. Especially now that I've seen how you've done right by Jodi. She's a great kid. You were a great father."

Moisture seeped through his jeans, chilling his knees. He struggled upright. He winced at the twinges in his back and tried not to tense up. Cold and tension often brought on spasms. He had too much work to do to be laid up right now. He shoved his gloved hands into his coat pockets.

"I wish you could have seen her at the rodeo. She took first place in barrel racing. And she's playing volleyball, too. She's the tallest girl on the team, and she can really spike the ball." He lifted his gaze to the stars. "I've been coaching her in basketball. Hate to admit it, but she's a better player than you or I ever were."

He frowned, washed in melancholy. "I can't ever replace you in Jodi's heart. I won't even try. I promise. But I'm glad I can be here for her. She sure misses you.''

An approaching vehicle caught his attention. Headlights bounced off the trees, drawing nearer. The sky was beginning to lighten, and the stars were growing faint.

Elaine walked up the hill. Ric stood taller, eagerness rising despite the circumstances. He couldn't help it. Every time he saw her, he turned stupid.

She wore a cowboy hat and a sheepskin coat, but looked unmistakably feminine. He'd spent the last four months working with Walt on the McClintock Ranch. He had seen her almost daily. She was warming to him, relaxing and acting friendly. Still, there was no sign she cared about him, or that she wanted to.

"Hi, Ric. I thought I recognized your truck.''

"Figured I'd beat the crowd,'' he said.

"Jodi's staying out of school today. We're going to have a picnic later. Mama, too.'' She stood beside him and looked down at the grave. "I figured I'd get all my crying done early.''

He tipped his hat. "I'll leave you to your privacy, then.''

"You don't have to go.'' She hugged herself, shivering. "In fact, I kind of wish you'd stay. Coming up here alone made more sense at home. It's pretty creepy in the dark.''

"Looking for Indian ghosts?'' he teased.

She mock-punched his arm. "Stop that.'' She dropped to a crouch and began gathering the chrysanthemums. "You shouldn't toss flowers. Bobby liked things tidy.''

"Those were here when I got here.''

She bunched the flowers into a neat bouquet and laid them next to his wreath. Dusting her hands, she rose. "I still listen for the sound of his pickup coming up the drive. I still reach for him in bed. I wait for the hurting to stop, but it doesn't.'' She looked up at him. ''Is your mother buried here?''

Her plaintive note made him want to sigh. ''She was cremated, and they sent her ashes to Walt. I don't know what he did with them.''

''I don't even remember what she looked like.''

He almost said, ''Look at Jodi and you'll know,'' but refrained. ''All my grieving happened after she left me with Walt. By the time she actually died, I'd gotten over her. Every once in a while I get a twinge. Wish things had turned out differently. Lucky for us, Bobby left us good memories. My mom never bothered with those.''

He felt ashamed of his bitterness. His mother had wanted to be a decent person. According to Walt, she'd quit drinking when she learned she was pregnant and managed sobriety for almost four years before the bottle hooked her again. Betsy Buchanan had been weak, not evil.

Elaine hooked an arm with his and leaned against him. It caught him off guard. He almost feared to breathe.

She laughed, a nervous note. ''Dawn was Bobby's favorite part of the day. He was always dragging me outside to see a colorful sunrise. I really thought it would be nice to come here at dawn, but this is too spooky. Would you walk with me up to the mausoleum?''

''Be my pleasure.''

He loved it, in fact, walking arm in arm with her, her trim body a beacon of warmth in an otherwise cold, lonely morning. The mausoleum loomed imperiously, a fitting final resting place for Del Crowder.

Ric almost felt like apologizing. Neither he nor Tate nor Tom had found one shred of evidence that Del had murdered Bobby. Whatever Bobby had stumbled across had gone with him into the grave. That didn't mean Del wasn't guilty, but it was easier for Ric to think, if not kindly, then without rancor about Elaine's father.

Elaine left him at the wrought-iron gate and walked up the path to the door. He turned his face east. The sky was turning pale pinkish-gold over the mountain peaks. Only the planet Venus was visible now.

"Ric? Look at this." Elaine hurried to the gate. She held a manila envelope. "Somebody put money by the door."

"Huh." Folks left the strangest mementos on graves. During the times he'd pulled funeral detail in the army, he'd seen, along with traditional flowers and wreaths, untraditional toys, tools, articles of clothing and even a vacuum cleaner. "Wasn't there some kind of charity people were donating to in your dad's name?"

"It's too much money for that."

He saw how much when they sat in her Jeep and turned on the dome light. The two of them counted out three thousand, seven hundred fifty-eight dollars and thirty-four cents. On the outside of the envelope, scrawled in black marker, were two words: *I'm sorry.*

"Isn't this just the oddest thing?" she asked.

He rubbed the back of his neck. He wondered if the scattered chrysanthemums on Bobby's grave and money were connected. "A debt? A tenant who owed back rent?"

"All debts were settled when Daddy's will was probated."

"A private loan, then. I doubt I could rest easy if I owed money to somebody who died." He shrugged. "I bet whoever left it welshed on a debt."

"I suppose," she murmured uncertainly. "What do I do with it then?"

"Buy me breakfast?" he suggested. Her hint of vanilla scent was filling the Jeep and his head. Images of breakfast in bed teased him.

She shoved the bills back in the envelope. "I'll give it to Pastor Rimes." She caressed the envelope. A lovely smile, soft and sweet, curved her mouth.

Ric thought his heart might explode.

"I think Bobby would like it if we have breakfast together. He always missed you, Ric. Missed your friendship." She lowered her face. "I missed you, too. It would be nice if we could be friends again. Do you think it's possible?"

He chucked her chin. "Not just possible, likely."

THEIR FRIENDSHIP grew, sort of. Ric and Walt worked at the ranch until Christmas. Instead of merely waving in passing while they renovated the bunkhouse, Elaine began stopping to chat. Cautious conversations, with an undercurrent of longing she tried to ignore. She relaxed about Ric and Jodi's friendship. He never missed one of her sporting events. If extracurricular activities kept the girl after school, Ric would drive her home. After Ric and Walt finished the bunkhouse, Elaine didn't see Ric very often. When she did see him in town or when he brought Jodi home or picked up the girl to attend a stock auction, her heart quickened, and she couldn't bear looking too long into his eyes.

She had to concede that a truly open friendship with him was impossible. She had too many secrets.

Now, a year and a half after Bobby's death, Elaine learned of a danger that threatened to thrust her deepest, darkest secrets into the light. And Ric Buchanan was part of it.

She drove too fast for the slush-covered dirt road. In the rearview mirror she glimpsed a driveway. She braked and the Jeep skidded. She backed up, then turned into the driveway. Up a hill, lights shone through the naked branches of scrub oaks. She prayed this was Ric's property.

The sun had settled behind the trees. Fields of snow, laced with animal tracks, spread to the forest's edge. Around a curve, she spotted a small trailer house mounted on cinder blocks and a two-horse barn with an attached corral. She recognized Ric's pickup truck, its bed filled with tools. She breathed a sigh of relief.

Ric and his buddies were going too far. If Ric didn't promise to put a stop to their ridiculous investigation, she was going to have to take drastic measures.

She stepped into the cold evening air. The month of April was following its usual pattern. Heavy, wet snow, followed by warm days that melted the snow into slush. Her boots squished in a muddy puddle. A darting movement startled her.

A dog woofed and did a little dance of greeting, his feathery tail whipping the air. She petted his ears. "Hey, Buster. How are you doing, boy?"

The black-and-white mutt had been a stray running around town until Ric adopted him. His friendly face hanging out of Ric's truck cab was now a familiar sight around the valley. It struck her as strange that Ric hadn't heard her drive up. She hoped he wasn't sleeping. On the other hand, she didn't really care if she woke him or not.

She rapped her knuckles against the trailer door. Lights were on inside, but no answer. She knocked harder.

Buster trotted around the trailer and disappeared.

Thinking Ric might have a workshop around back, she followed the dog.

The sight that faced her stopped her in her tracks. A rock-lined path meandered toward the forest, ending at a building with a pyramidal roof and fancy woodwork reminiscent of a Victorian gazebo. Golden light glowed through half-glass walls. It wasn't big enough for a house and it was too elaborate for a workshop. Buster stood before the door, his tail wagging. As Elaine approached, the smell of chlorinated water hit her nose. Through the glass door she saw a hot tub.

He lived in an old trailer, but had built the swankiest hot tub setup she'd ever seen. Men were so strange.

Eyes closed, Ric lounged in steaming water. He wore earphones on his head. Elaine knocked. Ric splashed water and jerked off the earphones. Trying not to giggle, Elaine waved. He beckoned for her to enter. When she opened the door, the swimming pool smell nearly knocked her backward, as did the sultry heat.

"Don't let the dog—"

Buster slipped past Elaine and hopped onto a cushioned bench. His muddy paws left tracks.

"—inside." Ric glowered at the dog who flattened his ears in apology, but made no move to leave. "Come on in and close the door. What brings you up here, Laney?"

The sight of him drove reasonable thoughts from her head. His hair clung damply to his forehead, framing a face far too handsome for any woman's good. It didn't help that practically every single female in the valley had a massive crush on him—a few married women did, too! Even Elaine's mother had commented about his good looks and shiver-worthy smile. Worse, his bare chest and arms were beautifully muscled, and his gold-tinged skin was flushed with heat. He was undeniably sexy.

Her hips loosened and heaviness settled in her pelvis. Grief had deadened her body and soul. She half-believed that her life as a sexual woman was over. Seeing Ric like this challenged that belief.

She tore her gaze away and focused on the tub's control panel.

"Laney?"

"Uhm, I need to talk to you."

Smiling, he crooked a finger. "Come on in, the water's great."

That she was so tempted to strip off her clothes and jump in appalled her. Fine, he was sexy and desirable and deep within her being were memories of how very much she once loved him. She wasn't, however, a starry-eyed teenager. She was mature, a mother and living in a very small community where widowed ladies who indulged in wild affairs ended up with poor reputations. Once in a lifetime for heedless madness was more than enough for her.

"No, thank you." The steamy heat was making her sweat. She unzipped her coat. She sat next to Buster and his tail whipped against the cushion. She kept her attention on the dog. Looking at Ric was too dangerous and meeting his eyes could prove her undoing. "This is quite a setup."

"It turned out pretty good for a first effort. Did you see my barn?" He winced, then smiled broadly as if trying to cover for it.

She understood the hot tub now. He needed it for his back. So he wasn't strange, but merely far too proud. "I saw it. Are you ever going to buy a horse or do you just like attending auctions?"

"Jodi and I are having a blast. You should join us sometime." He patted the tub side. "Sure you don't want to get in? Plenty of room."

She peeked, and regretted it. His grin was mischievous, compelling. Succumbing to the power of his smile could very well make her forget all the good reasons why she shouldn't get involved with him.

Forget niceties and small talk. "I know about the private investigator Tom hired. You and Tate are involved."

He reached for a wineglass. Lamplight danced against flexing muscles in a fascinating display. She wondered if he were completely naked and mentally kicked herself for even thinking it.

"Care for some wine? It's a nice Reisling a friend sent me from Germany. There should be another glass in the cabinet."

"Did you hear what I said?"

"I heard you."

"What are you going to do about it?"

"What would you like me to do?"

"For starters, put a stop to it! Tom and Gwen are not rich people. Hiring a private investigator for a wild-goose chase is expensive. Not to mention how it's stirring up a matter that's settled. My mother will be so hurt when she finds out. And she will find out."

"How did you find out?"

"From Axton Cross. A man who knew him back in Denver let him know someone is asking questions. It wasn't that difficult for Axton to figure out who was asking and why. He's very upset. It's hurting the realty."

He sipped the wine then smacked his lips. "Laney."

"What?"

"Look me straight in the eye. Tell me truthfully that you believe Bobby's death was an accident."

She squeezed her lips together and stared at her clenched fists. She couldn't blame Ric for wanting to know what had happened at the lodge. She wanted to know herself.

"Ric," she said, "I sympathize with Tom. I know he's hurting. But Gwen is so worried about him. She says he hardly talks anymore. He sleeps in Bobby's old bedroom instead of with her—when he sleeps at all. If not for my sake and my mother's sake, then stop this craziness for Gwen. It's killing Tom."

"I know what it's doing to him. If I could stop him, I would."

"What about Tate? If he wasn't egging Tom on—"

"That's not how it is. Trust me. Tom won't quit until he knows the truth. He just won't."

She sighed. Ric was her only hope.

His eyes caught and held hers. He'd always been easy to talk to. When he gave his attention, he gave it fully, never showing impatience. When he listened, it felt as if she were the only thing that mattered. At eighteen, she'd told him things she hadn't even trusted to her diary.

At thirty-one, she was about to do so again.

"I think Daddy might have shot Bobby on purpose." There. She'd said it out loud, confessed her terrible secret. Her muscles tensed and pain arced through her midsection. She waited for lightning to strike or the earth to open and swallow her whole.

Ric's gaze remained steady.

"Something was troubling Bobby a week or so before he died. You know him, how he always fussed and fretted. Like the world would stop turning if he didn't keep an eye on every detail. But this was different. He was acting funny. Snappish. He even yelled at Jodi, and he hardly ever did that."

"Do you have any idea what was bothering him?"

Like some horrendous relic too dangerous to dispose of, the note she'd found now lay buried in her lingerie drawer. If Ric ever saw it… "I pestered him to tell me what was the matter. All he said was that he wouldn't haul trash out of the realty for Daddy anymore. He said the trashman caught him."

"Why would Bobby haul trash?"

"Daddy could be sort of…cheap. Not about big things or gifts, but he'd reuse envelopes and haggle with workmen over the cost of supplies. Penny-ante stuff. He was always roping Bobby into doing odd jobs for free.''

''Did you talk to the trashman?''

''I did. He didn't know what I was talking about.'' In a funny roundabout way, it was almost a relief to confide the awful knowledge she'd been carrying for nearly eighteen months. She wiped sweat off her brow. ''But Bobby *had* hauled trash. I think he caught Daddy doing something.''

''What?'' he prompted.

''Nothing illegal, I swear. I looked everywhere. No shady deals. No bribing the zoning commissioners. No screwing around with water rights.''

''What did you find?''

She drew a deep breath. ''An earring in Daddy's car. It doesn't belong to Mama.''

He looked surprised. ''Del was cheating on Lillian?''

Her cheeks warmed and not because of the steaming hot tub. ''Bobby had absolutely no reason to be at the lodge that night. Or any night for that matter. He never went up there.''

Ric sipped wine, his expression thoughtful.

''Sometimes I *hate* my father.'' Misery weighted her shoulders. She wanted more than anything to crawl into the tub with Ric and let him hold her. ''I loved him. I can't stand thinking he might have murdered Bobby. Bobby didn't deserve to die. But no matter how many times I tell myself it was an accident, it doesn't feel like an accident. And it just wears on me and grinds me down.''

''Ah, Laney…''

''Whenever I see Tom, I want to tell him. I really do. But I'm so scared that he'll force Uncle King to investigate. Do you know what that would do to Mama? Daddy was her whole world. How can she live with knowing he's a murderer? And what about my brother and sister? Or Jodi? I feel like I'm betraying Bobby by not telling, but I don't know what to do. Please, Ric, don't let all this come out. Convince Tom to stop. Please.''

"Go on into the trailer and wait for me. I'm turning into a prune here."

She sniffed and swiped her hot eyes. She wished she could read his reaction. He didn't seem condemning or horrified, though, and it gave her hope.

RIC ENTERED the trailer. Before he could shut the door, Buster slipped inside. "Buster!" he snapped. "Feet." The dog froze in his tracks, his ears drooping and his eyes rolling. Ric reached for a towel and another spasm ripped through his lower back. A grunt escaped.

Elaine gasped. "Are you all right?"

"Do me a favor. Wipe off Buster's feet." He massaged the shrieking muscles with the heel of his hand. Deep, slow breathing helped some.

Eyeing Ric with concern, Elaine cleaned the mud from the dog's paws. "Did you hurt yourself? Are you okay?"

"Got too ambitious hauling lumber today. I'll be fine." He held the wall and used his toes and heels to work off his shoes. Hot spikes jabbed his spine. Nasty fingers of pain clawed paths through his thighs. Soaking in the hot tub had helped, but not enough. "Excuse me for being a poor host, but I have to lie down." Elaine grasped his arm.

Resentment pinged him. He was strong. He'd always been strong. He refused to let a few aches and pains turn him into a couch potato. She wrapped an arm around his waist. He let some of his weight rest on her. Together they hobbled into the tiny bedroom. She helped him lie flat on the narrow bed. He glowered at the ceiling.

"What can I get you?"

He pointed at the bathroom. "Big bottle in the medicine cabinet. Ibuprofen." He didn't want her seeing the prescription bottles, but he hurt too much to fetch his own pills. Fortunately these spasm attacks rarely lasted more than a few hours.

She brought the medicine and a glass of water. Without asking, she slipped an arm under his neck and gently raised his head. His cheek pressed her bosom. She had small breasts, but they were very nice. Not a good direction for his thoughts to travel, considering he wore knit sweatpants and no underwear.

He mustered thoughts about baseball and cutting wood, any non-sexual image, while he swallowed pills and gulped water. She dabbed at his wet chin with a tissue. He couldn't think about baseball when she smelled like heaven, and her big brown eyes trapped him like quicksand.

"Thank you, nurse." She lowered him to the pillow. He hungrily relished every millisecond of contact. He'd been celibate since his injury. Quite frankly, it sucked.

"You never did tell me about your accident."

He glanced at a shadow box hanging on the wall. It contained his Silver Star and Bronze Star medals. His Purple Hearts were in a box shoved under the bed. The sight dampened rising desire. Some hero he'd been. "It wasn't an accident, exactly. I got blown up."

She flinched and grimaced. "How?"

"I was on patrol when our Humvee hit a mine. I still don't know who planted it. Hard to tell the good guys from the bad guys anymore."

She stroked his arm. "That's so awful."

She didn't know the half of it. He still suffered nightmares. "I survived. Unlike the kid driving. He was only nineteen."

"Oh, Ric, that's so sad. I'm sorry."

Not half as sorry as he was.

"It's not so bad. At first the doctors weren't sure I'd ever walk again." He folded his fingers over her hand, reveling in the velvety softness of her skin. "Stuff happens. Nothing to do except pick yourself up and go on." He'd like to pick her up...

Just his luck. He got her alone in his bedroom, and he couldn't even move. Refusing to think about what might have been, he sniffed the air. The savory smell of chile made his stomach growl. "Can you stay a while? Where's Jodi?"

"She went to Steamboat Springs with some friends. A ski weekend. I can stay."

The girl had assured him that next to horses, skiing was her true love. He wished he could take her skiing. "You're a nice mom," he said.

Her lovely smile was a better reward than a thousand medals. "Thank you."

"Would you mind feeding me? I have a pot of stew on the stove. Join me. It's pretty good."

"It would be my pleasure."

He listened to her bustle around the trailer. Along with being a good mother, she'd been a good daughter, too. It must have cost her dearly to confess how she felt about her father. He knew too well what it was like to hate a parent. He'd been six years old when his mother deserted him. At odd moments, the old hatred popped up, accompanied by guilt and a bleak sense of betrayal. It never fully went away.

She brought a tray with two bowls, a plate of crackers, a jar of pickled jalapeño peppers and glasses of water. She set the tray beside him, left the bedroom and returned with a chair. All business, she helped him prop up on pillows. She handled him with an ease that didn't seem possible considering she couldn't weigh much more than a hundred pounds, and he weighed more than two hundred. He commented on her strength.

"You're a lot easier to manhandle than a calf is. Especially since you aren't bellowing for mama. Comfy?"

Not really, but he'd survive. "Food, please."

She handed him a bowl.

The first bite of chile made her choke. She gulped water. "I forgot how hot you like food. Whew! That's good stuff." Her eyes watered, and her face turned red.

"Jalapeños, please." He chuckled, and urged her to keep piling on the peppers. He ate a big bite. It wasn't as tasty as Consuela's, or even his uncle's, but still not bad. "So, do you really think your father is a murderer?"

She froze with a spoon poised before her mouth. She blinked rapidly. Her expression went stiff and cold. "Isn't that what you think?"

"Nope."

Her mouth fell open.

"Tate has talked to people all over the valley. Tom's private eye has been digging in nooks and crannies I didn't even know existed. We can't find any motive for murder."

"So why are you checking out Axton? He doesn't have a motive."

Ric considered carefully what he needed to say. He had a good relationship with Jodi. He had grown to treasure every moment he spent with her. He was also developing a nice friendship with Elaine. He didn't want to risk losing either by scaring her.

"On the day of the shooting, I talked to Bobby at the Track Shack. He told me he had a problem."

She dropped her spoon in the bowl. At her feet, Buster pricked his ears, while his nostrils sought the scent of spilled food.

"He didn't tell me what the problem was or with who. All he said was, it was personal. He called it shabby."

"Why would he tell you he had a problem without saying what it was?"

Careful, he warned himself. "I could see something was bothering him so I asked. He didn't want to tell me about it."

"I see."

She looked so relieved it hurt his heart. Logic said there were good reasons not to disrupt Jodi's life by revealing her paternity. He sure didn't want his daughter going through the same hell he'd gone through as a kid. Emotionally, however, it hurt that Elaine didn't trust him.

"An earring in your dad's car puts a whole new slant on things. If Del had a mistress, that's a motive."

She bristled. "The earring isn't proof of anything. He drove a lot of clients around to show houses."

"Don't get all defensive. Besides, it's hard to imagine your dad having an affair and nobody knowing about it."

She turned her head and fidgeted.

A hunch said she was remembering their secret affair. The first time he'd gone to her home to pick her up for a date, Del Crowder had pitched a fit. "No bastard like you is hustling my girl for his cheap thrills," Del had said. He'd flat out forbidden Elaine from having anything to do with Ric.

Someone had known Elaine and Ric had continued meeting on the sly, and she'd ended up pregnant as a result. That someone had threatened to tell Ric about Jodi if Bobby didn't back off. Ric had come to realize that it couldn't have been Del. He wouldn't have handed Ric am-

munition to make trouble for the McClintock clan—and
Bobby had known it. A mistress, however, might make
such a threat.

Or a greedy business partner. "Axton has a motive."

Her brows knit in a scowl, then she laughed. "That's
absurd! Axton Cross is the nicest man in the world."

Ric couldn't disagree about the nice part. During his
mission to scope out the realty, he'd enjoyed the hours
he'd spent with the real estate broker. The man had a
wicked sense of humor and a nose for ferreting out a bargain. Axton had gotten Ric a good deal on this property
and managed to make the seller feel satisfied, too.

"He might have stumbled onto a pretty good scam."

"He's sweet and generous. Everyone likes him. He even
kept the Crowder Realty name as a tribute to Daddy."

"Insurance." He paused, waiting for her to catch up.
"Twenty years ago, Axton's wife died in a car accident.
He collected insurance."

"He murdered his wife?"

He wagged an admonishing finger. "A few years after
that, he was a partner in an import-export business in San
Francisco. A warehouse containing their inventory burned
to the ground. The company had been in big financial trouble before the fire. Insurance paid off very profitably."

She shifted uncomfortably on the chair. "Accidents happen."

"Then, Axton moved to Denver. He formed a partner-
ship with a home builder. The market collapsed. The two
were scrambling to save their shirts. Then lo and behold,
the partner goes skiing, hits a tree and Axton collects insurance again."

Her slender throat worked with a hard swallow.

"Like Tate says, two incidents make a coincidence.

More than that forms a pattern. Axton collected half a million dollars when your father died.''

She snorted and flapped a hand. ''So what? That's standard business practice when the company is so dependent on its owners. The money went to business debts, not into Axton's pocket.''

Ric still hadn't figured out exactly how Axton could have known about Jodi. In retrospect, he and Elaine had been pretty dumb to think they'd kept their affair secret. King McClintock himself had caught them together and threatened Ric with jail and Elaine with telling her father. Anyone who could count could have figured out there was something fishy about the timing of Jodi's birth. Axton might have heard some gossip and on a hunch used it to blackmail Bobby.

''It seems kind of odd that Axton would move from Denver, a hot real estate market, to take a job as an agent in a piddly little town. Then, less than two years later, Del takes him on as a full partner.''

''But nobody murdered Daddy! It was a heart attack. And not exactly an unexpected one either. He had heart problems for years.''

''What if Bobby found out about the other partnerships and the insurance money? Was Del aware of Axton's history?''

Her gaze turned distant, and her forehead wrinkled in concentration. ''I really do not know. But if Bobby knew about it, he would have told me.''

''Unless he wasn't sure. Bobby never tolerated gossip. If he heard some dirt and didn't trust the source, I can see him talking to Axton about it. If the man turned mean or Bobby caught him lying, then Bobby would have gone to your dad.''

''And Axton shot Bobby to shut him up?'' She shook

her head so hard her hair whipped her cheeks. "Unbelievable!"

"Whether you believe it or not, Tom is pursuing it. If he finds one shred of hard evidence, then Tate will force your uncle to reopen the investigation." He snorted a dry laugh. "If King doesn't fire him first."

"If it turns out Daddy *is* a murderer and a cheat or a thief or whatever else, Mama will be crushed. Marlee and Davis will be devastated. Jodi will be, too."

"I can't let a murderer walk. Can you?"

She pinched the bridge of her nose and closed her eyes. He ached for her, but knew of no way to ease her pain. He touched her knee. The bedroom, small to begin with, felt far too intimate. He longed to touch her face, to kiss her.

"I don't want to cause you or your family any more agony than you've already suffered. Honest to God, Laney, I do not. I agree with you, if Del did murder Bobby, then justice hit fast and hard. Let it lie. But…" He stared, willing her to look at him. "If there's a killer running loose, he has to be caught. Talk to Tate. Tell him about the trash and the earring. In return, listen to what he has to say."

"Then what?"

"Then we'll decide what to do about Tom."

Chapter Five

Forcing a big smile, Elaine waved to her mother. Lillian drove out of the church parking lot. Usually they went to church in the same car. On this Sunday, Elaine claimed she was staying in town to have lunch with her friend Alice. That she'd refrained from mentioning she first meant to speak to Tate Raleigh sat ill with her. It worsened the tummyache she'd suffered since talking to Ric. There were too many secrets, too many lies, and all of them were spinning out of control.

She refused to believe Axton Cross had anything to do with the tragedy at the lodge. The note she'd found in Bobby's pocket proved it. Axton hadn't known Ric or the circumstances of Jodi's birth. The note was tucked in her purse. Revealing it meant explaining what Bobby and she had done to Ric. She'd only show it if she absolutely had to.

What a mess.

She drove up Main Street and parked across from the Track Shack Bar and Grill. The stubby building squatted next to railroad tracks that hadn't been used in over fifty years. It had been Bobby's favorite place to meet with other cattlemen for coffee and conversation. Elaine could count on one hand the number of times she'd been inside.

Forget it, she told herself. This was nuts. Who cared if Tom Greene hired a hundred private eyes and ferreted out skeletons in every closet in McClintock?

An opposing voice nagged that Bobby deserved better than dark secrets and shameful lies. If the possibility existed that a murderer had escaped, she was duty bound to pursue it.

She wanted to throw up.

Hugging herself against an icy wind, she crossed the street as quickly as her high heels allowed. At the door, she shied away from the handle. The bar was closed on Sundays. So, if it was locked, forget it. She'd go to Alice's house. If it wasn't locked, then it was a sign to continue. She tugged the door handle and it opened.

"God help me," she whispered and walked inside.

Ric sat at the only table that didn't have chairs stacked atop it. An aroma of strong coffee and hot grease made her stomach churn. Ric's gaze dropped to her legs. He raised an eyebrow. She tugged the hem of her suit jacket and smoothed a hand over her skirt.

"Hi," she said.

Ric stood. "I was afraid you wouldn't show."

She was relieved to see that though he moved stiffly, Ric didn't seem to be in pain.

"You look nice," he said.

The compliment made her fluttery. She patted her wind-blown hair, bemused by a sudden desire to apply fresh lipstick. He looked nice himself, with his lean, muscular torso emphasized by an olive green sweater. It wasn't right that the mere sight of him made her giddy.

"Where's Tate?" She settled on the chair he offered.

"Frying up some burgers. Have you thought about what we talked about?"

"I haven't been able to do anything else." She set her

purse on the floor and tucked it, and its damning missive, under her chair. She should tell Ric about Jodi, but she feared his reaction. If he got angry and cut himself off from Jodi, the girl would be crushed. Or he could do worse by insisting on telling Jodi the truth, then Lillian would know, and Tom and Gwen would know. Folks would whisper and gossip. Things were better the way they were.

Tate pushed backward through swinging batwing doors. He carried a tray piled with hamburgers, steaming French fries and bottled condiments. He wore his deputy's uniform: tan shirt, black tie, dark trousers, equipment belt and shiny badge. The uniform drove home how very serious this situation was. Were it only Tom Greene making noise, she could pity him for his grief and pray he'd give up his obsession and find peace. That Tate, who had no personal stake, involved himself at the risk of his job and standing in town, meant that no amount of hoping and wishing would make this situation go away.

"Hey, there!" Tate called. "Glad you could make it. Will you join us for lunch?"

She doubted if she could choke down a sliver of lettuce. "I'm not hungry, thank you. But do go ahead."

"Your loss. I fry a mean burger."

Ric began dressing a hamburger with mustard and ketchup. "I haven't seen Junior in a while. Where's he keeping himself these days?"

"Fishing. If he isn't fishing, he's thinking about it."

"You know, if it wasn't for Junior, I never would have made it through high school." Ric laughed softly and pointed to the end of the bar closest to the door. "I learned all I know about algebra sitting right there."

"I'm surprised Bobby didn't help you," Elaine said, thankful for the small talk. "He was a math whiz."

"That's the problem. It was too easy for him. I couldn't

follow what he was saying. You wouldn't have believed it, Tate, but Bobby could do calculations in his head faster than a computer.''

''He could have been a top accountant or engineer. But he hated being cooped up indoors.'' Elaine smiled at the good memories. ''It used to drive Daddy crazy. He'd have books spread all over the table, trying to figure out how come they wouldn't balance. Bobby would saunter by and say something like, 'You forgot to carry the two,' and he'd be right. He kept all the books for the ranch.'' She sighed, wishing Bobby were here, hating that he wasn't.

''I sure liked him,'' Tate said. ''Ric tells me you might know something about the shooting.''

Tension returned, and so did the tummyache. Elaine drew a deep breath, then repeated to the deputy what she'd told Ric. She pulled her purse onto her lap and opened it. The note was in an envelope, but she could not make herself bring it out. She found the earring and placed it on the table. It was a clip-on style with rhinestones glittering in the shape of a flower.

''You're sure it isn't your mother's?'' Tate asked. He turned the earring in the light.

''Mama wouldn't be caught dead wearing junk jewelry. Besides, her ears are pierced.''

''Hmm. And you went through all his papers at home?''

Unable to look either man in the eye, she confessed, ''I even searched his bedroom when Mama was out.'' She rubbed her aching throat. ''Daddy had a few enemies. He was a bit of a snob.'' A glimpse of Ric's skeptical expression made her face warm. ''All right, he was a horrible snob. He could be rather...nasty at times. If tenants were late paying rent, he evicted them. He was immune to sob stories. He liked to play one-upmanship games with agents from other realties. He was a good man, but he had his dark side. If he was doing something illegal, there are plenty of people who would love to tell you all about it.''

She gazed unhappily at the earring. ''He could be very charming. He liked to flirt. Mama didn't mind, she considered it harmless. I hate to think he'd cheat, but it's not impossible. He was handsome and aggressive. Not to mention, very wealthy. Some women might have taken his flirting seriously.''

''Does he have a history of affairs?'' Tate asked.

''I can't imagine Mama keeping quiet about something like that. She isn't shy.''

''I can attest to that,'' Tate said with a chuckle. ''She's a set of fireworks all by herself. So if she did catch him playing footsie with another woman, what would she do? Divorce?''

''I honestly don't know.'' It made her shudder to even imagine such a scenario.

''Del struck me as the sort who liked being rich.''

Elaine had to agree.

''A divorce would have cost him plenty.''

''Daddy made good money from the realty, and he owned fifteen rental properties. Still, it's a pittance compared to Mama's holdings.'' This was so awful. With every word out of her mouth, her father's motive for murder looked clearer. She turned on the chair to avoid the smell of food and the sight of the men eating.

Tate stroked his chin, and his eyes narrowed beneath a thoughtful scowl. ''If I caught my father-in-law fooling around, there ain't no way I'd confront him. The wife would have a fit. Be all kinds of yelling and crying. I'd end up being the bad guy. Uh-uh, not a chance. I'd pass the buck to my old lady and let her handle it. It's a guy thing. Why didn't Bobby tell you?''

Many a long, lonely night she'd lain in bed and asked

herself that very question. "I guess he wanted to protect my feelings. Or he didn't want me telling Mama. I don't know. I thought we talked about everything."

"I can't buy it."

She slumped on the chair. "Bobby probably wanted Daddy to quit before Mama caught him."

"Without you even suspecting?"

"Do you think I'm lying? Have you any idea how hard this is? It's my father we're talking about! I loved him!"

Ric took her hand and gave it a gentle squeeze. "We're looking for the truth."

She jerked her hand from his. "Don't play good cop bad cop with me." She swallowed hard against the thickness growing in her throat. "I adored my father. I know his faults. I'm not blind. But I still loved him. Now he's gone. He cannot answer for what he did. Mama will have to do that. Is that what you want? Do you want people whispering about her? Calling Daddy a murderer? A cheat? They were married thirty-five years. No matter what he did, he loved her. If Mama finds out about this, it'll be like killing him all over again."

She pushed the earring closer to Tate. "Suppose Tom's private eye finds a woman who claims she was Daddy's mistress. There's the motive. Then what happens? You force Uncle King to properly investigate the shooting as a murder? You find evidence that Daddy pulled the trigger on purpose, that he wanted Bobby dead? Tell me what good can come from it."

The men exchanged a look. Tate asked, "What about Axton—"

The door opened and Tate called over his shoulder, "Sorry, we're closed."

Sheriff King McClintock strode into the bar. He wore his hat pulled down low and his coat collar turned up. His boot steps made the floor vibrate. Elaine noticed the way Ric stiffened, alert and wary.

"Well, well, what have we got here?" King cocked back his hat with a thumb. He planted himself behind Tate's shoulder, forcing the deputy to twist in order to see. "I thought that was your Jeep, honey. Slumming?"

"Cup of coffee, sheriff?" Tate asked. He made as if to push his chair back, but King blocked him. Tate squeezed sideways away from the table. King propped a foot on the vacated seat and rested his arms on his thigh.

Irritated, Elaine cleared her throat. "Am I illegally parked, Uncle King?"

He chuckled. "I was just seeing what you're up to, honey. Seems to me you're keeping strange company. Don't think I've ever seen you in this place. Especially not on a Sunday."

King *knew* they were talking about Bobby's death. Elaine felt it vibrating in her bones. That he was acting so belligerent said he was afraid. She glanced at Tate. He looked a tad fearful himself. King could suspend Tate, or fire him. He could do worse, too, by harassing him about the bar, or even coming up with some pretense to shut it down.

"I'm visiting, talking with friends." She plucked a French fry from the basket. "Having lunch."

King wasn't paying attention to her. His flinty eyes bored into Ric. "Blood will tell. I can always find you in a bar."

Ric's neck and shoulders seemed to swell. Hot spots flared on his cheekbones.

Elaine straightened on the chair and tugged at her skirt. King had a special dislike for rowdy young men. He enjoyed nothing better than breaking up parties, pulling over souped-up cars and strutting through the video arcade in search of underage drinkers and smokers. His theory was, "Keep an eagle eye on the young, and by the time they can vote, they're good citizens." He took full credit for the valley's low crime rate.

Trouble was, he didn't know when to quit.

Tate handed King a cup of coffee. "Do you need me, sir?"

"Just satisfying some curiosity. What you got in that cup, Ric? Getting snockered on the Sabbath is bad form."

"Coffee," Ric replied. His voice was calm, but his eyes were stormy. He looked as if tossing the coffee at the sheriff were a distinct possibility.

Elaine seethed with embarrassment. Of all people, King had no call to be casting stones about drinking. He liked to pretend that no one knew his alcoholism had destroyed his marriage and lost him custody of his three children, or that he regularly attended AA meetings.

King had always hated Ric. It was unfair. Ric couldn't help what his mother had been. Perhaps he'd worn his hair a bit too long when he was a teenager. Perhaps he'd had an attitude. But what teenage boy didn't? Ric had never been a criminal. And look at the wonderful things he'd done with his life. A decorated soldier who'd served honorably and been wounded in the line of duty. He was gaining a reputation as a fine carpenter, and a hard worker who charged fair prices.

She stood. In high heels, she was almost King's height. "Is there something specific you want?"

He dropped his foot to the floor. His eyes widened. "I— I was just checking to see you're okay."

"I don't need you checking to see if I'm okay." She dropped a hand on Ric's shoulder. "I certainly don't need you insulting my friends."

His mouth opened and closed. Heady power coursed through her, putting steel in her spine.

"May I speak to you outside?" Without awaiting his answer, she stalked away, her heels cracking against the linoleum. She pushed through the door. The wind had increased, exhilarating her, fueling her indignation. She stomped her feet and slapped her upper arms.

Finally, King joined her on the sidewalk.

"You are embarrassing me!"

Wind, or perhaps discomfort, reddened his cheeks. His big mustache twitched. "I know what's going on, young lady. I don't like it."

"Oh? And what's that?"

"You and your mama both are going plum out of your minds. Bad enough Walt Buchanan's sniffing around Lillian like some love-sick calf, but here you are mooning over that trashy boy."

"Ric is not a boy. He isn't trash either."

"Ain't never been married, living out in the boonies like some survivalist nut. Every time I turn around, there he is with Jodi. Ain't there any sense in your head? Don't you know nothing about grown men with a taste for little girls? Hear about it all the time. Predators pick up lonely women just so's they can get at the kids."

She was horrified he'd even think such a thing.

"That boy hauled trouble like a tail when he was young. Leopards don't change spots, you know."

It struck her what his real problem was. He hadn't thought Ric Buchanan good enough for the high and mighty McClintock family when Elaine was eighteen. He didn't think Ric was good enough now. He sounded just like her father.

"I find it gross and disgusting that you'd even think such a thing, Uncle King. Ric likes Jodi."

"I bet he does."

She caught the undercurrent of fear in his words. A fear he was trying to cover with sarcasm and bluster. She guessed he knew about Tom's private eye. She bet he knew a whole lot of other things, too, such as what old secrets might be revealed if the full truth were known about the shooting. King either knew Ric was Jodi's father, or had a darned good suspicion. And it would just kill him if it became common knowledge.

"Ric and Walt are my friends. I will not tolerate your insults."

He shook a thick finger at her. "Don't be pulling that queen of the world act. You ain't your mama."

She lifted her chin.

"That boy's a troublemaker. I catch him even spitting on the sidewalk and I'll toss his can in jail."

She kept quiet. A car slowed in passing. King shot the driver a hard look. The car speeded up.

"You lie down with dogs, you end up with fleas, Elaine."

Thanks for the cliché of the day. "Will you be having supper with me and Mama at the ranch this evening? Perhaps we can have a family discussion."

He scowled and harrumphed. She'd called his bluff. Were he truly serious about suspecting Ric of pedophilia, he'd welcome the chance to voice his concerns to Lillian.

"See you later," she said and went back inside. Her muscles tensed. She half expected him to follow and drag her out of the bar. When he didn't, she let out a relieved sigh.

She met Ric's eyes. He was angry, and she didn't blame him. Her uncle had never treated him fairly. Nor had her father.

Her father... Daddy had never questioned Jodi's paternity. He'd never made a single comment about the hasty marriage. That he might have known was something she'd never allowed herself to think about.

She couldn't believe how stupid she'd been. Del Crowder hadn't written that desperate note to Bobby. He'd have cut out his tongue before handing Ric Buchanan an invitation to join the family.

"Laney?" Ric asked.

Daddy didn't write it! she almost cried out. She curled her lips between her teeth.

If her father hadn't written it, then someone else had. Someone with a motive for murder.

"I apologize for Uncle King," she said. "I'm really embarrassed." She slid an apologetic look at Tate. She suspected the deputy would be pulling onerous duty until King vented his vindictiveness. "Tate, is it too late to properly investigate the shooting?"

"There's no statute of limitations on murder."

"What do you need to do? What haven't you done already?"

He looked as eager as a cutting horse facing a steer. "I'd really like to get inside the lodge."

If her mother ever found out what she was up to, Elaine was dead meat. "You've got it."

Tate's eyebrows reached for the sky. His mouth curved in a surprised smile. "How much has the lodge been used in the past eighteen months?"

She shook her head. "Mama locked it up and chained the road. No one has been there since Bobby and Daddy passed away. I'll let you inside and you can take pictures or fingerprints or whatever else you want to do. But on one condition."

Ric folded his arms over his chest and cocked his head. He seemed skeptical. Renewed anger at her uncle flared in her breast. She decided she was going to talk to Mama anyway about King's rude behavior toward the Buchanans.

Tate looked ready to agree to anything. "What do you want?"

"That you find a way to make Tom Greene back off. His health isn't good and Gwen is worried about him. Not to mention the harm he can do to Axton Cross. Rumors have a way of turning into runaway trains around this valley. All that insurance stuff is very suspicious, but if Axton is innocent, gossip will ruin him. Tom won't listen to me, or to Gwen. He'll listen to you, though."

"That's debatable," Tate said. "But I'll give it my best shot."

She sneaked a peek at her purse and suffered a pang of guilt. The note was evidence. If Tate didn't find anything at the lodge, then she'd show it to him. She'd have no choice.

"Let me know when a good time for you is. It'll be easier for me if it's during school hours. That way I don't have to worry about Jodi." She checked her watch. "I need to run. Alice is holding lunch for me."

Tate gave her a funny look. He couldn't possibly be miffed at her mentioning Alice. Tate and Alice had dated for a short while, but she'd quickly tired of being squeezed into his busy schedule. Between the bar and the sheriff's department, he worked eighteen-hour days.

Ric stood and touched the small of her back with a hand. "I'll walk you to your car."

He opened the door for her. She leaned her head out to look up and down the street.

"Looking for someone?" Ric asked with a grin.

"King has it out for you. Better watch your step."

"He always has it out for me." As if it were the most

natural thing in the world, he slipped an arm around her shoulders, shielding her from the wind.

It felt natural, and right. He walked her to the Jeep and opened the door for her.

"I really do apologize for King. I don't know why he acts so obnoxious. Usually he's a nice guy. Are you still mad?"

"Nah. I am worried about Tate though. He could lose his job." He jerked a thumb over his shoulder. "He barely breaks even with the Shack. He needs the income."

"Worse comes to worst, I'll put in a word with Mama. She doesn't like it when King throws his weight around."

He rested an arm on the top of the door. Wind ruffled his hair. Sunshine sparked gold against the thick strands. The olive sweater deepened the blue of his eyes. Romantic notions tugged at her and she longed for simpler days.

"Uhm...?" He scuffed his boot against the asphalt. "I was wondering...?"

"Yes?"

"There's a restaurant in Durango. They bring in some pretty good bands on Saturday nights. The food isn't bad either."

"Are you asking for a date?"

His boot scuffed again. He tapped his fingers on the Jeep door. Finally, he lifted his head. "Sounds like we're kids again. Yeah, a date."

His bashfulness touched her and made her feel a little giddy, too. "I'd like that."

He seemed surprised, then his radiant smile took her breath away. "Next Saturday then." He stepped back and used both hands to shut the door. He gave her a little wave then crossed the street, his step jaunty.

A date with Ric Buchanan. She patted her breast, pleased he'd asked, and rather astonished she'd accepted.

She watched him enter the Track Shack. It struck her: she
liked him. Way back when, she'd fancied herself madly in
love, and certainly she'd been madly in lust. He'd been
her dream-lover, filtered through the stars in her eyes. She
hadn't truly known him. Over the past eighteen months
she'd come to know him as he actually was. She liked
very much what she saw.

She fumbled in her purse for her keys. The envelope
containing the threatening note transfixed her and good
feelings fled. She peeked at the Track Shack, then fumbled
the note out of the envelope.

Maybe some folks ought to mind their own business!
Especially folks in glass houses! Ric Buchanan is
back in town. How would he like knowing what you
really did to him? You don't know what you think
you know, so you better just keep your big mouth
shut! You go blabbing and I'll do some blabbing myself!

Gooseflesh prickled her arms. What a horrendous idiot
she'd been to even consider her father had written this.
Common sense said to give the note to Tate, let him find
the typewriter on which it was written.

Then she'd have to explain to Ric what she and Bobby
had done to him.

She looked up and down Main Street. On this quiet Sunday afternoon, everything was closed except the gas station. The town looked sweet and old-fashioned with its
hodgepodge of building styles and covered sidewalks. The
feed store had wooden hitching posts out front. During the
summer, it wasn't unusual to see horses tethered there.
She'd lived here all her life and never felt the slightest
urge to move anywhere else. If she were struck blind, she

could navigate by familiar sounds and smells. She knew everyone in the valley, if not by name, then by sight. Friends, relatives, neighbors, all of them generous folks willing to lend a helping hand. People she went to church with; people she sat on committees with for the Parent Teacher Organization and community events.

One of them might be a murderer.

Shivering, she locked the doors.

Chapter Six

Ric hadn't been to the lodge hidden up at the northern-most edge of McClintock Ranch in a long time. He drove nearly half a mile past the turn-off on a bumpy dirt road before realizing his mistake. He had to drive a ways before the road widened enough for him to turn around. All the while he watched out for ranch hands who might report his presence to Lillian, or to King.

The road to the lodge had nearly disappeared under weeds and encroaching scrub oaks. Branches slapped the truck sides. Pine cones crunched beneath the wheels. He inched over potholes and washouts. He reached a stout chain stretched across the road. He left the truck idling and examined the chain. It was rusty, but solid and locked. He settled in to wait.

It was quiet in this patch of forest, with trees so thick they blocked views of nearby mountains. Crows squabbled in the distance.

A chill rippled down his spine. People disappeared all the time in the Rockies. Planes went down and were never recovered. Hunters wandered away, never to be seen again. Bobby's murderer had killed once to cover his crimes; no telling what he'd do if he suspected Ric, Tom and Tate—and Elaine—were on his trail.

The sound of an approaching engine both relieved Ric and made him wary. He felt around in the jumble of tools on the passenger side floor and came up with a pry bar. He laid it on the seat beside him.

Elaine parked her Jeep behind the truck and hopped out. She waggled a set of keys at him. "I'd hoped to be early to open the place."

He drank in the sight of her while she worked a key into the rusty lock. In snug jeans and a chambray shirt, topped by a flannel-lined denim jacket, she appeared young and carefree. A pair of glitter-shot barrettes held hair off her face. Thoughts of murder faded, replaced by a memory of the time he and she had sneaked up to the lodge. It was the only time they'd spent an entire night together. She'd fallen asleep in his arms, and he'd awakened to the sight of her curled beside him. He'd loved her body, the alluring noises she made and the intoxicating scent of her silky skin. He'd loved the way she would prop herself on his chest and demand he reveal every thought going through his mind.

A few years ago he'd read an article that claimed married men made more money and lived longer than single men. He'd laughed when he read it. It didn't seem ridiculous now. With Elaine, any and everything seemed possible. Without her he was just marking time.

The lock opened with a rusty squeal. She hauled the chain off the road. When she turned around, the illusion of carefree girlishness shattered. Her face was so pale her freckles looked like ink spots. Circles beneath her eyes gave her a haunted expression. She waved for him to go ahead.

He drove up the rough road and around a bend.

Calling this place a lodge had been another of Del Crowder's affectations. It was a squat, rustic log cabin with a wide porch that was almost bigger than the interior. Ponderosa pines blocked the sun. Snow covered the roof despite temperatures in the forties.

Elaine joined him at the base of the porch steps. Frowning at the door, she jammed her hands into her back pockets. "I don't know if I can do this."

"No need to subject yourself—"

"I have to." She dragged the toe of her boot through the dried weeds. Thin blades of delicate green grass pushed through the thin soil. Her chin trembled as if she were fighting tears. "I keep having this recurrent dream where I see Bobby. He has his back to me and I call him. I know he hears me, but he walks away. He won't even look at me."

"He loved you, Laney."

"I know," she said with a sigh. "But this is all my fault. I could have pushed Uncle King. When I heard his ruling, I got so sick I couldn't even get out of bed for two days. I knew it was a lie. I can't even look Tom Greene in the face. At the same time, the idea of everybody knowing Daddy is a murderer makes me want to die." She swiped at her nose and sniffed.

"Marlee is graduating from veterinary school this year. She'll be working for Doc Colton. She's so excited, she calls me two or three times a week. 'I wish Daddy could see me graduate,' she says. 'Wouldn't Daddy be proud?'" Eyes closed, she shook her head. "My tongue is sore from biting it. To keep from yelling that he shot my husband and who cares if he's proud or not."

He slid an arm around her shoulders. "Ah, Laney."

"If I tell, I hurt people. If I don't tell, I hurt people. Sometimes I just want to run away and never look back."

"Does Lillian have any idea what you're going through?"

She lifted her face. "Sometimes I think she suspects. Once, she asked me straight out if I forgave Daddy for shooting Bobby. I chickened out and changed the subject. Then last Christmas my brother was talking about what to do with Daddy's gun collection. Mama got real angry. Totally out of the blue she pitched a royal fit. I was shocked. Afterward, when I thought about it, it seemed like she was terrified."

"She could have the same suspicions you do," he offered. "It might do you both good to talk about it."

"I can't. Unless I'm forced to, I just can't."

He didn't blame her for not wanting to be the bearer of bad news. He worked his fingers through her hair, separating windblown tangles, luxuriating in its texture. There were a few silver strands among the dark brown.

Her mouth fixated him. Her lips had a natural rose tint, and were sweetly molded, the indent in her upper lip barely there. The smell of flowery shampoo filled his nose, but beneath it, like some seductive undernote, he could smell her unique scent that always reminded him of vanilla. Her eyes were liquid, drowning pools, drawing him in until he no longer felt the chill breeze or heard the chirping, screeing, clacking and cawing of insects and birds.

He bent his head. The voice of reason told him to cut it out, but other urges yelled at him to kiss her or die.

When his lips touched hers, she stiffened under his arm. One slim hand pressed against his chest. Still, he couldn't make himself stop. He kissed her gently, his back muscles on the verge of shredding from the force it took to not sweep her into his arms and ravish her. Soft, so soft and so very sweet.

Then she was kissing him back. Her hand worked its tender way upward to rest beneath his shirt collar. When he opened his mouth, her lips parted, too. He inhaled her breath, mingling it with his own.

He kissed her harder, his mind awash with memories of the bed inside the lodge. The too-soft mattress that threatened to swallow them alive. The smell of pine sap and wood smoke and mice. The scent of her arousal burning his blood and waking every nerve.

The intrusion of an approaching vehicle almost made him cuss. He dropped his arm. She stepped away. Color had returned to her face. She nervously patted her hair, then the base of her throat. Her lips glowed with faint moisture. When she licked them, his pulse rattled his eardrums.

Kissing her was even better than he remembered.

Tate arrived in his old beater Ford Bronco. The man was a nickel away from the poorhouse. That he was willing to risk a steady income and public censure drove home how very seriously the deputy believed there was more to the shooting than an accident.

"Am I late?" Tate called. He carried a large Styrofoam cup of coffee and a nine-volt flashlight.

"We just got here," Elaine said.

Tate sipped coffee and wandered around the yard. He appeared aimless, but Ric guessed he was studying the layout.

"Is there any other way a vehicle could get here?" he asked Elaine.

"Not unless it has wings." She pointed east. "There are two big ravines between here and Branch Road. Up north it's all national forest. You can make it here cross-country on foot or horseback, but not in a vehicle."

"Who's been inside since it happened?"

"As far as I know, only the ranch manager. He closed

it up and made sure there was nothing around to attract bears. It doesn't look as if anybody has been here since.''

Tate gestured at the door.

Elaine swallowed hard. She sorted through the ring of keys and climbed onto the porch. She unlocked the door, pushed it open—the hinges creaked as if in pain—then stepped aside. Tate handed them each a pair of latex gloves. He turned on the flashlight and entered.

"Going in?" Ric asked her.

"I have to know," she whispered and walked inside.

Ric passed a nervous hand through his hair; his throat felt tight. The gloves made his hands look eerie in the gloom. The lodge was as dark as dusk except where Tate's flashlight shone. It smelled musty, rousing images of ancient tombs.

Elaine opened wooden shutters. Window panes were so dirty the light seeped inside with a yellow tinge. Dust swirled whenever one of them moved. A large stain marked the wooden floor planks. He recognized the unmistakable rusty brown of dried blood. Bobby's blood. Ric's gut lurched.

"Are you okay, ma'am?" Tate asked.

Elaine was staring at the stain on the floor, too. Ric touched her shoulder. She shuddered and turned away.

"Tell me about the lodge."

She hugged herself and kept her gaze fixed on the ceiling. "My grandfather built it in the thirties. At that time the only way to get here was on horseback. He'd bring friends up here for hunting parties. That's how Mama and Daddy met. He was the son of one of Granddad's hunting buddies."

Ric cast a baleful eye on the trophy heads mounted on the walls. There were several elk and deer heads with soot darkened antlers and a snarling bear showing ivory fangs.

His philosophy was, if it wasn't shooting at him, leave it be. Even if he did hunt, there was no way he'd have glass eyeballs staring down at him.

"I heard he came up here all the time," Tate said. "Even out of season."

"At the office, people were always coming in to discuss business. At home, there's Mama." She shrugged. "Mama likes to talk. And a shut door is a challenge to her. So when he wanted privacy, he came up here. He just seemed to need solitude every so often."

Tate studied an old-fashioned rotary telephone on a desk. "Did your mother ever come up here?"

"No. She calls this the boy's clubhouse."

"Did she ever suspect he was having an affair?"

Eyes wide and wary, she faced the deputy. The fingers on her right hand tip-tapped against her arm.

"I know it's unpleasant," Tate said. "But this is the perfect setup for a guy who's fooling around. And you're the one who found the earring."

"There was one time…" She turned away and bent as if to examine a dusty rocking chair. She kept her gloved hands away from her sides, as if uncertain what to do with them. "Daddy and Bobby took Jodi to a boat show. Alice came over. She and I and Mama were drinking wine and, you know, girl stuff. Mama said the funniest thing. Not funny ha-ha, funny strange."

"Which was?" Tate prompted.

"She said if Daddy ever left her, it would be for a girl like Alice." She added quickly, "She didn't mean it, though."

"Then why do you bring it up?"

"Because you're asking!"

Ric could hear her agitation rising and took a step, but

stopped. Tate had to ask these questions. Elaine had to answer. Even if it caused her discomfort.

"Daddy flirted with Alice, and she flirted back. It was harmless. You know she isn't the type to fool around with a married man."

"How did Alice react to your mother's comment?"

She lifted a shoulder in a quick shrug. "She laughed it off."

"Any other women he seemed chummy with?"

"Linda." She laughed, sounding strained. "Linda was Daddy's right hand. She was his office manager for more than twenty years. I can't see them having an affair."

Ric chewed his inner cheek to keep from saying something obnoxiously sexist. No way would Del Crowder have risked his marriage for a rangy old sourpuss like Linda Pallo. The woman had all the charm of a drill sergeant. He couldn't imagine her even kissing a man, much less having an affair.

Tate made a shooing gesture. "If you would, wait outside for a little bit."

Ric took Elaine's arm and escorted her outside. She seemed relieved, but puzzled. She pulled off the gloves and eyed them in distaste.

Through the open door Ric watched Tate settle cross-legged on the floor near the place where Bobby had died. Tate set the coffee cup beside him.

"What is he doing?" Elaine asked.

"Some kind of detective magic, I guess."

They watched for a while, but all Tate did was sit, his back to them. Ric began to get cold so he wandered away. Elaine trailed him.

Behind the lodge was a corral and shed for pack horses, and the falling down remains of an ancient outhouse. He spotted the tracks of a black bear in a patch of snow. He pointed them out to Elaine. Hard packed trails led away through the forest in several directions. A squirrel chattered at them.

"I can't imagine how Daddy could have an affair," Elaine said. "You know how some people are. Always looking for dirt to gossip about. Besides, Tate is right. If Bobby had caught Daddy with a woman, he wouldn't have dared keep something like that from me."

"What would he have kept from you?" He'd like to have an affair. Right now. All this quiet and fresh, earthy forest air made it too easy to ponder kissing her again.

She walked aimlessly, her hands in her jacket pockets. "That's a tough one to answer. I don't think he ever deliberately withheld information from me." She turned to him. "He didn't tell me you were back in town."

They made a slow circuit around the lodge. Tate was still sitting. So they wandered and made small talk and finally ended up inside his truck. Ric hated the circumstances, but he enjoyed the opportunity to spend time with her. He desperately wanted to kiss her again.

TATE ASKED Ric and Elaine to come back inside the lodge. His brow furrowed in a scowl. "This is not right."

Ric and Elaine waited for him to elaborate.

Tate turned a slow circle, one arm outstretched, seeming to indicate each table and chair and the desk. He stopped, pointing at the door. "You might not want to listen to this, ma'am."

Elaine drew herself stiffly erect. "I have to."

"The sheriff called me to say he had a shooting and to bring my evidence kit. When I got here, another deputy was already inside and so were the paramedics. They were working on Del." He pointed to the floor. "Bobby was laying right there." Small stains led away from the big stain. "It was a mess. Men tracking blood, stuff moved around." He scowled ferociously at the door. "Del's revolver was laying on the floor over there. You can still see the chalk marks I made. I tried to do damage control, keeping people away from Bobby and making sure the scene wasn't contaminated any worse than it was. Everybody swore up and down they hadn't moved Bobby."

Tate made it too easy to see what had happened that night. Ric began feeling sick.

"I shot a roll of film. Del had passed by then, but the paramedics kept working on him while they took him away. Always the faint hope, you know? So anyway, the sheriff comes back in and sees me marking the floor. He flips. He'd already thrown the other deputy out and he ordered me out, too."

"What reason did he give?" Ric asked.

"He didn't."

"So why were you sitting on the floor just now? Did you see something?"

"Trying to make sense, that's all. Getting my memory straight. When I first saw Del he was covered with blood. I thought he'd been shot, too. Then I figured out he'd been trying to resuscitate Bobby."

Ric glanced at Elaine. Her face was pasty.

"So Bobby was laying on his back." He tapped the center of his chest. "Dead on shot, right through the heart. He was a fairly big guy, so Del wouldn't have done much more than rolled him over. I'm pretty sure by his position that he was facing the desk when he was hit. Except Del's gun was by the door, behind Bobby." He turned on the flashlight and swept it slowly over the floor and wall around the door. "The medical examiner didn't find a slug. There was an exit wound." His voice dropped to a husky whisper. "Ha."

Ric followed the flashlight beam. Something in the wall gleamed dully. "Bullet?" he asked.

"Bingo. So if he's shot while facing the desk, why is the gun behind him?" As if holding a debate with himself, he answered, "Someone could have kicked it. Or, Del could have started for his car, remembered he had a phone in here, and dropped the gun—"

"No," Elaine said. Her face was still white, but her expression was determined. "I might, if there is no other possibility, believe Daddy had *one* accident with his gun. But two accidents? You don't know how fanatical he was. He'd no more drop his revolver than a mother would drop a baby."

"Why would he bring the weapon inside in the first place?"

She showed her palms in a helpless gesture. "He always carried it in his car. As far as I know, he never took it out." She studied the desk. It was covered with papers. "The only reason I can think of, would be if he was cleaning it. But no cleaning supplies."

"I don't recall seeing cleaning supplies at the time. Huh. Take a look around while I get my kit. Put your gloves back on. Look for anything unusual or out of place."

After Tate left, Ric touched Elaine's arm. She shuddered. "Are you okay?" he asked.

"Other than wanting to toss my breakfast, I'm just fine." She swiped a sleeve across her lips then straightened her shoulders and focused on the desk.

The papers scattered across the desk were dusty and parched looking. Several were smeared with rusty stains. Ric narrowed his concentration to the task at hand. He studied a map and a large drawing that seemed to correspond with the map. He asked Elaine about its meaning.

"It looks like a plat map," she said. "Here's the river.

Oh, it's the southeast corner of the ranch. This is the high-way.''

"So what are all these puzzle piece-looking marks?"

"Just guessing, but it looks like a housing development. This must be a golf course here. What do you think?"

Having never seen a plat map, Ric wasn't certain what exactly he was looking at. The meandering pencil lines did vaguely resemble a golf course.

"This isn't Daddy's handwriting. He drew a lot better than this, too." She made a squeaky noise, clamped her hands over her biceps and backed a step. "Axton wanted to buy this portion of the river so he could subdivide it into ranchettes. King owns this part of the ranch."

"Axton and King had a deal going?"

She shook her head, but seemed uncertain. "I really don't know any details. No one has mentioned it since Daddy died."

"What are all these receipts and stuff?"

"Bank slips." She peered closely at a green ledger sheet. "It looks like it's for one of his rentals." She shrugged it off and turned her attention back to the maps. "Daddy talked about development in the valley. Go to places like Buena Vista and Durango, almost any small town, and the residential building is astonishing. With te-lecommuting and retirees looking to escape the cities, mountain property is a hot market."

"Del and Axton were full partners, right? So Axton could make deals with anyone he wanted. He didn't need Del's okay."

"I guess…"

"So Bobby goes to the realty to pick up trash. He catches King and Axton in cahoots."

"Now my uncle is involved in murder?"

"I didn't say that. Bobby said he'd discovered some

shabby information. Not illegal. Not immoral. *Shabby*. That could describe a guy stabbing his business partner in the back. Not to mention a brother selling the family legacy out from under his sister.''

''If this is such incriminating evidence, why would King leave it here?''

He opened his mouth, but had no rebuttal. King was a jackass, but he wasn't stupid.

Tate returned with a plastic box. He set it on a chair and popped the lid. ''What have you found?''

''Maps of the ranch and sketches for what might be a proposed housing development.''

''This ranch?''

''Uncle King's portion.'' Elaine chewed her lower lip. She looked worried. ''Mama and King own the ranch half and half. Mama pays King for grazing rights and he gets a share of profits from cattle and hay sales.''

''Tell the rest,'' Ric prompted.

She sighed, put upon. ''Apparently King had been making noise about selling some acreage to Axton for development. He couldn't have been serious. Even if he were, he'd have been in for a huge fight with Mama.''

''Are we talking big money?''

''Probably.''

''Interesting.'' Tate turned to the bullet in the wall. First, he took several photographs, both with and without Ric holding a ruler to show how far it was from the floor and door. Then with a dental pick, Tate pried the slug from the wood and it dropped into his palm. A colorful expletive slipped from his mouth. He shot a sheepish grin at Elaine. ''Check this out, ranger.''

Ric peered at the misshapen bullet. It had a faint rusty streak on it. ''Is that blood?''

''Probably. But that's not what's so interesting. What is

interesting is that Del's revolver was a .38 special Smith & Wesson. Model called a Body Guard. Fairly small. Easy to handle. A nice little piece.''

Ric got it then. The implications made his insides constrict. "This isn't a .38 round."

"It's a .44," Tate said. He dropped it into a zipper-top plastic bag and wrote a notation on it. "When I picked up Del's weapon it had recently fired one shot. Start looking for more bullet holes."

Elaine inspected the furniture and window panes. Ric and Tate checked the walls. Ric found a small hole rendered nearly invisible by soot-darkened chinking between the logs.

"I think this might be it," Ric said.

Tate put his nose nearly to the wall. Again, he shot photos, with and without measurements. He again used the dental pick to probe the hole. A slug popped into his waiting palm.

"Well, well, well. We've got ourselves a .38. How many handguns did Del own?"

"Only the revolver he carried in his car," Elaine answered. "Oh, and a pair of matched Colt .45s. Antiques. I don't think they've ever been out of their display case."

Tate brought out a telescoping pointer and worked it into the bullet hole. He fiddled with it, his brow furrowed in concentration, until the metal rod protruded at an angle. He looked between it and the other side of the cabin. He pointed at the door. "I'd say this was fired from somewhere right over there." He fetched a spool of white string from the plastic box.

He had Elaine hold one end of the string against the bullet hole, then unrolled a length to follow the angle of the pointer. He hemmed and hawed like a mechanic seeing something interesting underneath a car hood.

"A midget shot Bobby?" Ric asked.

"Hold this, ranger. Ma'am, make sure the string stays lined up with the pointer. How tall was your father?"

"Just under six feet."

Tate's broad shoulders blocked the doorway. "Here's a possible scenario. Bobby comes up here to tell Del about some *shabby* information. But the bad guy got here first. He's standing in front of the desk, trying to talk his way out of trouble. Bobby walks in, the guy panics and shoots. Bobby falls. Del runs to his car and grabs his weapon. The heart attack hits." He clutched his chest with his left hand then raised his right hand cocked into a gun shape. He dropped to one knee and bent over as if in pain. His gun hand lined up perfectly to the bullet hole in the wall.

Elaine dropped the string. It fluttered to the dusty floor.

"The shooter hightails it out of here. Del doesn't have the strength to hold the gun. He drops it. He crawls to Bobby, tries to give him CPR, but he's hurting too much. He makes it to the desk, hauls himself onto the chair, calls the sheriff, manages to choke out that Bobby's been shot, then he collapses."

"Murder," Ric said.

"An honest to God whodunnit. Oh, man, I *hate* whodunnits."

Elaine clapped a hand over her mouth and raced out the door.

Chapter Seven

Elaine sat on a stump. Sunshine warmed her body, but she felt cold and numb inside. She waited for Tate and Ric to finish collecting evidence from inside the lodge. Through the open doorway she could see occasional flashes from the camera. If she had her way, she'd never step inside the lodge again for as long as she lived. She wanted to burn it to the ground.

The forest was conducive to contemplation. Big trees and blue sky and the clean smell of snowy ground made self-delusion impossible. One thought kept returning over and over again: Daddy wasn't a murderer; he was a hero who had died trying to save her husband. It should have alleviated her anger and despair. Instead, guilt swarmed like buzzing flies. Her cowardice had allowed a murderer to escape.

A double-murderer. For surely, if not for the stress and trauma of seeing his son-in-law gunned down, Daddy wouldn't have suffered a heart attack.

If King had searched the lodge, he would have found the bullets. If he hadn't been able to bear being in the place where his brother-in-law and nephew-in-law had died, he should have allowed Tate to collect evidence. Perhaps his refusal had nothing to do with squeamishness or the fear of exposing Del as a murderer. Maybe it had to do with prime riverfront property and housing developments and a big money deal being worked out behind Del and Lillian's backs.

Why had Daddy even called King? She distinctly remembered her uncle saying he'd taken the call. The old rotary phone didn't have speed dial or programming capability. It would have been faster to dial 911. Unless Daddy hadn't made any calls at all. Which would mean King hadn't raced to the scene—he'd been there already.

Imagining her beloved uncle involved in murder was as sickening as believing her father capable of it.

Ric and Tate emerged from the lodge. Tate carried the plastic box. Atop it was a stack of plastic bags containing the bullets and fingerprint cards. Ric carried several brown paper sacks with the tops neatly rolled and sealed with tape.

"We searched both bedrooms and the bathroom," Tate said. "If he had a woman up here, she didn't leave anything behind." The men loaded the kit and evidence into the Bronco.

"Is there any way to check phone records from the night of the shooting?" Elaine asked.

"If I can get a court order to demand records from the telephone company. If they archived the records. Some companies don't. Why do you ask?"

"I was wondering why Daddy called King instead of 911. Or why didn't he call home? Or if he called anyone at all? What if King was here all along?"

Tate smiled dreamily at her. The smile caught her off guard. She'd never thought him attractive before; big and beefy held no appeal. Now she understood why many women in town had tagged him as "yummy."

"Points to the pretty lady," he said, his tone admiring. "Those are real good questions."

Ric scowled at his friend. Elaine sensed a definite rise of testosterone. It both amused and annoyed her. One kiss did not give Ric dibs on her.

Although, it had been a pretty hot kiss.

"I hate thinking Uncle King had anything to do with it." She drew a deep breath. It was appalling how much sense this line of reasoning made. "I can't conceive of him hurting Bobby, but he's certainly in a position to hide evidence."

"She's got a point." Ric draped an arm around her shoulders, ignoring her look askance. "If we turn the evidence over to King, it could disappear. Then where are we?"

"Let me talk to Linda Pallo," Elaine said. "If anyone can explain about the maps and sketches, she can. If she doesn't know about them, then that tells us plenty. Tate, do you know anyone who can help us process the evidence without Uncle King knowing?"

"The old man's got friends all over the state. I couldn't make a move in any official capacity without him finding out." He snapped his fingers. "Unless...I might be able to plead my case with the FBI. I hate bringing feds into a local matter. Not to mention how the sheriff will react when he learns he's the target. I'll talk to that private eye Tom hired and see if he can come up with anything. He works for a large firm. Maybe he can get the phone records."

"Without a court order?"

"Hey, where gumshoes get their info is none of my business."

"Now might be the time to speak to your mother," Ric said.

Eyes closed, Elaine breathed, "No, not yet. Especially if King is involved. Let me talk to Linda first and see if I can figure out the deal with the maps."

Tate was agreeable. Elaine watched him drive away, then deliberately removed Ric's arm from her shoulders. "Don't assume liberties with me," she said tartly.

He struck an aggressive pose with his thumbs hooked in his jeans pockets. "Liberties?"

"I'm not a fence post, and you aren't a hound marking territory. You don't have to get all jealous because of Tate."

He laughed mockingly. "Jealous of Tate? Right."

"Then why did you put your arm around me?"

"You looked cold."

"Ha! Big fibber." She jerked a thumb at his truck. His jealousy shouldn't flatter her, but it did. "You drive out first. I have to chain the road."

He muttered something she didn't quite catch. She thought it might have been, "...a little jealous." A glance at her watch showed almost the entire morning was gone. If she hurried, she could take Linda to lunch and still get home before the school bus dropped off Jodi.

"What's your phone number?" she asked.

Ric paused in the midst of opening his truck door. Her gaze slid down his backside. A calendar containing only photographs of his taut, sexy backside would probably sell millions.

"Call the shop. I don't have a phone hooked up yet at home."

He looked reluctant to leave—she didn't want him to leave.

"I'll find you after I talk to Linda." She climbed into the Jeep. She reached for the door to pull it closed when Ric stepped to her side.

He hooked a hand around the back of her neck and pulled her close. He kissed her hard, close-mouthed, but passionate. Her senses reeled with pleasure and instant arousal. All her joints seemed to liquify. He broke off as abruptly as he'd begun. His smile was crooked, wicked and warm. His fingers teased her neck then the line of her jaw. He tapped the tip of her nose, winked and walked away.

He fired up the truck engine, tooted the horn, then drove off.

She pressed a fingertip to her lips. All doubts as to whether she could ever feel sexually aroused again vanished. She wanted him, all of him. She wanted a second chance to love him.

Ric Buchanan is back in town... How would he like knowing what you really did to him?

If she knew Cedric Buchanan at all, he wouldn't like it one little bit.

THE FIRST THING Elaine saw when she pulled into the Crowder Realty parking lot was the last thing she wanted to see. Axton Cross and Tom Greene were having an argument at the realty's side door.

Axton was a slender man and not very tall. If pressed, Elaine would call him a dandy, especially given the double-breasted suits and tastefully subdued ties he always wore. Tom had lost weight since Bobby's death, going from lean to skinny. He looked wiry, coiled like a compressed spring. He loomed over the real estate broker. He shook a fist at Axton's face.

"Tom!" Elaine called. Her father-in-law whipped his head about. Seeing his sunken eyes and gaunt cheeks made her heart ache. It was as if grief and anger were burning him up from the inside out.

"Tom." She reached his side and placed a hand on his arm. "What is going on here?"

"I want this son of a bitch to 'fess up." He shook a sheaf of papers in the air. "I got all the proof I need right here!"

Axton backed up a step, shaking his head, but never taking his gaze off the older man. "I don't know what you're talking about. I have nothing to confess, Mr. Greene."

"I got some options now."

The side door opened and Linda Pallo stuck her head out. "What is going on out here? Axton, is everything okay?"

"Not for long," Tom said. "I hired myself an attorney. He says I got grounds for a civil suit."

Linda said, "How about I do some suit filing of my own, Tom? There's customers awaiting Mr. Cross and calls on hold. You're impeding the progress of a legitimate business. I can throw in trespassing and harassment, too."

"Don't you care this no-account carpetbagger was scheming to murder Del? Huh? That he killed my boy to shut him up?"

Elaine tugged on Tom's arm, but he was as unmovable as a bull.

"I'm filing a wrongful death suit. You just wait 'til I open up your life like a can of beans, Cross. Everyone will see what a murderous, scheming low-down dog you really are."

"That's enough." Elaine dug in her heels and pulled Tom. "Come on. Let's go on over to Walt's."

"Gonna go over your life with a microscope," Tom growled. "I'll own you! I'll ruin you!"

"Tom, *please!*"

"I'm calling the sheriff." Linda ducked back inside.

"You murdered my boy, and you're gonna pay." Tom finally allowed Elaine to haul him away from the door.

She shot Axton an apologetic look, then hustled the old man across the street. He kept muttering about lawsuits and the promises his attorney had made. She practically shoved him inside the wood shop.

Walt Buchanan shut off a table saw and pulled goggles off his eyes. Ric emerged from a painting booth. Buster trotted over to greet them. Seeming to sense Tom's agitation, the dog slunk under a bench.

"Talk some sense into him, Walt," Elaine said. "He was practically assaulting Axton. He's going to end up in jail."

"Stay out of this, girl," Tom grumbled at her. "You might be happy with your uncle's conspiracy to make everything nice and neat, but I'm not." He slapped the sheaf of papers on a table. "I got the full report from the investigator. Axton Cross is up to his ears in muck. He's a con man and a killer. My attorney says I can file a wrongful death suit. It'll all be public record then. If King doesn't change his ruling and open an investigation, then I surely have enough to go to the state attorney."

Elaine dropped her face on her hand and groaned. When Tom Greene grabbed hold of an idea, he was like a snapping turtle—he wouldn't let loose until his head was cut off. She held not the slightest doubt that Tom would sell off every material possession he owned in order to finance a legal battle.

Ric guided Tom to a stool. Though the older man resisted, Ric pushed until he sat. Ric tossed a significant look at Elaine. "It might be even more complicated than you think, Tom."

Elaine tensed. Ric was going to reveal what they'd

found at the lodge. She didn't consider it wise. There was no telling what Tom might do with the information.

"Take a break, Uncle Walt," Ric said. "You might want to hear this, too."

Ric explained how he, Tate and Elaine had examined the lodge and collected evidence. When he talked about the bullets, Tom's eyes widened and his weathered cheeks paled.

"You're saying it's a solid fact Del didn't shoot my boy?" Tom asked.

"I'm not saying anything is a fact except what we found. You need to back off. If you go off half-cocked after Axton, King will stomp you. He'll shut down Tate and the evidence we collected will disappear."

"He's right," Walt said. He handed his friend a mug of coffee. "I can't quite believe King is crooked. I do know the man will not tolerate being embarrassed. No matter how this turns out, he's in for a big old cherry face. No sense poking at him before we have to."

"The attorney says he's never seen such a blatant cover-up," Tom argued.

Elaine cleared her throat, catching Tom's attention. "I hate admitting this, but I have spent the last eighteen months scared to death that some evidence would turn up that proves Daddy is a killer. I'm as guilty in the cover-up as Uncle King. I am so sorry."

He refused to look at her.

"But I won't close my eyes any longer. No matter what happens, or what comes out. Not even if it hurts Mama. So, please, hold off on filing a lawsuit. And stay away from Axton. I promise you with all my heart, on Bobby's grave, that if Axton murdered Bobby, justice will be done."

"I got a case. Once I get it rolling, I'm going to the

state attorney. If I gotta sit in his office forty days and forty nights, I'm gonna make him see what kind of corruption infests this valley.''

Elaine considered briefly calling Gwen. All that would accomplish would be to deepen the poor woman's worries. Gwen wasn't the type to defy or argue with her husband.

She threw her hands in the air. "Talk sense into him, Ric. I'm going across the street. Maybe I can convince Axton not to press charges.''

''Gonna let that slick-talking con man convince you the sky is orange?'' Tom asked with a snarl. ''He fooled your daddy and he'll fool you, too.''

''I intend to convince him to not file a restraining order against you.''

She left the wood shop, her mind churning. Talking Linda into having lunch, and getting her to talk was probably impossible now. Linda had worked at the realty for so long, she'd assumed a proprietary interest. Elaine felt duty bound to try anyway.

It relieved her to see only Linda and Axton were in the office. Not that she felt comfortable around Axton. At least the other agents, all of them eager for gossip, weren't around as witnesses. Elaine forced a smile she didn't feel.

''Oh, Axton, I'm so sorry about Tom.'' It gave her eyestrain trying to look convincingly contrite.

He sat on the edge of a desk, sorting through mail. He harrumphed. Elaine had never figured out his age. His hair was thinning and nearly white, but his face and hands were smooth. He looked extremely irritated.

Axton Cross could have put a bullet through her husband's heart and left her father to die. Suddenly, the air felt oppressive and the office way too small. She remained near the door.

''That old codger is nuts,'' he said. ''He's been harass-

ing me up and down ever since Bobby died. I'm sorry.
Really sorry for his loss. And yours, too, Elaine. But I
didn't have anything to do with it. I'm fed up with him
acting like I do. People are starting to take their real estate
business elsewhere."

Linda was seated at the receptionist's desk rather than
in her cubicle. Her fingers moved rapidly over a computer
keyboard. Elaine could tell the woman was paying close
attention. Elaine wondered if Linda had transferred all her
loyalty to Axton now that Del was gone.

Axton dropped the mail and indicated a door. It led to
the private office her father once occupied. "Come on in.
I've been so busy lately, I've been neglecting you. Forget
Tom Greene. He'll come to his senses eventually. How are
you doing? Staying out of trouble?"

If only you knew. Her face ached from the effort it took
to keep smiling. No way was she going behind a closed
door with Axton Cross. "Actually, I came to see Linda.
Uhm, I never properly thanked you for taking care of those
busted pipes in the Fourth Street house. I'd like to take
you over to Daisy's for lunch."

"All I did was call a plumber," Linda said.

"At three in the morning. You've been a godsend to
me and Marlee and Davis the way you take care of the
rentals."

"That's what I get paid for. Besides, I can't leave until
Kay gets back."

"If you girls want to go to lunch, I can man the
phones," Axton offered. "Go on, Linda. I'll be more than
happy to eat your tuna fish sandwich for you." He winked
at Elaine. "Woman makes the best tuna salad in the world.
If we could figure out a way to sell her sandwiches over
the Internet, we'd make a fortune."

Linda huffed and stomped into her cubicle. She returned

with a paper bag that appeared much reused. "If you want my sandwiches so bad, Axton, say so, and I'll bring extras."

He hid a smile behind his hand.

The woman's grouchiness was all show, her way of expressing affection. She used to snap and snipe at Del the same way. Elaine made a mental note to not say a single negative word about Axton.

It took a bit more coaxing, but Linda finally agreed to trust Axton with the telephone. Elaine sensed the woman was flattered by the invitation. Although Linda had been born and raised in McClintock, she didn't have many friends. She had an abrasive personality, plus had spent so many years caring for two no-account husbands and her elderly parents that she'd never acquired the habit of socializing.

In Daisy's Cafe, Elaine and Linda sat next to the window where they could watch people passing by. The cafe had seven small tables. It was open for lunch and breakfast only. The aroma of their signature cinnamon rolls permeated the walls. Rolls so good that tourists made special trips to McClintock merely to pick up a dozen or so. Fresh flowers on the tables and tole-painted tinware on the walls gave it a homey feel.

"We haven't talked in ages," Elaine said. "How are you doing?"

"Well as can be expected." Linda scanned the menu.

Elaine's tongue felt thick and clumsy. Linda intimidated her. An annoying fact, but true. Linda intimidated a lot of people. She was taller than most men and had big shoulders and large, muscular hands. Though in her fifties, she looked as if she could run people half her age into the ground. Elaine had always suspected her father had admired the woman so much because she was kind of scary.

She searched for something complimentary to say. Linda's gray hair was skinned back in a clumsy bun. Her muddy-gray suit looked like something a prison matron would wear. ''Your nails sure are pretty,'' she said, relieved to mean it.

Linda actually blushed and hid her fingertips in her palms.

''Who does them for you?'' She displayed her short, unpolished nails. ''Mama says professional manicures would do wonders for me. I hate to shell out the money just to break my nails while I'm working.''

''I wear gloves when I'm doing housework or tending the garden.'' She shyly opened her hands. ''You're looking well yourself, Elaine. Course, you McClintock girls always do. Speaking of which, I heard Marlee is taking a job with Dr. Colton.''

''Yes, she is.'' How, she wondered, would she ever gracefully work in references to those maps? ''Doc Colton is making noises about retirement.''

''Don't you believe it. He'll work 'til he's a hundred or until a cow stomps his head. Course he's about a hundred now.''

The waitress greeted them both by name. Elaine ordered chicken breast sandwiches for them both, a fruit platter to share and hot herb tea. Linda seemed pleased by the royal treatment.

''I hear you've taken up with that Buchanan boy again.''

It vaguely annoyed Elaine that everyone over fifty in this town insisted on calling anyone under fifty either *boy* or *girl*. It also irritated her to be caught off guard. ''Ric? He's a nice man. We're good friends.''

''Gotta watch them fine-on-the-eyes fellahs. Both my husbands was real handsome. They were as worthless as three-legged cow ponies.''

Elaine bit her lip to keep from laughing. Ric would die if he learned that Linda Pallo thought him handsome. "I haven't taken up with him. He and Walt have been doing a lot of work for Mama."

"Lillian." Linda sniffed. "I swear, does she think folks don't see her making moon-eyes at that old man? Woman her age ought to show some dignity."

Elaine bit her lip again, but this time to stop a sharp comment. Walt and Lillian were good friends, nothing more. Their friendship was nobody's business except their own.

"That Buchanan boy seems real taken with your daughter, too."

Reminding herself that she'd known full well how narrow-minded and tactless Linda could be, Elaine kept smiling. Their food arrived. The distraction gave her time to order her thoughts. Steering this chat away from anything personal was her top priority.

"Is the realty really losing business?" she asked.

"Wish I could say no, but the strain is showing." Linda clucked her tongue while she cut her sandwich into four neat pieces. "For instance, Ole Ingmar got himself the cancer. Prostate. It won't kill him, but it did get him thinking about that hundred acres he owns. Man has five kids and not a one of them is interested in working land. So Ole decided to sell before he died and the government takes it for the taxes. Did he ask Axton to list it for him? No he did not. Trotted himself down to Durango." She snorted, a bitter sound. "Ain't had a single offer yet. Serves that traitor right."

"What about developing land for houses? There's good money in that. Axton and Daddy used to talk about it all the time."

"Pie in the sky blathering. Ain't nobody wants this

place to turn into another Durango. All the good grazing given over to ranchettes and high taxes forcing out the natives. Bad enough the EPA is coming out with new regulations every day and grazing fees are shooting to the moon.''

''Hmm. I thought they were serious. I even saw a plat map. It showed a golf course and everything. Riverfront property.'' She bit into the sandwich to keep from saying too much.

Linda chuckled. ''Oh, that. The Aspens.''

''You know about it?''

''More pie in the sky. Axton was trying every which way to convince your uncle to sell him two hundred acres down by the river. Del and I had a bet going about how many offers Axton would make before King convinced him that he wouldn't sell.''

''Oh, so it was all Axton's project?''

''His big dream. Poor dear. Still talks about it every so often. The day is coming when the building boom will hit this valley. But that day ain't now.''

So, if her father had known all about the big plans to turn King's riverfront property into a housing development, then it wasn't a motive for murder. ''I'm surprised. Daddy never turned up his nose at making money.''

Linda laughed out loud. The sound brought the waitress to their table where she topped off their water glasses. She asked if they had a good joke to share.

Only if murder is funny, Elaine thought. After the waitress left them alone, she said, ''Well, I feel for Axton. I'd hate to see him have to close up shop.''

''It won't come to that. 'Sides, that boy is a whiz with investments and such. Might have to pay from his own pocket to keep things going until that fool Tom calms down, but keep going he will.'' She speared a piece of pineapple from the fruit plate and popped it in her mouth. "*Mmm-mm.* Pity fresh pineapple costs so dear. I'd eat it every day if I could afford it."

Investments, Elaine mused, from principle supplied by insurance payouts.

"Is Tom serious about a lawsuit?" Linda asked.

The worry in her voice, more than the question, made Elaine wary. Linda should worry. Even a whiz with investments could be wiped out by a legal battle. Linda could lose her job. "It's grief," Elaine answered. "He can't get over losing Bobby."

"Stubborn old so-'n-so." She jabbed at a slippery piece of pineapple, sending it skittering across the plate. "Your Daddy had himself his share of legal tangles. Fortunate he never actually went to court, but a few times things got ugly."

Elaine shrugged. "He always said every contract is a lawsuit waiting to happen. Never seemed to bother him."

"Axton told you Tom hired a private eye."

"Surely Axton doesn't have anything to hide. After all, Daddy trusted him, and he was an excellent judge of character. Or was Daddy upset about the, what did you call it? The Aspens?"

Linda jabbed the pineapple so hard the fork rang against the plate. She waved her pale yellow prize. "Del wasn't a bit upset. Especially considering how your mama would fight tooth and nail to prevent carving up the ranch. Why do you keep bringing it up? Do you know something I don't?"

Elaine considered how much she dared to say. Her father had trusted Linda implicitly, with every aspect of his business. They'd been friends. "Do you think there is any possibility that Axton had anything to do with what happened at the lodge?"

"No."

The flat answer took Elaine aback. "Tom's attorney will dig deep. He'll take depositions from all the employees. Including you. If there was anything remotely shady going on, the attorney will find out."

Linda slowly set down the fork. Her expression grew tight and solemn.

Elaine refused to quail under that flinty gaze. She wondered how the woman would react to the news that Daddy hadn't shot Bobby. Caution kept her quiet. All it would take would be one word from Linda to Axton, and if he owned the murder weapon, it could disappear forever.

She leaned forward and lowered her voice. "Here's what I think, Linda. I think Bobby was murdered. If Tom Greene goes ahead with the lawsuit, I'm going to help him anyway I can."

If Linda had bristles, every single one would be standing on end. "You'd do that to Axton? To your daddy's realty?"

"I like Axton. But if he had anything to do with what happened at the lodge, he has to pay." She searched Linda's angry expression. "I know you loved Daddy. He sure thought the world of you. For his sake, please, if you know anything, tell me."

"Lawyers make fortunes by making folks miserable. They'll swarm all over this valley looking at private records and disrupting lives. Not a person living doesn't have some sort of skeleton in his closet."

"Is Axton hiding something?"

Linda exhaled, long and heavy. Her broad shoulders relaxed. She called over the waitress and requested a box to take the remainder of the fruit salad home. "Del used to say, lawyers are like mildew. Once they get themselves a toehold, it doesn't take long before they're all over everything. Might remind Tom that if he starts a lawsuit, Axton will get himself a lawyer, too. Dirt digging goes both ways.''

The barely veiled threat rattled Elaine. Daddy used to joke that Linda had missed her true calling—she should have been a Mafia don's enforcer. The joke didn't seem funny in the least right now. Linda had enough insider knowledge about everyone in the valley to heavily arm Axton if he decided to counter-sue.

"Fine lunch, Elaine. Thank you. But I best get back to the office before Axton starts routing phone calls to China.''

Chapter Eight

On an overcast afternoon, Ric and Elaine met at the Greene ranch. Ric studied signs of neglect around the property. A few shingles littered the yard. A tiller had been left to rust. It was painful to see ruts in the driveway and tools stacked carelessly on the front porch. Tom Greene used to take pride in his property. Even his pickup, which he'd babied into lasting nearly a quarter of a century, looked as if it hadn't been washed or waxed since Bobby died.

Elaine stared at the century-old house where Bobby had grown up. "I don't know if this is such a good idea," she said. "Tom is pretty mad at us."

He dropped a hand on her shoulder. "Look at this place. It's going to pot. He can't afford a lawsuit. Not financially, not emotionally. He'll end up losing the ranch."

"I don't think he cares anymore. And he's so paranoid..." Her voice trailed, and she shook her head sadly.

Ric understood what she left unspoken. After Elaine told Tom about her conversation with Linda Pallo, Tom had accused Elaine of conspiring with the enemy. Then he'd blown up at Ric and Walt. The topper was, when Tate explained his reasons for not wanting to force the sheriff's hand just yet, Tom had accused the deputy of corruption and dereliction of duty.

"Tom should have calmed down by now." Ric hoped.

Gwen Greene stepped onto the porch. Once, she'd been a pretty woman, slim and dark-haired with big gentle eyes. Every time Ric saw her, she seemed smaller, older, and grayer. She waved at them.

"If he doesn't hand over the private investigator's report," Elaine said. "And if he doesn't agree to hold off on the lawsuit, then what?"

Ric didn't want to consider failure. "Let's assume he'll be reasonable."

They walked up to the house.

Ric and Elaine kissed Gwen's cheek. The front of her housedress and her cheeks were dusted with flour. She smelled of cinnamon. "Using up the last of my peaches," Gwen said, inviting them inside. "I'll be bringing cobbler out of the oven in a half hour or so."

In passing through the parlor, Ric noted the many framed photographs of Bobby and Jodi. Large and small photos perched on tabletops and hung on the walls. His insides clenched. If Jodi's paternity came to light, the Greenes would be crushed. He supposed he could deny his daughter. Then Jodi could despise him for not only embroiling her in scandal and making her the subject of taunts and gossip, but for shirking responsibility.

Life would have been better all the way around if he'd never returned to McClintock.

Tom was sitting in the kitchen. Without a hat covering his lank hair, the way he was neglecting not only his ranch but himself was clear. Gwen gazed at her husband and sighed.

"How are you doing, Tom?" Elaine asked.

He glowered into a coffee cup.

Ric sat. He leaned so close to Tom that the old man

either had to look at Ric or leave the table. He lifted bleary eyes.

"Listen to me," Ric said. He noted the flicker of heat in Tom's eyes. He took it as a good sign. "You are not alone in looking for justice. You never have been."

"You're all against me. You're siding with that—"

"I said listen to me."

Tom snapped his mouth shut. His bushy eyebrows lifted high.

"If you file your lawsuit, Axton Cross will counter-sue. The realty is losing business in good part because of you. An attorney won't have any problem finding witnesses who'll testify you're guilty of slander. As it stands, he has a better chance of winning than you do."

"I know he killed my boy."

"No, you don't. Tate needs time to figure out who did."

"You got proof there was another shooter. You got bullets."

"Which mean nothing by themselves. In order to run ballistics tests, Tate has to have the weapons that fired them. Del's .38 is locked up in the sheriff's station cellar. We don't know who owns the .44."

Gwen timidly cleared her throat. "The kids are right, honey. That report you got is full of questions, but no answers."

"The insurance angle is suspicious," Ric said. "But it isn't proof of anything."

"My lawyer says I got a case."

"Even if you do, is that good enough? A civil suit could take years to resolve. And what if Axton isn't the murderer? You'll be responsible for ruining an innocent man's life."

Tom crossed his arms and hunched into himself. His

chin thrust forward at a stubborn angle. "If you'd married this girl, my boy would be alive today."

Low blow, Ric thought. From the corner of his eye, he caught Elaine's flinch.

"Tom," Elaine said. "I want to catch Bobby's killer. I want him to pay with everything he's got. I promise you, if any hard evidence turns up against Axton, I'll join you in a wrongful death suit. I'll finance it, no matter what it takes."

For the first time Tom looked more interested than angry.

"But I won't do it unless I know for sure Axton is guilty. And I will not jeopardize a criminal case. I want the murderer behind bars. Please, cooperate. Give us the investigator's report. Back off from making threats."

"I ain't threatening, I'm promising."

"You can't do this on your own," she said.

Ric echoed the sentiment, then shut up. Elaine and Gwen both seemed to be holding their breath. Finally, Tom rose. He left the kitchen, then soon returned. He slapped a thick envelope on the table before Ric. The investigator's report.

"Tell Tate he's got a week. He don't come up with something, I'm filing the lawsuit."

At seeing Elaine readying for a protest, Ric warned her with his eyes to keep quiet. Tom was nearly at his breaking point and further arguments might push him over the edge.

Gwen saw them out. Elaine pulled a folded check from her pocket and urged Gwen to take it. Gwen's eyes filled with tears. She tried to give it back, but Elaine shoved her hands beneath her armpits.

"It's made out to you," Elaine said softly. "Buy groceries, pay bills, put it in the church collection plate. It makes no difference to me. I know what Tom is doing to you. Please, take it. A gift from Bobby. Okay?''

Nodding, the woman slipped it into a dress pocket.

Ric kissed Gwen goodbye, then walked Elaine to her Jeep. "That was a nice thing to do," he said.

"It's blood money," she said bitterly. "If I hadn't been such a coward, Tom wouldn't be in the state he's in now. Sometimes I just hate myself." Her eyes grew moist with tears. "Will we ever prove who did this?"

Unable to resist, he cupped her face in both hands. Her skin was so soft he could barely feel its texture through the calluses on his fingers. "Trust Tate. He knows what he's doing." He brushed a tear from the corner of her eye. "Are we still on for tomorrow night? I think we can both use a change of scenery."

"I'm looking forward to it."

He'd have kissed her, but standing in Tom Greene's driveway was not the right place. Reluctantly, he turned her loose.

"Ric!" Jodi pushed open the screen door. Giggling, her eyes shining, she invited him inside the house. She wore her hair in two long braids. Her delicate ankles showed beneath jeans she was clearly outgrowing. "Flowers, oooh."

Flustered, he handed her a pink tin box of Almond Roca. Giggling anew, she scampered toward the kitchen. Tonight was the night, he'd determined. He would tell Elaine that he knew about Jodi.

"Mommy isn't ready yet." She searched through a cupboard. "Way she's going, she's never gonna be ready. She's changed clothes about a hundred times. Boy, you sure look nice."

"Thank you." The collar on the brand new shirt was

scratchy and the tie felt too tight. Since Jodi approved, the discomfort was worth it. "You aren't staying alone, are you?"

She plunked a crystal vase onto the table. "No." She dragged out the word in dramatic disgust. "Mommy says I have to go to Grandma's. I'm almost thirteen, old enough to stay alone. Don't you think so?"

Images of house fires, tornados, freak accidents, mad ax murderers and swarms of killer bees paraded through his mind. "Being alone isn't what it's cracked up to be."

"Grandma won't let me watch music videos."

Good call. "She'll come up with something fun to do."

With a harrumph and a snooty expression, she took the bouquet of pink roses. She smelled the flowers. The snootiness disappeared. Like her mother, apparently, she couldn't resist the sight, texture or scent of flowers. Ric unbuttoned his jacket, and took a seat at the table. He watched her artfully arrange the baby roses in the vase.

"How's school?"

"Boring. I can't wait for summer vacation. If you'd buy a horse, we could go riding together."

"I saw my physical therapist last week. She says as long as I'm not bulldogging or jumping fences, riding won't hurt. It might even help my balance."

"I saw an ad at the feed store. Erles Harbaugh is selling his Morgan gelding. Sue Harbaugh rode him in pleasure trials. He's got nice manners. Mr. Erles is asking sixteen hundred, but I bet you can talk him down." Appearing satisfied with her arrangement, she stepped back from the flowers. "Want a drink? Mommy bought some beer."

He almost said yes, but changed his mind. "I'm driving. Not a drop if I'm getting behind the wheel."

She hooted laughter. "You sound just like Daddy! But

you forget the part where he says, 'and always wear your seat belt.'''

She set to work on removing the lid from the candy box. "Hey, Ric, can I ask you a weird question?" She slid a surreptitious glance at the doorway then lowered her voice. "Missy Gullman called her daddy a sperm donor. Why would she say that?"

He nearly fell off the chair. "Uhm, why do you ask?"

"Missy was sad 'cause he didn't even call on her birthday. Not a card or nothing. She was crying in the bathroom at school."

"Poor kid."

"I know when Grandma artificially inseminates cows, the bulls aren't even around 'cause they got their sperm took by the vet. That's a sperm donor, right? So how come Missy says her father is one? He's not just a number in a bull registry."

His ears grew hot. He worked a finger under his shirt collar. "Uhm, well, you see, some men are careless. Like, they don't bother marrying the mothers or they take off and don't have anything to do with their kids. I guess that makes them nothing more than sperm donors."

"Doesn't Missy's dad love her? He's all the way in California, and she doesn't even know his phone number. She's a real nice girl. How come he's so mean to her?"

"The world is full of stupid people." *Like me.*

Having removed the lid of the tin box, she slowly unwrapped a piece of candy. "Sometimes," she said, now solemn, "I get kind of mad at Daddy for leaving me. I know he didn't want to and it isn't his fault, but I get mad anyway. Then I get mad at myself. Daddy never would have left me on purpose."

"I know, honey. It's hard."

She lifted a skinny shoulder. "But if he did do it on

purpose, I wouldn't be crying in no bathroom. Uh-*uh!* I'd
make him look me right in the eye and explain himself.''

Ric held not the slightest doubt that she'd do exactly
that. ''It's never the kid's fault when the parents are
jerks.''

She bit into the toffee candy. Her eyelids lowered to
half-mast. She offered him the tin, but he declined. He
didn't want chocolate or almond bits stuck in his teeth
when Elaine finally showed.

''How come you don't have kids?'' she asked.

He couldn't meet her eyes. ''I, uhm, it never happened.''

'''Cause you were in the army?''

''I traveled a lot.''

''You thinking about getting married?'' Her tone was
high and far too innocent.

''Jodi,'' Elaine said. Both turned on their chairs to face
her. ''What have I said about being so nosy?''

''Sorry, Mommy.'' She wore a gleefully hopeful expression.

Ric could not breathe. His mouth hung slack.

Elaine wore a dark green velvet dress, with the hem a
few inches above shapely knees encased in black stock-
ings. Over her shoulders she'd draped an open-knit shawl.
The simple outfit wowed him and made his heart beat faster. Her hair framed her face in a halo of soft, sable curls.
Her lips were red and glossy.

''You look nice, Mommy,'' Jodi said, watching Ric's
reaction.

Elaine executed a little twirl. She peered coquettishly
over her shoulder at Ric. ''Thank you.''

An ankle bracelet of such fine gold links it was more
sparkle than substance drew Ric's gaze to her sexy high
heels. He was going to die right here. A happy man.

''Run on over to Grandma's,'' Elaine said. She leaned

toward the vase of roses. A hint of creamy cleavage tormented Ric. She moved her face back and forth so the rose petals caressed her cheeks. "Are these for me?"

Ric remembered his manners. He rose from the chair and buttoned his jacket. "That dress is worth a few dozen more roses. You look…incredible."

"Thank you." She fluttered her eyelashes. Then, she kissed Jodi's cheek, leaving a lipstick print. "Don't keep Grandma up too late. I'll see you in the morning."

Jodi shook a finger at her mother. "Don't keep Ric up too late. He's an old guy, you know, and needs his sleep." Snickering, she snatched up a backpack and skipped out the door.

"I'm sorry," Elaine said. "I never know what will come out of that child's mouth. I have to remind her daily about not gossiping."

Tell her, he thought, while she's smiling and safe in her own kitchen. Jodi's talk, however, about Missy and sperm donors had him rattled. So did Elaine's loveliness. He didn't want to spoil one second of their date. "Shall we go?"

They walked outside into an overcast evening. He suggested she bring a coat. She twirled an end of her shawl and assured him she'd be fine. He opened the truck door, and wished he drove a Mustang or Corvette, something worthy of her. He walked around the truck, stepped in a depression and twisted his ankle. A sharp twinge shot up his back.

Not tonight, he thought angrily. He took an experimental step. No real pain. He made a mental note to watch his step. He wanted his back strong enough for at least one dance with the lovely Elaine.

When he took a seat behind the wheel, she said, "I saw you stumble. Are you all right?"

"Right as rain."

He drowned in her eyes, enchanted by her long lashes and a faint shimmer of powder on her eyelids.

He reached past her. He smelled a light perfume reminiscent of vanilla and honey. Senses reeling, he opened the glove box. He brought out a short handled plastic flyswatter emblazoned with the feed store's logo. He handed it to her.

She turned the swatter over. "It's too cold for bugs."

"Not for bugs." He started the engine. "It's for me. I can't be trusted to keep my hands off you."

She playfully tapped his hand with the swatter. "Such a gentleman."

If only she knew how very ungentlemanly he felt at the moment. He glimpsed Jodi standing at a window in the big house. She waved to them. The girl obviously approved of her mother dating. He wondered how much she'd approve of knowing Elaine dated a sperm donor.

In Durango, he had to drive up and down Main Street three times before he found a place to park. Hand in hand, they walked up the sidewalk. Her high heels slowed her step. At least, he hoped it was her shoes and not that she worried about his back.

The restaurant was packed. Tables were squeezed together to make room for the band and a dance floor. A heady aroma of hickory wood smoke and grilled meats filled the air. Ric could barely hear himself think. He spoke against Elaine's ear, asking if she'd cared to go somewhere quieter. Her eyes matched the jewel-sparkle of her drop earrings. She assured him she thought this was great.

He slipped the hostess twenty dollars to put them in an intimate booth. They had to wait an extra fifteen minutes. It was worth it to be in a secluded corner lit by candles that gave Elaine a mysterious glow.

He ordered wine for her and iced tea for himself.

She suddenly grasped both his hands. "Do you know how long it's been since I've dated?"

"Guess it depends on how liberal Bobby was."

Her laughter rang sweetly against his heart.

"I feel like a kid again." She shyly lowered her eyes.

Maybe tomorrow he'd tell her he knew about Jodi. For tonight, he wanted to hear her laughter and admire her beauty and feel gloriously alive.

"It's been a long while since I've dated, too," he said.

"I bet you were a real ladies man in the army."

He scrubbed his fingernails against his chest. "I got around."

He kept her laughing through dinner—trout for her, Black Angus filet in brandy sauce for him, then creamy tiramisu for dessert. The band began playing. Couples crowded the dance floor. He watched Elaine tap her fingers and bob her head to the oldies but goldies rock 'n' roll. Fast dancing in that crowd meant risking injury, so he waited. His chance came when the musicians launched into a sultry slow song.

He rose and offered a hand. "Care to?"

She set the shawl aside, revealing creamy shoulders covered by the thinnest of spaghetti straps. "Love to."

The dance floor was so tiny and crowded, they could do little more than hold each other and sway. He stared into her eyes. He debated inviting her for a soak in his hot tub, but that would be moving too fast. They'd moved too fast before, and he'd lost her. He wasn't taking that chance again, even if he was so dizzy from arousal that he half-feared his head was about to float away.

When they finally left the restaurant, the temperature had dropped. Springtime in the Rockies often brought frost or even snow well into June. Many of the cars parked along the street sported ski racks. He draped his jacket over her shoulders. It hung almost to her knees.

On the drive home along the dark highway, she leaned her head back and hummed the tune they'd danced to. Content to listen, he concentrated on watching for deer or elk.

He turned off the highway toward McClintock.

"Ric," she said, "there's something I need to tell you."

He tensed. Pain thudded through his back. He knew what she was going to say. He wanted her to say it, clear the air, and give them a fresh start with no secrets between them. He didn't want to spoil the evening. "Sing some more."

"I wasn't singing."

"Humming, then. You've got a great voice." He grinned. "Especially for such a little squirt."

She regarded him solemnly. "It's important. Something...something I should have told you a long time ago."

Red and blue lights flared in the darkness. A cruiser pulled out of a side road behind them. Muttering a curse, Ric glanced at the speedometer. He was going five miles under the speed limit.

"If that's Uncle King." Elaine twisted on the seat to see out the back window. "I'll shoot him."

If Ric had a gun, he'd oblige her.

Ric tapped the brakes until he could safely pull off the road. He asked Elaine to find his registration and insurance card in the glove box. The cruiser stopped behind them. King McClintock emerged. He took a moment to adjust the fit of his hat before swaggering toward the driver's door.

Ric rolled down the window. "Hey, sheriff. Is there a problem?"

Elaine leaned over Ric's arm. "Yes, Uncle King, is there a problem?"

King looked startled to see her. His bushy mustache twitched.

Ric kept his hands on the wheel. He thanked heavens he hadn't had anything alcoholic to drink tonight. He hoped like hell his proof of insurance card was the right one. He'd received a new one in the mail a few weeks ago and couldn't recall if he'd stuck it in the truck or not.

King looked between Ric and Elaine. Then he stepped back as if examining the truck. He brought out a small notebook and flipped through pages. "I got a report of stolen tools. Just so happens that a pickup matching the description of this very one was seen in the vicinity."

"You're making that up!" Elaine cried. "Let me see that report."

Ric could have groaned. A box in the truck bed was full of tools.

"Official business, young lady. Be quiet."

"Horse hockey," Elaine said. "You know darned good and well Ric didn't steal anything."

"I don't know any such thing. What are you doing with this boy anyway? Seems to me you're keeping poor company these days."

Don't say anything, Ric urged her mentally.

When Ric was a teenager, King had pulled him over at least once a week. Twice, Ric had been handcuffed and taken to jail. Once because King insisted Ric had been drinking—which he hadn't been—and hauled him in for a blood alcohol test. Another time it had been for bald tires. King had impounded Ric's car. He'd had to shell out nearly a hundred bucks in towing fees and another hundred for the unsafe vehicle fine before his car was returned.

With a hand on the butt of his sidearm, King ordered

Ric out of the truck. Ignoring her uncle's commands to
stay in the vehicle, Elaine jumped out the other side. She
stomped around the truck. She was a furious little hen
facing down a coyote.

"This is harassment and you know it, Uncle King. I will
not stand for it."

"It's all right, Laney," Ric said. "I've got nothing to
hide. He's just doing his job."

"Oh, no he's not! You're being a big jerk!"

"If you don't get back in the truck, girl, I'll arrest you
for interfering with a law officer."

She clamped her arms over her bosom and lifted her
chin. "Go right ahead."

"Laney…"

"Get back in the truck."

"No."

Ric knew that if not for Elaine he'd be in handcuffs
right now while the sheriff took a pry bar to his truck in
a search for "stolen" goods. He also knew that if the man
wasn't given a graceful way to save face, this was going
to turn ugly. He doubted if he and Elaine would be sharing
a cell.

"Hey, Laney, it's okay." He modulated his voice into
a friendly, nonchalant tone designed to soothe and hold
attention. "Tool theft is quite a problem around here. It
seems some folks can't resist picking up whatever they
find. What *exactly* was stolen, sheriff?"

King shuffled his feet and tugged at his hat brim. He
consulted the notebook again even though the lighting was
so poor he would have needed night vision goggles to read.
"Uhm, one of them…handheld power tools. You know
what I'm saying. A saw and drill. Cordless tools."

Ric decided exposing the sheriff as a liar in front of his

niece was too dangerous, no matter how satisfying it might be. "Those are expensive. What brand?"

"Brand?" King tugged his hat again, and consulted the notebook. His mustache twitched like a nervous ferret. "Lemme think. That brand Sears sells. That's it, the Sears brand."

"Ah, Craftsman. Good tools." Ric waited for the sheriff to nod agreement. He sorted through his key ring and found the key to his toolbox. "You're welcome to look, sheriff."

King had no choice except to play this charade to the finish. He shone his flashlight at the truck box. Ric offered to hold the flashlight. Grumbling, King handed it over. He opened the box. All of Ric's power tools were DeWalt's.

"Happy now?" Elaine called. She was hugging herself and shifting her feet. "Can we go? I'm freezing."

King slammed the toolbox lid and twisted the key. He all but threw the ring at Ric. His expression said he knew he'd been manipulated. "You can go."

Elaine climbed in through the driver's side and scooted over.

With his back to Elaine, King lowered his voice to a menacing growl. "You're engaging in some real unhealthy behavior, boy."

"I'll remember to take my vitamins. Sir."

"A regular smart ass, aren't you? How smart will you be if I go on up to that land of yours and take a look around? Or take a peek at your uncle's shop? No telling what kind of fire hazard he's created."

Ric understood the threat. If King could cover up a murder, there was no reason he wouldn't stoop to planting drugs or other nasties on Ric's property. Anger climbed through his chest. His forehead tightened.

"Safest way to stay clean is to keep your nose out of places it don't belong. Get my drift, boy?"

King strolled back to his cruiser. He cut off the bubble lights and gunned the engine. The tires sprayed Ric with gravel in passing.

Nice thing about small towns, Ric mused. Not much ever changed.

Chapter Nine

Elaine rode in silent, seething humiliation. Near home, she finally made herself look at Ric. His profile seemed set and stony, harsh in the lights from the truck dash. *She* was the reason King disliked Ric. Her uncle either knew, or suspected, Ric was Jodi's father. King would deprive his grand-niece of a father rather than let everyone know a man he considered trash was a part of his family. Miserable and torn, she tugged her shawl tighter around her shoulders. "About my uncle—"

"One question," he interrupted. He glanced her way. "If Tate finds proof King is involved in the murder, what's your position?"

She blinked rapidly. "Position?"

"Will you defend your uncle?"

Her heart sank. "How can you even ask that?"

They'd reached the entrance to the McClintock Ranch. He slowed the truck. Far in the distance, pale bowls of light glowed around buildings in an otherwise pitch-black landscape.

"Your uncle threatened to plant contraband on my property. Or maybe he'll go after Walt. He's real nervous that we're getting too close to the truth."

She groaned and let her head fall back against the seat.

The truck left the paved road. Gravel pattered beneath the wheels.

"If you hadn't been with me," he said. "I'd be in jail right now."

"I know. And I'm sorry. But he isn't evil. I swear to God, Ric. He's just scared."

"Of me?" He laughed, a bitter note. "Right."

"Don't you understand? King is scared of being embarrassed, of losing his job. It's all he has. Did you know he has three kids? They hardly talk to him. I can't remember the last time any of my cousins visited. He lives alone, and he's lonely. His whole identity is being sheriff. He knows he botched the investigation. That's why he's acting so mean."

Ric focused on the road ahead. His cheek twitched. He chuckled deep in his throat.

"Why are you laughing?"

He loosed a long breath. "Ah, Laney, do you have any idea what a good person you are? You give everybody the benefit of the doubt. You're always willing to look beneath the surface."

His words discomfited her. "I try to be fair."

"And my question was unfair. I know you'll do the right thing. I'm sorry." He groped for her hand, found it and squeezed. "I really am sorry. Forgive me?"

"Forgiven."

"Good. Because I refuse to let King ruin the best night I've ever had."

At her house, he hopped out of the truck and hurried to the passenger side to help her down. Even when she was firmly on the ground, he kept holding her hand.

"The best night ever?" she questioned.

"If there were better nights, I can't think of any."

He walked her to the door. The porch light cast alluring

shadows over the strong lines of his cheeks and jaw. His eyes were dark, compelling. The last remnants of anger at her uncle wisped away. Her heart began to thump with the possibilities. Jodi was staying all night at the big house. She and Ric were adults. It might be uncomfortable for both of them to share the bed she'd shared with Bobby, but there was always the guest room—or the kitchen floor.

She wanted him. Lord have mercy, but she wanted him bad.

He ever so slowly, ever so gently tucked a strand of hair behind her ear.

Knowing exactly what would happen if she invited him inside, she despaired. If they made love before he knew about Jodi, it would seem as if she seduced him in order to protect herself. He adjusted the shawl higher on her shoulders. His actions were so tender her hips went heavy and loose.

"Would you care to come inside? Have a nightcap?"

Had she actually said that? Was that her voice sounding so smoky and seductive? She couldn't believe how deep a hole she was digging for herself.

He turned his gaze to the night. His chest rose and fell in a silent sigh. "No."

Her mouth fell open. Every look he turned her way radiated desire. She *knew* he wanted her. Maybe King's harassment made him realize she was more trouble than she was worth. She searched for means to regain a shred of dignity.

He took her right hand in both of his. "I see tonight as starting over. We made a lot of mistakes in the past. Our relationship back then was based as much on rebelliousness as it was on mutual desire."

She struggled to make sense of what he was saying. "Do you think so? I don't. I—I cared so much about you."

"I want you to care again. The right way, for the right reasons. So how about it? You and me, a clean slate."

His thumbs were doing delicious things to her wrist and palm. The air temperature might be close to freezing, but within her skin an inferno blazed. Her knees were wobbly.

"I want to do it right this time. Up front and out in the open." He caught his lower lip in his teeth, looking thoughtful. "You hold an important place in this community. A lot of people look up to you."

Hell of a time for him to worry about her reputation. "Um, thank you, I think."

He chuckled. "I want people to look up to me, too. Especially the most important person. Jodi."

Uncertain where this led, she drew warily aside, beyond the intoxicating influence of his scent and vibrant masculinity. When she withdrew her hand from his, her skin tingled, aching to reclaim his touch. "She does look up to you. She thinks you're a hero." She needed to tell him the truth. She needed to tell him now.

"How heroic would it be for us to sneak around?" Now solemn, he lowered his face. "Your uncle isn't the only one who thinks I'm not good enough for you."

"But—"

"Ah-ah, hear me out. I need to say this, for you to understand. When I was growing up, all I wanted was out of this place. I hated McClintock. I hated how people made me feel like a stray dog. Kids teased me about my mom, about not knowing my father. Teachers always expected the worst from me."

"Oh, Ric, that doesn't matter."

"It *does* matter. It's why I thought I found a home in the army. A place where I was somebody. When I got hurt, I found out I was just a number, a broken cog in the big machine. They threw me away like so much garbage.

Whoop-di-do, I get a retirement check. A monthly reminder about how much they don't want me.''

All her life she'd known exactly where she belonged.
She'd never doubted the love of her family, friends and
community. She couldn't conceive of feeling like a root-
less outcast.

''I came home to McClintock because I had no where
else to go. My only plan was, get better and beat it out of
here. But things have changed. Now, when I walk into the
hardware store, Paul calls me over to ask my opinion about
hot-dipped nails or some new brand of wood putty. Every
time old Mrs. Whitehorse sees me, she goes on and on
about what a great job I did on her kitchen cabinets. Just
the other day, Pastor Rimes personally invited me to attend
church services.'' His teeth gleamed. ''Your mom calls me
honey.''

''You're a nice guy,'' she murmured.

''I want to be more than that, Laney. I want to be good
enough for you.''

''You are!''

''Good enough to walk hand-in-hand with you down
Main Street. Good enough to sit next to you in church.
Good enough so that when folks see us together, nobody
is thinking you're slumming with that Buchanan boy.''

She felt the chilly air now along with rising emotion.
She didn't know how he'd react if he knew she wasn't
good enough for him.

''I want to set a good example for Jodi. She's growing
up to be a beautiful young lady. We have to show her how
she should be treated. She needs to see me treating you
like the lady you are.''

If only he knew what unladylike thoughts were racing
through her head. ''I see.''

He touched a fingertip to her lower lip. Shivers raced

up and down her spine. She wanted to tear off his tie and rip open his shirt and plant kisses all over his broad, beautiful chest. She wanted to tell him about Jodi. She couldn't make herself do either.

"So, no more kissing until the third date. That's properly respectful, right?"

He was killing her. The wicked twist of his smile proclaimed he was enjoying himself immensely. "You're assuming," she said tartly, "that there will be a second date."

"Next Friday? A movie?"

"Okay."

He shook her hand with exaggerated formality then stepped off the porch. "I'll see you in church." Whistling, he sauntered to his truck.

Not one kiss until the third date? She might burst into flames and explode before that happened.

ELAINE OPENED her eyes after the final prayer. She sat with her mother, Jodi and Uncle King in the McClintock family pew. It was at the very front of the Maya Valley Church of Christ. A place of honor for the family that had provided the stained glass windows, organ and marble altar.

People sidled out of pews. Pastor Rimes meandered toward the doors to make sure he had a word with every member of his congregation. Elaine leaned past her mother and smiled at her uncle. "May I speak to you for a minute, Uncle King?"

In uniform, he held his hat over his chest. He glared at her from the corner of his eye.

"It'll only take a minute," she said, sweetly.

"Come on with me, Jodi," Lillian said. "I need to remind Pastor Rimes about reserving the meeting room."

Elaine kept her voice down and her mouth smiling, but

inside she seethed. "I will not stand for you harassing Ric Buchanan. Or making threats. Or threatening Walt."

He opened his mouth, but she snapped up a hand to halt his speech. She smiled and nodded at a neighbor who called a greeting.

"I know you don't like him. You might even think you have good reasons. But he's a law-abiding citizen. I will not put up with you throwing your official weight around."

"You best remember who you're talking to, young lady." His face was turning an alarming shade of purple.

"You best remember who you're talking to," she shot back. "If you want to play power games, I can play just as hard and dirty as you want."

"I never—"

"Need I remind you that I've known every single member of the county commission and the town council all my life. Every one of them is a good friend. You don't even want to go head-to-head with me over who has more pull in this town."

"Oh, so now you're threatening me? For that no-account boy?" He sneered. "Gonna sic your mama on me?"

"I don't *need* to sic mama on you."

"Don't you see what's going on here, honey?"

She crossed her arms. She thought she'd made it perfectly clear that she knew exactly what was going on. "I know that traffic stop last night was a total fabrication. If I hadn't been with Ric, you'd have trumped up some charge to throw him in jail."

"You'd be better off if he was in jail. He's out for vengeance. He hated Del, always has. All his snooping around and riling Tom Greene is pure troublemaking. Trying to make our family look bad."

Incredulous, she shook her head. If she were holding

anything other than a Bible in her hand, she'd have smacked him with it.

"He's the one driving that poor old man crazy. Is that what you want? Tom dead of a stroke? Gossips calling Del a mad dog killer?"

"Your investigation was shoddy, Uncle King." Afraid she'd start shouting, she whispered. "That was my husband who was shot. My father who died trying to save him. But you do a better job investigating poachers. Tom has every right to question your ruling. So do I."

He glanced at the people clustered near the church doors. "I know what happened at the lodge and it's ugly, damn it."

His admission startled her. "You do?"

"It wasn't an accident. Is that what you want to hear? Huh? How about we catch up to Lillian and tell her, too? How about I get up in the pulpit and announce it to the whole dad-blamed town?" His ears had turned crimson and his eyes blazed. "I loved that damned Del. I loved Bobby, too. What happened makes just sick in the heart." He dropped a heavy hand on her shoulder. "I know how bad you feel about losing Bobby. But how's it going to make you feel better seeing in black-and-white that your daddy is a killer?"

His absolute certainty confused her and made her wary.

"I don't know why Del did it. We'll never know. I do know the law can't take him to task for it. I do know it'll break Lillian's heart. It'll tear this town in two. That would make Buchanan happy as a pig in mud."

"You're wrong."

He leaned in close enough for her to smell Old Spice aftershave and breath mints. "You think I'm an old coot, going senile, not a lick of sense in my head. But I know people, honey. I know *hombres* like Buchanan. They twist things up and light little fires that start big conflagrations.''

''What if Daddy didn't shoot Bobby?''

King snorted a wry laugh. ''So who did? Santa Claus?'' He slid his gaze toward the doors. His eyes narrowed and his mustache twitched. ''Or could be some fellah with a grudge against Bobby. Now that I recollect, I got some witnesses that says Buchanan and Bobby had themselves a big old fight in the Track Shack right before Bobby was killed.''

She followed his gaze. Ric walked up the aisle. He wore a dark suit and tie. His tawny hair was neatly combed. He'd meant what he said about seeing her in church. He hesitated about halfway up the aisle, his expression questioning.

''You can't be serious,'' she whispered.

''Reckon it might not be such a bad thing to take another look at my ruling. I could have overlooked something. Like Buchanan having a motive for murder.'' He tugged an end of his mustache, his grin sharky. ''Yep, he might have been mad enough to go gunning for our boy. Now wouldn't that be something?''

''Uncle King—''

''I got work to do, honey.'' He nodded curtly and turned away. He strutted down the aisle. He nodded at Ric. ''Nice to see you in church, boy. Scrub a few black marks off your soul.''

She turned her eyes to the wooden cross hanging behind the altar. *Oh dear Lord, what have I done?*

Ric joined her at the end of the pew. He watched King shaking hands with the pastor. ''What was that all about?''

She sighed. ''I told him to stop harassing you. He just promised me it's going to get worse.''

''Huh.''

"I'm sorry, Ric."

"Don't worry about it."

"Oh, really? He threatened to produce witnesses who'll testify you had a motive for murder. He'll convince somebody to lie about you fighting with Bobby the day of the shooting."

"I did fight with Bobby and there were witnesses." He slid a hand around the nape of his neck. "We had an argument in the Track Shack."

"About what? Why didn't you tell me?"

"I don't see what difference it makes." He glanced at the back of the church again. King was gone. "At the time I couldn't even walk, much less drive. I don't own a handgun either. King is blowing smoke."

"What were you fighting about?"

He took her hand. "Give it a rest." He squeezed her fingers. "Your mother invited Walt and me to have lunch at the ranch. I was wondering if I could make a detour first with Jodi. Erles Harbaugh is selling his daughter's show horse. He said I could come by and take a look today."

She wanted to know what Bobby and Ric would have to fight about. They'd made their peace about her and Bobby's marriage years ago. Ric had only been in town a day or two, so they hadn't had an opportunity to get on each other's nerves.

"Why don't you come, too?" he asked. "It'll be fun."

Jodi came skipping up the aisle. "Mom! Grandma invited Mr. Walt and Ric to lunch. Come on, Grandma's waiting at the car."

Elaine looked between her daughter and Ric. Jodi wore a skirt she'd received last Christmas; already it was too short. She seemed to be growing an inch a day. A beautiful young lady who needed a good example as to how to be treated like a lady. Ric acted more like a concerned parent than a mere friend.

Ric Buchanan is back in town...how would he like knowing what you really did to him?

He knew. Call it intuition, call it a hunch. Whatever it was, she knew without a doubt that he knew he was Jodi's father. He and Bobby had argued because of it.

"Well?" Ric asked.

"Lunch will be waiting," she said. "How about if we look at the horse afterward?"

"What horse?" Jodi asked. "The Morgan?"

"I spoke to Mr. Harbaugh earlier," Ric said.

"You know that horse, Mommy. Sue Harbaugh rode him in pleasure trials. Don't you think he'd be just perfect for Ric?"

"Could be. We can look at it after lunch."

Jodi tugged Ric by the hand toward the door. Elaine followed them out of the church and into the sunshine. A fool's gold day with a blinding blue sky and a wicked wind that dropped the temperature into the thirties. She turned her face to the wind, letting it cut across her cheeks and clear her thoughts.

Ric knew. He'd argued with Bobby because he knew.

Sunday lunch at the ranch turned into its usual noisy affair. Along with Ric and his uncle, they were joined by the ranch manager, his wife and their three children, and a pair of ranch hands who were so shy around Lillian it was almost painful to watch their fumbling and mumbling.

While the gathering ate pot roast and new potatoes, Marlee telephoned from college. Elaine could tell from Lillian's side of the conversation that her little sister was in a panic over upcoming final exams. Lillian finally convinced her middle child that the stress wasn't going to kill her, and she didn't have a brain tumor. She would actually pass her finals and graduate on schedule.

Somehow, Elaine managed to eat and talk and laugh.

After lunch, Elaine said, "I need to change my clothes before we look at horses. Ric, would you walk over to the house with me?" Lillian gave Elaine a questioning look. Elaine pretended not to notice.

On the way to her house, Ric worked off his tie and unbuttoned the top button of his shirt. He rolled the tie and stuck it in his jacket pocket. In her kitchen, Ric asked, "What's going on, Laney?"

She was shaking inside. "Have a seat. I have something to show you."

She walked to her bedroom, but slowly, studying the white on white striped paper she'd put up in the hallway. Groups of framed photographs hung on the walls. She passed Jodi's room where her unmade bed was piled with stuffed animals and clothes. This house had been a wedding gift from her parents. She and Bobby had turned it into a home.

She didn't regret a minute of her marriage. She regretted the lie it was based on, and the pain it had caused Ric. If she had to do it all over again, however, under the same circumstances, she would.

Still, if she were wrong, and Ric didn't know about Jodi, what she was about to do could destroy their relationship.

Her hands trembled as she reached into the back of her lingerie drawer and found the envelope. A sudden impulse to slam and lock her bedroom door, to hide, held her frozen for a moment. She had to do this. Ric deserved better than lies. Bobby deserved better than having her conceal evidence because she was a big fat coward.

She slipped off her pumps. In stocking feet she returned to the kitchen. She placed the envelope in front of Ric.

Her throat choked up and her eyes burned with impending tears. The urge to cry confused her. She pinched the bridge of her nose. When he unfolded the note, she turned away and hugged her aching belly.

"Where did you get this?" he asked.

She opened her mouth and a sob escaped. She gulped hard until she could speak. "Bobby's pants pocket. The day before the funeral. For the longest time I thought Daddy had written it. But he didn't. He wouldn't have. That's what you and Bobby were fighting about, isn't it? Who told you about Jodi? Who killed my husband to shut him up?"

She ripped a paper towel off a roll and jammed it against her eyes. Ric touched her back. All she could do was shake her head.

"It's all right, Laney."

She blew her nose and scrubbed her eyes. "It's not all right! What you said last night...it touched me, Ric. It really did. I want so much to start fresh, to be with you again. Truth is, I'm not worthy of you. I don't deserve your respect."

He gently turned her around. He seemed so calm and accepting.

"Who told you, Ric?"

"Bobby."

Dumbfounded, all she could do was stare.

"I meant to tell you, but I didn't know how." He enfolded her in an embrace and held her head against his chest. She snuffled into a wadded up towel. She felt guilty about accepting his comfort, but was unwilling to give it up.

"Bobby caught me off guard. I lost my temper. Said some ugly things." His voice dropped to a broken whisper. "Then he was gone."

Her thoughts raced over the past eighteen months. How wrong Uncle King was about Ric. If he'd wanted revenge, he could have embroiled her family in scandal or legal battles. Instead, he'd become Jodi's friend. The glee-club-unto-himself who shouted himself hoarse at volleyball and basketball games and track meets. The devoted fan who sat in the sweltering sun on hot bleachers, watching Jodi race her horse around barrels. The dependable guy who picked her up after school when she missed the bus because of sports practice or drama club.

"I understand why you married Bobby."

She looked at him then. "Do you?"

"He was here, I wasn't."

She pushed at his chest until he released her. "Stop being so understanding. I feel terrible. I loved you. I really did. I dreamed about us getting married and traveling the world. Then I found out I was pregnant. I was so scared."

"Laney, I—"

"Daddy just hated you. I don't know why, but even mentioning your name made him lose his temper. I was scared of what he might do."

"I know—"

"Bobby said let's get married, and it sounded like the perfect solution even though I knew you would hate me. I just didn't know what to do."

He caught her shoulders with both hands. "I know! If it makes you feel better, hell yes I was mad. I wanted to beat the snot out of Bobby. I wanted to confront you and let you know—" he gave her a little shake "—how much you hurt me. But then he was gone. I couldn't hurt you. I couldn't hurt Jodi. So I got over being mad. I even got over being hurt."

She searched his eyes, wanting to believe him. Deep and wise, the dark blue depths were warmed by kindness.

"When I got to know Jodi, I saw what a great father Bobby was. He did more for her, and for you, than I ever could have." He grinned crookedly. "It would have been a huge mistake if we got married. You'd have hated the army. You'd have ended up hating me."

She didn't believe that; she refused to believe it. "I wanted to tell you. I couldn't figure out how."

"Come on, sit down." He pulled out a chair for her. "Bobby said I needed to hear about Jodi before I heard it elsewhere. I guess this note is the reason why." He set a glass of water before her.

She pressed the cool glass against her hot forehead. "God, I feel so guilty. I should have shown it to Tate. I should have told—"

He stared out the window over the sink. "Uh-oh, Jodi's coming."

Not wanting her daughter to see she'd been crying, Elaine scrambled to her feet. She snatched up the note. "She doesn't know, Ric."

Still watching out the window, he said, "Then let's not tell her. Go change your clothes."

She hurried to the bedroom. Weeping had left her drained and wobbly, but oddly lighter. She stripped off her dress and panty hose, then pulled on socks, jeans and a flannel shirt. When she saw her blotchy face in the bathroom mirror, she groaned. She scrubbed her face clean of cosmetics.

She picked up the note from the bed. Lunch shifted unpleasantly in her stomach. Tate was going to have to see this.

What might happen from this point on, she hadn't a clue. At least there were no more lies between her and Ric.

When she joined Ric and Jodi in the kitchen, Jodi had already changed out of her church clothes and into jeans.

She was telling Ric how she and Elaine, Lillian and Uncle King were going to Greeley to attend Marlee's graduation. Ric listened to his daughter as if her every word were a precious jewel.

Elaine felt Bobby's presence now, in this cozy kitchen where he'd spent hours helping Jodi with her homework. Where he'd eaten countless meals. Where they'd shared laughter and small talk and philosophical discussions and arguments. His presence seemed to say to her, ''Let the past go and get on with living.''

Somehow, some way, she'd make amends for what she'd done. Elaine cleared her throat to catch their attention. ''Shall we go see a man about a horse?''

Chapter Ten

Ric rested his forearms on the corral's top rail. His daughter put the Morgan gelding through his paces. A fine example of the breed, the horse had big intelligent eyes and trim ears. He was a dark russet bay with black legs and an extra long mane and tail. In the midst of shedding his winter coat, he was scruffy but looked and acted healthy. He loped in a neat figure-eight, kicking up dust in the corral.

"She rides like a dream," Ric said.

"Amazing considering how fat that pony is," Elaine replied. She turned a teasing grin to Erles Harbaugh. "How long since he's been ridden?"

The middle-aged man hawked and looked about to spit, then cut his eyes at Elaine and swallowed. He thumbed back his cowboy hat. "Not since Sue went off to college. Old Savvy there is worse than a beagle dog. Eat anything that isn't nailed down."

"He looks good," Ric said. Jodi looked wonderful. He thought his heart might burst with pride.

Jodi tugged the reins. The gelding obediently tucked his hindquarters and stopped. One dark ear remained swiveled toward his rider. He wore a hackamore instead of a bridle with a bit. It struck Ric as a sign of a gentle animal.

"Rides real easy, Ric," Jodi said. She patted the animal's neck. "But needs some exercise. Listen to him blow."

Elaine reached through the fence and tugged a long whisker. The Morgan snuffled hungrily around her hand. "You say he's twenty years old?"

Erles laughed. "I ain't playing horse trader with you, missy. Uh-uh, not with no McClintock gal. He's fourteen, in his prime. Yeah, he's a butterball, but like the little lady says, just needs exercise. I got his pedigree, properly registered. And a vet certificate, too. Get him in shape and he'll do wonders in pleasure trails. He's one of them show-off critters. Loves it when a crowd is watching. Acts like the king of England when he goes prancing into a show ring."

"I hate to sound like a greenhorn," Ric said, "but does he have any dangerous quirks?"

Frowning in concentration, Erles scratched beneath his hat. "He's pretty darned good at picking latches. I suggest a padlock on your feed shed. He's been down for colic twice 'cause he's gotten into grain. Didn't founder, though." He rapped his knuckles on the fence. "Knock on wood."

Jodi offered, "Ric has a bad back. He can't have a horse that'll buck or spook."

Ric flinched at the artless explanation.

"Ah, that's right." Erles clapped a horn-textured hand on Ric's shoulder. "Brave man doing what you did for your country, son. Real proud of your sacrifice. I promise, won't give you no knucklehead horse."

Erles climbed over the fence into the corral. He asked Jodi to take the gelding at a canter in a wide circle. Erles whipped off his hat and, shouting, waved it at the horse's face. The Morgan cocked an ear toward the man, but never broke stride. Then Erles whistled, loud and piercing. A pair of hounds squirmed beneath the corral fence. The horse noticed the dogs, but didn't react, not even when a dog trotted after him. Erles then flicked a rope at the gelding's hindquarters, earning a rippling twitch and an annoyed look, but no shying or loss of concentration.

"That's one calm animal, Ric," Elaine said. "If you like, you can keep him at the ranch for a while. Jodi can get him in shape. You can ride him in the arena until you feel comfortable."

"Is he worth sixteen hundred dollars?" He was still reeling over Erles calling him a hero.

"He's worth a lot more than that. But I'm sure Erles is sick of feeding him."

"You don't think he's too short for me? He looks short."

"Fifteen hands is about right. Make it easy for you to mount and dismount. Besides, Morgans pack a lot of power. Look at the depth of chest on him. Iron legs, too. Once he's in shape, he'll be unstoppable."

He smiled down at her. "I'll take you at your word."

"Offer Erles twelve hundred. He'll be insulted if you don't dicker."

"You're joking."

"Nope."

So Ric tossed out the low-ball offer. Elaine was right. The man looked delighted, though he tried hard not to show it. In the end, Ric agreed to pay seventeen hundred and fifty dollars for the horse, the saddle and hackamore. Erles went to fetch the paperwork. Jodi led the horse into the barn to unsaddle him and rub him down. Ric and Elaine sat in his truck.

He was writing out a check when Elaine asked, "Are you sure you aren't mad at me?"

Her cheeks were pink from the cold wind and her hair
was tousled. She looked young enough to be Jodi's sister.
Gorgeous. He took his time signing the check. "I got over
being mad. I told you that."

"I'm not over being mad at myself." She sighed
heavily. "We need to tell Jodi."

"Nope." He tore the check out of the book and examined it. This made him the official owner of an eating
machine that required vet check-ups, grooming, daily feeding, exercise and shoes. The pride on Jodi's young face
for helping him select the perfect animal made it all worth
it.

"We have to, Ric. She needs to know."

"No, she doesn't. There's no point to her knowing.
Bobby was her daddy. And if you and I," he shrugged,
"get together, there's no sense in confusing her about
things she has no control over."

She fiddled with a coat button. "Wouldn't you want to
know?"

"I *don't* want to know. If I opened my door today and
some guy said he's my father, I'd probably punch him in
the nose."

"It's not the same thing."

"It is as far as I'm concerned. I'm not going to turn her
whole life upside down. Fill her up with questions I don't
know how to answer. What we did, we have to live with.
I don't see why she has to suffer."

She placed a slim hand over his. Even an innocent touch
was pure torment for him. If only she knew how very
difficult it had been for him to walk away from her last
night.

"She loves you," she said.

"As a friend. I love her too much to make her life any

harder than it is now." He longed to gather her into his arms. "The person we have to tell is Tate."

She drew back, her eyes growing wide. "The note?"

"We have to, Laney. I suspected all along Bobby was being blackmailed. The note is proof."

Erles approached the truck. Ric handed over the check. Erles handed over an envelope containing the Morgan's pedigree, registration and vet certificate. "I'm gonna hate seeing that old chow-hound go. He's friendly as a lap dog."

"I'll send a man with a trailer to pick him up tomorrow," Elaine said. "What's the best time for you?"

"Any old time in the afternoon, hon. Either me or the missus will be around." He shook hands with Ric. "Does my heart good to know Savvy is going to a good home. Just don't forget padlocks, son. And cut his grain in the summertime to nothing unless you're working him hard."

Flattered the old rancher thought he was giving the pampered Morgan a good home, Ric said, "I will, sir. Tell your daughter, if she gets nostalgic, she's welcome to ride him any time."

Ric drove Elaine and Jodi home. The girl made excited plans about getting the Morgan in shape. She listed the many places she could take Ric riding. When they reached Elaine's house, Ric noticed his uncle's truck was still parked in front of Lillian's. The old bachelor had finally been heart-snagged. It amused him.

Elaine lingered next to the driver's side of the truck while Jodi ran into the house. "I really think it's better if we tell her. I'd hate for her to hear it from someone else."

"Trust me on this, will you? I'm going to find Tate. I'll call you."

He rested an arm on the open driver's window. He didn't want to go. He'd be happy to sit in her kitchen and drink coffee and watch her do laundry or read the Sunday paper. Listen to Jodi talk about the thousand and one things that utterly fascinated her this week. Shoot a few baskets with his daughter. Elaine seemed reluctant to end the day, too.

Her smile quirked. She walked her fingers along his forearm. Her expression turned impish, her big eyes shining. "So, does today count as our second date?"

He bit back laughter. "Why, Miz Greene, I'm shocked and appalled by your eagerness."

She batted her eyelashes, her smile far too innocent. "Just asking."

He kissed her cheek, lingering with his nose in her hair. She smelled of fresh air and sweetness. Desire jolted him, weakening his resolve. He pulled back and started the engine. "You be a good girl."

She stepped back, sighing dramatically. "It's hard."

"Tell me about it," he muttered and shoved the transmission into reverse.

EARLY ON Wednesday morning, Elaine drove through town. The windshield wipers swiped at steady rain mixed with sleet. It was so early none of the shops were open. Icy rain kept pedestrians off the sidewalks. She pulled around behind the Track Shack and parked next to Tate Raleigh's Bronco.

She darted through the rain to the back door. By the time Tate answered her knocking, water was streaming from the brim of her hat. She hustled inside, shivering, chilled to the bone.

"Good morning," Tate said. He helped her out of her coat. He hung it and her hat on a wooden peg. "Crazy weather. Don't you ever get spring around here?"

"Wait until you see your first July snowstorm. Is Ric here?"

"Not yet."

She followed him into the tiny apartment tacked onto the back of the bar. Age-darkened pine paneling covered the walls. Indoor-outdoor carpeting was worn through in spots. A rack holding free weights crowded an entire corner. What snagged her attention were the books. Shelves made of planks on cinder blocks sagged beneath the weight of countless volumes. Books were piled on the floor and in a precarious looking stack atop a table next to a sofa. Tate moved books from a kitchen chair.

"You like to read." She felt dumb for stating the obvious.

"When I have time." He plunked a steaming mug of coffee on a table in front of her. He winked. "Hopeless bookaholic."

She never knew what to make of Tate. Her first impression had been of a big, dumb jock, but once she stopped being distracted by his accent, she'd realized he was highly intelligent. If the eclectic collection of books indicated anything, he was cultured as well.

"I imagine you miss book stores," she said.

"And a library. This town needs a library, what do you think?" He jerked a thumb at a computer squeezed into a corner. "The Internet is useful, but libraries are better."

"Why did you move here?"

He joined her at the table. "When I was twelve my family took a cross-country vacation to California." He laughed. "Station wagon, crap tied on top, fighting with my brothers and sisters, Dad making time, Mom whining about bathroom stops, the whole schmear. What I remember best was the Rockies. I fell in love. Everything is so big. It's…*grand!* So when I got a chance to move, I took it.''

Elaine got a funny sense that he wasn't telling the whole story. She shook off the feeling. His personal life was none of her business.

When Ric showed up, he was soaking wet after walking from the wood shop. His hands were red. He gratefully wrapped both of them around a hot coffee mug. He lowered himself to a chair as if fearing he'd break in half.

"Are you okay?" she asked.

"Fine," he answered sharply.

Her mothering instinct probably irritated the dickens out of him. She curled her lips inward against the urge to fuss.

"Ric says you have something to show me," Tate said. The rickety table dipped when he rested an arm on it.

She pulled the note from her shirt pocket. The time was past for shame. She handed it over.

Poker-faced, he read it. "Where did you get this?"

She told him about finding it in Bobby's jeans pocket. She added, "I had it in my head that Daddy wrote it. I even searched his house for a typewriter, but didn't find one. I was scared to death it was proof that he was a murderer. But now I realize it's impossible."

Tate looked between the note and Ric. "Why is that?"

"Because the threat…he threatened to tell Ric that he's Jodi's biological father."

Tate's expression remained bland. What was a huge scandal in McClintock probably didn't mean diddly to a New Yorker.

"Bobby told me that day in the Track Shack," Ric said. "He wanted me to hear about it before I heard elsewhere. Laney is right. Del would have shot himself before letting me know I had a claim on his granddaughter."

"So, who else knows?" Tate asked.

Elaine slumped on the chair. She was a fool to think she could keep any secrets in a small town. "I never told anyone, and I doubt if Bobby did, but our hasty wedding caused some gossip. So did the timing of Jodi's birth."

Tate frowned. "I'm surprised Bobby didn't tell you that he told Ric."

She supposed not even the intimacy of marriage meant knowing another person inside and out. "He must have wanted to talk to Daddy first."

"How would Axton Cross know about Ric and Jodi?"

Elaine looked to Ric, and he looked to her. In sync, they shrugged. She said, "He must have heard some gossip. Do you still think Axton is involved?"

"He owns a revolver."

Elaine's belly lurched. "What kind?"

".44 magnum."

"Oh my God," she breathed.

Ric sat taller. Suddenly, he looked very dangerous.

"The weapon is registered, and he has a concealed carry permit. The sheriff issued it. I talked to the M.E. who autopsied Bobby. Bobby's wound was consistent with a .44 round fired at close range. I also did what I could with the phone records, but I don't think anything will come out of it. The under-sheriff was on desk duty when Del's call came in. He swears the sheriff was at the station."

"Good old Gil Vance," Elaine muttered, relieved her uncle had an airtight alibi from his under-sheriff. To Ric's questioning look, she added, "Gil thinks King is a blowhard, and King thinks Gil is after his job. Gil wouldn't lie for my uncle. So, what about Axton? Does he have an alibi?"

"Don't jump the flag," Tate said. "There are more handguns than mice in this valley. Unless we can put the gun and the bullet together, we've got squat."

"Can you get a warrant to search Axton's house?" Ric asked.

"Based on what?" Tate tapped the note. "No offense, Elaine, but all we have is your word that you found it in Bobby's pocket. This is a very small piece in a very big puzzle."

"What do we do then?" Ric asked.

"We've got some serious problems," Tate said. "At the top of the heap is the sheriff."

"He'll reopen the investigation." Elaine spoke with more confidence than she felt. King had made it clear that he wasn't about to take any chances that Del would be exposed as a murderer. "I'll tell him I found the bullets. I'll show him the note, too. He'll have to do the right thing."

Tate cocked an eyebrow. His twisted grin struck her as unnecessarily patronizing. "I can count on one hand the number of times I've seen the sheriff out of uniform. I've known a lot of cops like him. They live for the job."

"I know how he is."

"You don't know what you're asking for. His reputation is on the line. Folks are already squawking about corruption. Tom Greene could slap a lawsuit on him. The sheriff won't like lawyers lining up for a chance to dip into his pockets."

"If he realizes he made a mistake…"

"I know a D.A. who pushed through a capital murder case knowing damn good and well that his witnesses were tainted. He put a man on death row rather than admit making a mistake. I've known cops who planted guns after bad shootings. Others who ignored contradictory evidence. It happens all the time."

"So, you're saying we're stuck?" Ric asked. A most unpleasant glitter made his eyes look like glass.

"We have to handle this real careful. I've got a plan."

Ric and Elaine were all ears.

"I sent the fingerprints we lifted to the Colorado Bureau of Investigation. Their techs are backed up. We have to wait until they get around to running them. Good news is, being a licensed Realtor means Axton's fingerprints are on file. So if we get a match, then we'll take the sheriff up to the lodge. I'll lay out the photos, the measurements we made, show him the bullets."

"What if we don't have Axton's fingerprints?"

"Then we'll figure out another way to get the sheriff up to the lodge."

Ric swung his head side to side. "It could blow up in your face, man."

"A risk I'm willing to take. What about you two?"

"I'm in," Ric said.

Elaine swallowed hard. "What if Uncle King tries to turn this back on Ric?"

"If he does trump up a charge against me, then he has to reopen the investigation, right?" Ric grinned at her.

She imagined he'd rather enjoy going head-to-head with her uncle. As long as both of them were on equal footing.

"I can't believe I'm going to say this," she muttered. "If he knows Axton killed Bobby, and he's covering it up, then what?"

Tate waggled his eyebrows. "Then we're in trouble."

Ric patted her hand. "We have to do this, Laney."

She hoped like crazy that her uncle wasn't involved in her husband's murder. "You're right. I'm in."

Elaine insisted on driving Ric back to the wood shop. He didn't protest too strenuously. The rain had turned into snow. It was sticking to roofs and vehicles. When he climbed into the Jeep he grunted and winced. Taking care to avoid potholes, she parked as close to the wood shop door as possible.

"Scared?" Ric asked.

"I can't believe Uncle King is a criminal, but he sure is acting like one. And what about Jodi? We have to tell her."

"I know," he grumbled, looking none too happy about it. "One way or another, it's going to come out. Damn it."

"She's a tough kid. Smart. She can handle the truth."

He waved a hand at nothing and everything. "What about this town? Can they handle it?"

"Nobody is going to blame Jodi for what we did."

"Yeah, right."

She caressed his shoulder, leisurely examining the powerful round of muscle and heavy bone. She ached for the boy he'd been, suffering for the sins of a careless mother and absent father. "The first real fight Bobby and I ever had was about you."

He peered at her from the corner of his eye.

"It was after Jodi was born. I felt so guilty about not telling you. Bobby kept insisting no, no, he couldn't hurt you worse than he had. It wasn't that he convinced me he was right, but that I was so ashamed of myself. All those years I avoided you. When you visited Bobby would say, come on, let's go have a drink with Ric. But I couldn't face you."

"I understand."

Her chest hitched. "I think I'm finally beginning to understand. We go around saying we don't want to hurt people's feelings. We're really trying to protect ourselves."

"I'm not ashamed of Jodi. Or you. I loved you, Laney. I really did."

It stung a bit to hear him speaking in past tense. "Jodi

needs to know. Especially if you and I are to have any kind of future. To keep the truth from her is merely protecting ourselves from shame. That's not fair.'' She paused in order to gather her emotions. ''If I hadn't been such a coward, Bobby might still be alive.''

He clunked his head against the window glass. ''Don't go there, Laney.''

''Well, it's true! I always thought if a person had good intentions, then everything would be okay. But I hurt you, I hurt Bobby. I could hurt Jodi.''

''Stop. Just *stop*.''

His fierceness made her freeze. Her throat was growing tight with impending tears. She swallowed hard to keep them at bay. She was so darned sick of crying.

''We're not saints. Not me, not you, not Bobby. We muddle along trying to make the best of things, and sometimes we mess up. Do I feel responsible for Bobby's death? In some ways, yeah, I do. He was the best friend I ever had. I miss him.''

She dug through her pockets for a tissue. Whenever she began to believe she'd gotten past her grief, it sneaked up on her again. It felt as if an anvil weighted her chest.

His expression softened. The corners of his mouth turned in a hint of a smile. ''When we were about sixteen, Bobby told me he'd discovered the meaning of life.''

''What's that?''

''He said, if you can figure out what's worth dying for, then you'll always know what's worth living for. You and Jodi were it for him, Laney.''

''I didn't want him dying for me.''

''He did anyway. If he were here right now, he'd do it again. You know it's true. So get off the guilt-trip. Let's get on with what we have to do. Okay?''

He slid a hand behind her neck and drew her forehead-to-forehead with him. She kept her eyes closed, afraid if she looked at him she'd burst into tears. He smelled of rain and wet wool. His hand was hot against her skin.

"Are we still on for Friday night?"

"Yes," she whispered.

"Good. Now get out of here before I forget you're a lady."

Chapter Eleven

On Friday afternoon, Elaine drove Jodi over to the Greene's ranch. The storm had blown itself out. Late day sun warmed the earth, leaving patches of dirty snow. Brave little purple crocuses poked out of the wet dirt. Gwen had promised to give Jodi a lesson in how to quilt. Elaine suspected much of the girl's excitement about the lesson had less to do with learning sewing techniques than that her daughter was delighted about Elaine's date with Ric.

Elaine was delighted, too. Going to a movie and sharing a bag of popcorn with a sexy man offered much needed respite from stress. For a little while she'd be able to feel normal. She might even be able to stop worrying, for an hour or two, about murder and loss and suspicious characters.

After she'd opened the door, but before she left the Jeep, Jodi gave her mother a hard looking over. "You aren't going to wear that shirt, are you?"

Elaine looked down at herself. "What's wrong with this shirt?"

Jodi rolled her eyes and sighed dramatically. "It's a guy shirt, Mom. You should wear the pink sweater. The cashmere with pearl embroidery. And don't wear jeans either."

Exactly what she needed, Elaine thought with amusement. Fashion tips from a teenybopper. "We're just going to a movie. What's wrong with jeans?"

Again with the big sigh. "*Mah-ahm.* Jeans are only okay if they're *designer* jeans. Otherwise you look like a hick."

Elaine crossed her heart. "I promise not to embarrass you with my hickness. Okay?"

"You can borrow my khaki skirt." She bobbed her head and snapped her fingers as if to a beat. "You'll look really with it."

Elaine gave her daughter's skinny hips a once over. "I doubt it will fit, but I'll try it on."

Gwen, clutching a ragged old sweater around her thin shoulders, approached the Jeep. "Everything okay, girls?"

"Hi, Nana!" Jodi hopped out of the Jeep. She slammed the door, making both women flinch. On her way to the house, she yelled, "Tell Mommy she has to wear something nice tonight!"

Elaine laughed into her hand. "How is Tom doing?"

"He's been on the phone most of the day. Actually talking about buying some calves." Gwen smiled while she watched Jodi run into the house. "Maybe I'll get Jodi to roust him so he stops talking and starts doing." Her smile faded. "How is the investigation going?"

Elaine clasped her mother-in-law's hand, dismayed by how thin and fragile the woman felt. Dismayed, too, by the idea of what might happen when Gwen learned the truth about Jodi. "One way or another, we'll find justice. Tate is working really hard." She studied Gwen's face and saw Bobby in her features. Grief sneaked in and nipped her. "Does it bother you that I'm dating Ric?"

"My lands, why would you say that? Life goes on, honey, whether we want it to or not. 'Sides, he's a good boy. I'd hate to see him end up all alone like his uncle. Loneliness is a sorry state for a man."

Sorry state for a widow, too.

When she returned home, her answering machine light was blinking.

Ric, sounding tight and unhappy, said, "Laney, I'm sorry. I can't make it tonight. I'll call you as soon as I can. All right? I miss you. See you later."

She called the wood shop. When Walt answered, she said, "It's me, Elaine. What's the matter with Ric? Is he all right? Uncle King didn't do anything to him, did he? Oh, I'll skin him alive if he did."

The old man's laughter warmed the telephone line. "Calm down, honey. Ric is fine. It's just his back."

"Where is he?"

"I reckon he's in bed right about now. He'll be laid up for a day or two. But he's okay."

Foolish, stubborn man, stuck all the way out in the middle of nowhere, alone. She paced as far as the phone cord would allow. "Walt, tell me the truth. How bad is his back?"

The old man hemmed and hawed.

"I'm not asking you to reveal state secrets. I just want to know if it's safe for him to be home alone. He doesn't even have a telephone in case of emergency."

Walt remained silent for a few beats. He sounded grim when he spoke. "That mine he hit done broke his spine. All told, he spent fourteen months in hospitals. It pains him sometimes."

"I'm going over there."

He made a worried noise. "Best not, honey. He's in a mood. He don't like company when he's in a mood."

"I'll take my chances."

"Don't say I didn't warn you."

She stomped around the kitchen and gathered the fixings for a meal. Ric might fancy himself a loner, but nobody was that independent, or that proud. Taking care of him was the right thing to do. Whether he liked it or not.

BY THE TIME Elaine reached Ric's place, the trees were casting long shadows across the trailer and barn. The trailer was dark, abandoned looking. A flicker hopped on the aluminum roof. The woodpecker gave the metal an experimental tap before taking off in a flash of orange underwings.

Elaine suffered a moment of wrenching fear that Ric hadn't hurt himself. Instead, he'd packed up and left the valley for more peaceful surroundings.

Buster trotted up to the Jeep. His tail wagged so furiously, his entire body wriggled. Ric wouldn't desert his dog. He wouldn't desert Jodi either. The valley was home for him now. She carried a bag of groceries to the trailer and knocked. No answer.

"Is he soaking in the hot tub, Buster?"

The dog sniffed hungrily at the grocery sack. Elaine tried the door knob. It opened easily. She called for Ric. Hearing nothing, she set the groceries and her purse inside the door. Then she used her cell phone to call the Greene ranch.

Gwen answered. Elaine explained that her plans had changed. She'd called to make sure the cell signal was strong enough. If Gwen or Jodi needed her, they had the number.

"Up to Ric's?" Gwen sounded amused.

"He's hurt himself. I'm going to fix him supper."

"Sweet of you. You'll be glad to hear, Tom went to look at those calves after all. He took Jodi with him."

Elaine smiled at the image of her daughter talking Tom's ear off. "That's great to hear. Tell her I'm wearing the cashmere sweater. Talk to you later."

She walked around back. Lights were on inside the hot tub house. Through the glass door she saw that the water didn't merely steam, it bubbled. Sinking deeper into the water, Ric scowled at her. She ordered Buster to stay, then entered.

"Didn't you get my message?" Ric asked. "I told you I couldn't make it tonight."

"I hate being stood up." The chlorine smell made her eyes sting. Steamy heat made her a little dizzy. She pulled off her jacket. "I'm going to fix you some supper. How about oven-fried chicken, mashed potatoes and my world famous biscuits? Which, by the way, really are better than Walt's."

He pushed a button on the control panel. The bubbling, Whirlpool action stopped. The water calmed. "I don't need you babying me."

She sat and primly crossed her legs. She studied his flushed face and damp, golden hair, and drank in the shape of his skull and cut of his jaw. His grumpy tone and the fact that he didn't attempt to coax her into the tub indicated how much his back must be hurting. "We all have crosses to bear."

"Right."

Walt had understated Ric's mood. He was acting like a bear with a toothache. "You're not the only one who's suffered."

He rolled his eyes.

"I'm not trying to one-up you on who got the worst deal out of life. All I'm saying is, we make do with what we've got."

"If you're trying to make me feel better, it isn't working."

"Only because you don't want to feel better. Is that why you bought land so far out of town? So you can brood in peace? The big bad lone wolf licking your wounds in private?"

"I'll be okay by tomorrow."

"You won't, and we both know it. You might be able to stand up straight. Go to work. But you'll still hurt. You hurt all the time, and it isn't going to get better."

His expression tightened. Cords stood out on his throat. "I am not a cripple."

"I didn't say you were. You're an amazing man. I admire your strength, your determination."

He groaned and let his head fall back. "Now you sound like a physical therapist, or a shrink. Quit it."

"I will not. I don't think any less of you because you have a wonky back. What bothers me is this tendency of yours to hide. You don't even have a telephone. What if there's an emergency?"

"So what?"

Incredulous, she huffed. "Fine, tough guy. You can take care of yourself. Big jerk."

His eyes opened wide.

"You're a selfish jerk. You don't care that I worry about you. That I need to know you're okay and properly fed and have everything you need. Only a totally inconsiderate jackass pushes away the people who care about him."

"I can take care of myself." He didn't sound so sure.

She snatched up her jacket. "So I'm going to fix you a proper meal. If you don't like it, haul your butt out of there and stop me."

"Laney..."

Grinning to herself, she left him to soak.

She was kneading biscuit dough when he limped into the trailer. She waited for the savory smell of baking chicken to work its magic on him. Nobody could stay in a bad mood in the midst of such a delicious aroma. He settled gingerly on a kitchen chair. She'd already set the table and had even found a candle to cast some romantic light. She could feel him watching her every move. Unable to find a biscuit cutter, she used a flour dusted water glass to cut the dough. She turned up the heat on the oven.

Ric petted Buster. "Made yourself right at home. Bet it's not what you're used to cooking in."

"I've worked in worse. What can I get you? Ibuprofen? Something stronger? Do you want to lie down?" He wore gray sweatpants and a gray T-shirt with ARMY printed on the front. His feet were white and water-wrinkled. His hair stuck out every which way. She wanted to comb it with her fingers.

"I already took something. I feel okay sitting." He sniffed the air. "Smells good." He lowered his gaze to his hands. "Sorry I growled at you."

She decided not to press her advantage. "Apology accepted. Are you sure you don't want to lie down?"

"I'm doing better. No spasms."

She pulled the chicken, golden brown and sizzling, from the oven, then slid in the biscuits to bake. "What can I get you to drink? A beer?"

"There's iced tea in the fridge."

The kitchen was so small she had only to turn to reach the refrigerator. "I hope you don't mind, but I looked at the drawings you made." She indicated a stack of sketches on the coffee table. "Is that a project for Walt?"

"It's for my house. I'm hoping to break ground this summer."

She liked the sound of that. It was so permanent. "Those are really nice." She set a glass of tea before him. He smelled of chlorine. His eyes were dark and solemn, arresting. She couldn't help it. She pecked a kiss on his forehead before whirling away to tend the potatoes.

"Laney?"

"Yes?" She poured off the water from the potatoes. Steam wreathed her face.

"I am a selfish jerk. I just…I hate being weak. My worst nightmare is that I'll end up with a big pot belly from sitting around watching TV all day and feeling sorry for myself."

She added butter and milk to the potatoes. She began mashing them smooth.

"Every ache, every twinge reminds me that I'm not the same. That I'll never be the same again. I don't want to end up all twisted and confined to a wheelchair. Useless. Want to see what they did to me?"

She wasn't sure but intuited that she needed to. Ric's fears were nothing new to her. All her life she'd been around strong men who reacted poorly to any sign of weakness. Her father had been a prime example. Del's heart disease had been diagnosed when he was in his forties, but he'd refused to slow down. His philosophy had been, no sense living to be a hundred if he had to act like an old man in order to get there.

"Sure. Show me."

He grasped the hem of his T-shirt and pulled it up to his shoulders. She peered at his back. Ridges of scar tissue, pink and shiny, tracked along and across his spine. A flash of revulsion rippled through her, then was gone. Visions of him bleeding and broken choked her up. She traced a long scar with a fingertip. When the mine exploded, had he screamed? Shook and trembled, his eyes glazed with shock, terrified of dying and hurting so much he wished for death? Had he crawled through mud and blood and tears in a hopeless attempt to save his dying driver? His flesh quivered when she touched the scars.

"Is this supposed to scare me?" she asked.

He tugged his shirt down. "Doesn't it?"

She crouched and rested her forearms on his knees. "You're not as scary as you think."

"What if I have to have more surgery?" He worked his fingers through her hair, his strong fingers tender against her scalp. "What if I end up paralyzed?"

"Well, then you do need me, now don't you?"

"I don't know if I'm man enough for you, Laney."

"If all you could move was one eyelid, you'd be more than enough man for me." She rose and leaned close to his face. When her nose nearly touched his, she paused. "This is only our second date, right?"

Finally, blessedly, he smiled. "You're one hot little number, aren't you?"

"You don't know the half of it, Cedric Buchanan." She bustled away to finish putting the meal together.

He winced a few times while he ate. Once he froze in the midst of lifting the bowl of mashed potatoes, the cords standing out on his neck and his eyes strained. She refrained from commenting. Instead she encouraged him to talk about the house he planned to build. His house plans were simple, but elegant with clever usage of space and interesting flow.

In the midst of washing dishes, she asked, "Have you ever thought about going back to school?"

"I never was a scholar." He sneaked half a biscuit to Buster.

She glanced at a book shelf containing a decent collection of classic novels and non-fiction books on design, building and history. "Surely you've taken some classes since high school? Learned some skills in the army."

"I jumped out of airplanes and chased guerrillas. Not much call for that around here."

"What about architects? There's always a call for those. You have an incredible talent."

He appeared surprised. "Do you think so?"

"All you have to do is ask the women you've renovated kitchens and bathrooms for. Don't get me wrong, you're a terrific carpenter, but drawing designs for a living isn't nearly as strenuous."

"I do like to draw." He turned a thoughtful gaze on the pile of sketches. "You really think those are good?"

She hung the dishtowel on the oven handle. "I think they're wonderful." She finger-combed his hair into a semblance of order. "I think you're wonderful."

He slid an arm around her waist and held her loosely. His hand was warm against her hip. "Maybe buying Savvy was our second date. What do you think?"

She answered with a kiss, a soft press of her lips against his. He made a pained noise deep in his throat and winced. She drew back. He averted his gaze. The corners of his mouth pulled down.

"Your hair is making me crazy," she said.

He smoothed one side with a hand, making the other side look worse by comparison. "We should call it a night."

"Not until I do something with your hair. Sit still."

"Laney, it's not—"

She was already out of the room and in the bathroom where she found a comb. Odd recklessness gripped her. She didn't intend to seduce Ric, though a wild affair based on sexual passion held its own appeal. She wanted more. She wanted to be with him. What she really wanted was for him to want to be with her, even when he didn't feel his best. She wanted to prove to him that she found him desirable no matter what.

Ignoring his half-hearted protests, she combed his hair.

Years ago, when he'd been a sharp-pressed young soldier with a crew cut, he'd been incredibly handsome. Now his hair was longish, dark at the roots, golden wherever the sun had touched. Its unruliness added a raffish element to his attractiveness. The comb caught in its thickness. She drew it slowly through the strands. He watched her every move.

"You smell like chlorine," she said.

"You smell like chicken." He waggled his eyebrows. "Wonder if you taste like chicken." He slid both hands seductively over her hips.

She gave his nose an admonishing tap with the comb. "Behave. If you have videos, we can still watch a movie."

"No VCR," he said. "No TV either."

"Hmm." She critically eyed her handiwork. One thick hank of hair insisted on falling over his forehead.

"Can't get any reception up here. I had to decide between buying a horse or a satellite dish."

"You made a good choice. Oh my, but your skin is all dried out. Hold on." She dug through her purse until she found a tube of hand and body lotion.

"No, Laney, uh-uh. No pink stuff. I'm not smelling like a girl. Put that away."

"After long soaks in the tub, and with this dry air, you need lotion. Now hush. Give me your arm."

He growled and grumbled, but finally extended his left arm. She squirted a blob of lotion into her hand, gave it a few rubs to warm it, then went to work. Nice, nice arm, she mused, with well-defined muscles and forearms like steel. He wore the grouchily abashed expression of a dog suffering through a bath, but eventually, as she worked her way over his elbow, triceps and biceps, his brow smoothed and his mouth relaxed. When she demanded his other arm, he instantly complied.

She had to slide her hands beneath his T-shirt sleeves to reach his shoulders. She asked him to remove the shirt. When he pulled off the shirt, her knees went wobbly. His belly was flat and smooth. His chest was broad, marked by whorls of dark hair. Gooseflesh rose on his arms and back, but she doubted he was cold. She felt as if she were burning up.

"You are really turning me on," he said, his voice smoky.

Grinning, she squirted more lotion into her hand. "Do you know we have a masseuse in McClintock?"

"I met her."

"Mama goes to her once a week. She swears she's a miracle worker. Did she give you a massage? You don't like her?"

"She's okay, but all the candles and aroma therapy oils and pingy-dingy music freaks me out."

Laughing, she kept her touch light across his scars. She could feel bumps on his spine where it had been broken and subsequently fused. He creakily leaned forward until his elbows rested on his knees. Bobby had always been wrenching muscles; being stoved up and sore was the cowboy way. So she knew one or two tricks about how to warm skin and muscles to ease the knots.

"You have good hands." He practically purred.

"Thank you." His skin was gleaming from the lotion. She felt as if she were glowing from the inside out.

"Nice legs, too."

"Thank you again."

"And your butt—"

"Ric."

He laughed. She'd never tire of listening to his laughter. At that moment she realized what was different about tonight. It wasn't his sore back, or that she'd insisted on feeding him, or even that she was indulging in touching his body. It was that there were no more secrets between them, no more shame.

He'd been at least partly right in calling their former relationship rebellious. The more her father had railed against him, the more she'd wanted Ric. Now, there was no sneaking around. No terror-thrill of getting caught. She'd come to know Ric as a person rather than as an object of desire. He was a good man, with a good heart. He was everything she expected a man should be: honest, generous, affectionate and strong.

She slid her hands over his shoulders, up to his neck where her fingers met in a vee, then down his spine gently, across the tough muscles banding his ribs and his waist. His breathing had a ragged quality.

"Sit up," she said. "Let me do your chest."

"No."

"Come on. I won't hurt you."

"No."

She tried to see his face, but he kept it lowered. Then she understood. He was aroused. Feeling absurdly pleased to have such an effect on him and touched that he was shy about it, she screwed the cap on the lotion tube. "I didn't bring any dessert. Do you have anything sweet?"

"You're driving me crazy, Laney."

"Am I?"

"You know you are."

He lifted his head and grinned. He seemed dazed. His pupils were so big the irises were thin rings of sapphire. She no longer smelled the hot tub, but an intoxicating mixture of baby-powder scented lotion and something darker, sultrier, uniquely him.

"I'm putty in your hands, honey."

"I bet that's not putty in your britches."

He was startled.

"Does that shock you? Well, if you don't want me ravishing your body, then tell me where you stash the sweets."

His laughter filled the trailer and her heart. She rummaged through the refrigerator and freezer. With an "Ah-ha!" of triumph she pulled out a carton of chocolate, chocolate-chip ice cream. "Holding out on me," she said, working off the carton top. "You should be punished."

She presented him a spoonful of ice cream. Then pulled it back, just out of his reach. "Hmm, now what shall I have you do to earn this?"

"Now you're just being cruel." He opened his mouth and she relented, allowing him the ice cream. He made a show of licking the spoon clean.

"I wasn't thinking cruel and unusual," she said, her voice low and husky. "I was merely considering...unusual." She brought ice cream to her lips and slowly worked the blob of chocolate sweetness in and out of her mouth. "Did the army teach you anything—" she waggled her eyebrows, "—interesting?"

He stared so hungrily, a jolt of desire made everything jump inside her. "I know a trick or two you might consider interesting," he said. His voice and the intensity in his eyes were powerfully erotic.

She fed him more ice cream. He finally straightened, revealing that he was indeed aroused. Perhaps she was being a tad cruel.

She used a finger to wipe a smear of ice cream from his lower lip. "Do you know what I'd really like to do?"

He wagged an admonishing finger. "Please don't say it. If you do, I'll agree then I'll really mess myself up."

She dipped her eyes significantly to his crotch. "I just hate to leave you suffering."

He grasped her shoulders, his long fingers splayed and burning hot through her sweater sleeves. "Listen to me. I want to make love to you. Really want to make love to you. I dream about you all the time. Holding you. Kissing you."

She was melting inside. "Oh, Ric, me, too."

"Then let's do it right. Not in this crappy trailer. Not when I'm scared to make a wrong move. How about a suite in the General Palmer Hotel down in Durango? A whole weekend."

"Marlee's graduation is next weekend."

"The weekend after that then. What do you say?"

"I don't know if I can wait that long."

He chuckled, a wicked note. "Two can play the teasing game, sweetheart." He slid his hands boldly, firmly over her breasts. She gasped. When he flicked his thumbs across her nipples, she gasped again. "Say yes."

"Yes," she breathed. When he tenderly squeezed her breasts, she saw double.

"Now you move over to that side of the table."

An impish impulse to continue the love play made her hesitate. But he was right. It couldn't be pleasurable for him to worry that any wrong move could send his muscles into spasms.

A trilling noise made Buster leap to his feet. He barked once. Ric looked around in confusion.

"You are saved by the bell, mister," she said. She fetched the cell phone from her coat pocket. "You ought to get one of these. The reception is fine. And then I can find you when I...*want* you." She opened the phone and pressed it to her ear. She expected to hear Jodi, but it was her mother. "Hi, Mama, what's going—"

"Thank God I found you! Where are you?" Lillian sounded in a panic.

"I'm at Ric's. What's the matter?"

Lillian seemed to be struggling for breath. "There's been an accident. It's Tom, up on Branch Road. He's hurt bad."

Elaine groped for a chair. She dropped onto it. Ric reached for her arm. "Car accident? Oh my God, Mama, was Jodi with Tom? She went with him to look at calves. Is she all right? Is she hurt? Where is she?"

"She's gone! Gwen said she was with Tom, but she's disappeared!"

Chapter Twelve

Ric and Elaine made it to the accident site on Branch Road in time to see the Flight for Life helicopter lift into the sky. It had been a harrowing ride for them on icy roads. Ric drove the Jeep, clenching his teeth against the pain every time he worked the clutch. Elaine spoke to her mother on the cell phone. Whenever they drove through a low area and transmission failed, Elaine would clutch the phone in both hands and yell, pleading for information.

The helicopter rose, the turbulence from its blades making tall trees sway. Seeing it, knowing what it carried, hearing its chuffing, chopping engine noise filled Ric's heart with dread.

Ric steered through knots of trucks and utility vehicles and horse trailers. It looked as if the entire population of the valley had mustered out to search for the missing girl.

A sliver of moon rising over the mountains only served to drive home how very dark the night was.

A deputy waved a flashlight, ordering them to stop. Ric rolled down the window. ''I've got Jodi Greene's mother. We need to find the sheriff.'' The deputy waved them through. Ric spotted Tom's pickup truck parked on a turnout. Official vehicles, all of them with emergency lights strobing, blocked the road. Before he turned off the engine, Elaine was out and running in search of her uncle.

His daughter, his Jodi, was out there, lost in the wilderness on a cold night that was getting colder by the second. He couldn't bear imagining her frightened or hurt. Elaine couldn't survive losing her child.

He eased out of the Jeep. The muscles along his spine felt as fragile as hot cellophane, stretched tight. He pushed the pain aside. He spotted Tate Raleigh and shoved through the crowd.

"Ranger," Tate said, his expression grim. "Bad situation."

A knot of people gathered around King McClintock. He shouted orders. Men and women, several holding excited dogs, were fanning out into the forest on either side of the road. Flashlight beams danced and bobbed like a drunken laser-light show. Radios crackled and spat.

"What happened?" Ric asked.

"Somebody beat hell out of Tom Greene. Fractured his skull, busted his ribs. Lucky for him, the sheriff was on patrol. Damn near run over him on the road. I don't know if he'll make it." Tate stared at the distant sky where the helicopter had disappeared.

"Did Tom say who did it?"

"Couldn't talk. What we're hoping is that Jodi saw the attack and ran."

Not a year passed without some hapless hiker or hunter disappearing into the mountains, never to be seen again. His frantic brain rattled off dangers: bears, mountain lions, deep ravines, hypothermia, rock slides, starvation, dehydration. "You *hope?*"

"Better in the forest than with a kidnapper."

"Raleigh!" the sheriff bellowed.

Tate hurried to the sheriff's cruiser. Ric followed. Shell-shocked and blank, Elaine sat on the cruiser's driver's seat. Kidnapped, Ric thought, numb and cold inside. Beautiful, lively, funny Jodi kidnapped by a maniac who'd beaten an old man into unconsciousness. He reached for Elaine's hand. Silent tears streamed down her cheeks.

"We'll find her, honey," he said. "I swear to God, she'll be safe and sound."

The sheriff had a large map spread out over the cruiser's hood. An electric lantern cast harsh white light. With a red marker, he slashed and circled areas on the map. "Coordinate with the State Police and Highway Patrol," King told Tate. "I want roadblocks set up all the way around the valley. I'll coordinate with the park service to block the forest trails." He waved over a stocky man wearing a tribal police uniform. The two consulted in low voices.

Tate bent over the map. He spoke slowly and clearly into a radio mike.

King McClintock seemed to notice Ric for the first time. He scowled beneath his hat.

Just happened to be on patrol, Ric thought. Right.

The sheriff turned his attention to Elaine. "Honey, Gwen told me Tom was visiting folks tonight, but she didn't know who exactly. Start calling everyone you can think of. Find out who he visited, who he might have talked to and how long he's been where."

"How will that help find Jodi?" Ric asked.

"Well, Mr. Sherlock Holmes, we got one of two scenarios here. Tom pulls into the turnout, gets out to admire the view or take a leak, and some yahoo driving by decides to just beat the snot out of him. Got no reason but meanness, 'cause it sure ain't robbery. Didn't take Tom's wallet or his truck."

"How do you know Tom wasn't run off the road?"

"Because he was parked. Keys in his pocket. No skid

marks, no damage to the pickup. So here's what's more likely. Tom knew his attacker well enough to pull off the road and get out for a chat. Felt safe, too, 'cause he had Jodi in the truck.''

Elaine turned a frantic circle, looking up and down and all around. "Nobody has calves up here. It's all national forest." She shoved Tate out of the way and bent intently over the map.

Search coordinators called the sheriff away.

"No calves up here," Elaine muttered. "What the hell were you doing, Tom? Damn you."

"He was investigating the murder," Ric answered. He felt so cold inside he barely noticed the icy air against his face and hands. He prayed Tom lived, so Ric could get a few shots in. The old man had no right searching for a murderer with Jodi in tow.

King returned with a man. He was skinny and bowlegged, and wearing a huge hat. Ric recognized him, but couldn't recall the name. Elaine called him Herb.

Herb spat a stream of tobacco juice. "Tom and your girl come by around six o'clock," he said. "Checked out some weanlings.''

"Did he say where he was going? And why?" the sheriff asked.

"Borrowed my phone," Herb said. "Weren't trying to eavesdrop, but couldn't help hearing some of what he was saying. He was asking, sure you got it? Sure it's the right one? Things like that. He was all excited. Said the justice train was pulling into the station." He spat again and glared at the sheriff. "He was talking about his boy, weren't he? Doing *your* job."

Ric leaned against the cruiser and shut out the chaos around him so he could think. Tom had spent the last eighteen months showing not the slightest interest in his ranch or livestock. All of the sudden he decided to look at calves.

"The gun," he said, sotto voce, to Tate. "He must have gotten a lead on the .44."

Tate gave the sheriff a long, considering look. "Do you think Axton Cross set him up? Lured him out here to kill him?"

Ric's stomach clenched into a knot almost as painful as his back. If Axton meant to murder Tom, what was to stop him from getting rid of a young girl, too? He beckoned for Elaine. "Where does Axton live?"

Clutching at her throat, she swayed. "He ambushed Tom? Ohmigod. He lives just south of town. We've got to get over there!"

"Don't panic." Tate snatched up the radio handset and got through to dispatch. He requested a unit to check out Axton Cross's residence. He added the warning that the man was possibly armed and possibly holding a hostage. As soon as he finished, he said, "It doesn't make sense. In the first place, Tom couldn't even say Cross's name without practically having a stroke. I can't see him meeting in a secluded place. Second, if Axton had a gun, why beat him up? Why not shoot him?"

Ric shut out the cacophony of vehicles, shouting people, crackling radios and barking dogs. He put himself in Tom Greene's head, envisioning what the old man was thinking and feeling. Blinded by obsession, Tom wasn't rational these days. He knew about the bullets found at the lodge. He knew it was a likely possibility that there was a third party at the lodge the night of the shooting. Could Tom keep that information to himself? Ric doubted it. So word of the suspect .44 was probably drifting around the valley. If Cross heard about it, who could he induce to help him take care of Tom?

He watched the sheriff consult with Elaine. She'd stopped crying. Though she looked shocked, her expression was determined. She nodded grimly at whatever the sheriff said.

Try as he might, Ric couldn't convince himself that the sheriff would harm Jodi. Nor could he believe the sheriff would allow Tom to live. Ric knew of only one person who was loyal enough to Cross to lie for him. One person, too, Tom might trust.

Tate signed off the radio. He said to Ric, "No one's home at Cross's place. His car is gone. I've got an APB out on him and a man checking out the realty in town."

"Elaine!" Ric called. He beckoned for her to come closer. "Do you know Linda Pallo's home number?"

She seemed confused by the question. "Why?"

"She's loyal to Cross. And she's mad at Tom. She could have lured Tom up here."

"She would not do that."

"She would if Cross convinced her he was going to get Tom off their back."

Red and blue flashers gave her face an otherworldly look. Her eyes were huge, full of fear and fury. She punched a number into her cell phone. "Busy." She slapped the unit closed. "Have we heard back from the officer checking Axton's house?"

Tate answered in the affirmative. "Cross won't risk driving around too long with Jodi in the car. Does he own any other property?"

Elaine thought about it. "Homes for sale. Empty listings will have a lockbox to which Axton has access." She turned her attention to the map and loosed a groan so full of despair it choked up Ric's throat. "I don't know which houses."

"Linda will know." Ric stabbed a finger at the map. "She lives about a mile from here."

Elaine turned a circle. "What if Jodi is here? Lost?"

"What if Cross has her?"

Again the heart-wrenching groan.

"Run over to Linda's," Tate said. "If we find Jodi, I'll get on the horn immediately. If you get even a whisper that Linda is involved with this, you call me right away. In either case, get a list of all the empty houses to which Cross has access." He lowered a hard look on Ric. "If you spot Cross's car, contact me. Don't go in playing hero. Got it?"

Ric snapped off a grim salute. "Got it."

Tate dropped a hand on Elaine's shoulder. "We'll find her. I promise."

Ric and Elaine looked at each other. He suspected the same question was going through her mind as was his: What if they didn't?

They made their way through the chaos back to the Jeep. Elaine slid behind the wheel. Ric questioned her ability to drive.

"I'm okay. Axton won't hurt Jodi. I know he won't." She started the engine. "He probably didn't mean to hurt Tom either. We'll find her."

Ric tried several more times to call Linda's home. The phone stayed busy. He imagined her gossiping to some other lonely woman about who wore what to the grocery store, unaware of the missing girl or the badly wounded old man. Unaware, possibly, of what damage her loyalty to Axton Cross had wrought. At least the busy signal offered assurance that they would find her at home.

Elaine turned into Linda's driveway. The ruts and potholes were so deep that the Jeep bounced and rattled as if they were climbing boulders. A few times the wheels spun in mud before slithering onward.

There were lights on inside Linda's house. Her old Wagoneer was parked beneath a lean-to. When they pulled up, the front door opened. Linda appeared.

Elaine breathed a prayer of relief.

While Elaine ran up to the front porch, Ric followed more slowly. There was a sodium arc lamp mounted on a pole in the front yard, but it wasn't turned on. Or else, it had burned out and the bulb hadn't been replaced. Ric guessed it was the latter.

Linda stood behind the screen door. She made no move to welcome them inside. Used to seeing the crisp, almost military woman in her severe suits, Ric was astonished by her appearance. Her hair, the color and texture of steel wool, hung in disarray to her shoulders. Her face looked even craggier and more dour than usual. She wore a man's cardigan sweater over her broad shoulders.

"Thank God you're home," Elaine said. "May we come in?"

"I'm not set up for company," Linda replied.

"This isn't a social call." Elaine pulled open the screen door.

Linda stood her ground. Behind her, the parlor held sparse, shabby furniture. The walls were dark with age and water stains. The rugs were threadbare. Elaine pushed her way inside. Ric disliked the sour, old smell of the place.

"I've got nothing to offer," Linda said, her tone belligerent. "Haven't been to the store yet this week."

Ric could see into the kitchen. It had old steel cabinets and ancient linoleum. It was neat, but tired looking. The whole house seemed weary, as if it were worn out by merely standing. There were muddy tracks on the floor from Linda's rubber galoshes. It struck him as wrong. If she were chatting on the telephone, there should be no reason her boots were muddy. No reason for her to be wearing boots.

Elaine launched into a rambling, disjointed tale about what had happened on Branch Road. Linda stood stiffly. Her cheeks were flushed. The more Elaine talked, the redder Linda's face grew. It might have been from the heat. A fire in an old potbellied stove turned the room stuffy. Under the cardigan, Linda wore a flannel shirt. At her throat the gray-white neckline of thermal underwear showed. A coat lay crumpled on a chair, as if carelessly dropped.

Ric unbuttoned his coat and rubbed his aching back. Prickling suspicion made him want to scratch. The longer Linda stood silent and unmoved, the more high-pitched and frantic Elaine sounded. Her hands flailed like panicky birds.

Ric sidled closer to the kitchen doorway. A rolled sleeping bag and a coil of rope lay upon a metal table. A wall-mounted telephone caught his attention. The old-fashioned harvest gold receiver hung there, but no cord or handset.

When Elaine paused for a breath, Ric asked, ''Might I bother you for a glass of water, ma'am?''

Linda glared, her eyes narrow and hate-filled. He could almost smell her fear. She looked about to flatly refuse him, but seemed to gather herself. She stomped into the kitchen.

Ric snatched the coat off the chair. Listening to water running from the faucet and anticipating Linda's heavy footsteps, he examined the front and sleeves. Mouth agape, Elaine tugged at his arm, demanding in a whisper to know what he was doing. There were streaks and spatters on the fabric that might be dirt, might be paint, or might be blood. Linda's return made the floor vibrate faintly. He dropped the coat. Linda's hand shook so water sloshed from the glass.

If she had a handgun, he reasoned, she'd have shot Tom instead of beating him. Or perhaps she hadn't intended to kill him. Still, a woman living alone in bear country probably kept a rifle or shotgun within reach.

A short hallway led off the parlor. Both doors he could see were closed.

"Might I bother you again, ma'am? I need to use the restroom."

"This ain't a service station," Linda snapped. She was hugging herself, backing away, shaking her head, emphatically negative. "'Sides, the toilet's busted. I have no information for you, Elaine. I haven't seen Axton since five o'clock. I left him yakking on the telephone. Doubt I'll see him until Monday. And it's just plain ridiculous thinking he has anything to do with your daughter. So you'll have to leave now. I've got, uh, I've got—" Her movement had taken her close to a narrow door.

A coat closet, Ric thought. If she owned a weapon, it was in there. In two long strides, Ric blocked her way. She was a big woman and in an instant seemed to get bigger.

"Get out of my house!"

"Where is she?" he asked.

"Ric?" Elaine stared as if he'd lost his mind.

"She knows where Jodi is. Give it up now, Linda, before things get out of hand. I know you don't want to hurt Jodi. You probably didn't want to hurt Tom either. We can clear this up, make things right. Did you help Axton? Is he behind this?"

If he were wrong, it would end now.

"Get out of my house!" Linda screamed. Her face

blazed crimson and veins throbbed in her temples. Her hands clenched in white-knuckled fists.

A loud thump, as if something heavy had hit the floor, startled all three of them. It came from the rear of the house.

"Jodi?" Elaine headed for the hallway.

Screeching, Linda jumped on her, tackling her to the floor. Elaine hit the ground so hard the wooden planking rocked. Ric had a glimpse of Elaine's wide, stunned eyes before Linda reared back and swung a wide roundhouse punch aimed at the much smaller woman's head. Elaine grunted with the blow.

Ric grabbed Linda's arm. Her weight and strength astonished him. He dug in his heels and hauled her off Elaine. Still screeching, the woman writhed and twisted. She locked her arms around his knees, driving him backward. He felt something tear in his lower back. His left leg went numb. He hit the floor so hard that he feared his teeth had shattered.

Disbelief stunned him. She was incredibly strong, and she had murder on her mind. Unable to gain any reliable movement out of his lower body, he caught her in a bear hug and squeezed with all his might. He heard her teeth snapping close to his ear, felt her hot, angry breath against his neck. She stank like an animal, rank and vinegary. Her arms strained against his. Her fingers clawed.

Elaine grabbed fistfuls of Linda's hair. Ric gained enough leverage to get his good leg under him. He managed to roll, wrestling Linda beneath him.

"Stop it!" he roared into Linda's face. He jerked his right arm from beneath her bucking body. He jammed his forearm against her throat. She gagged. Her heels drummed the floor. He tightened the pressure on her throat. Her eyes began to bulge from the sockets.

"You're killing her, Ric!"

He heard Elaine's cry as if from far, far away. She grabbed his shoulder and shook him, begging him to stop. Linda finally went limp beneath him. Carefully, praying she wasn't playing possum, he relaxed his hold on her throat. She gasped raggedly and coughed.

"Rope," he grunted. "Kitchen. Get the rope!" The pain along his spine had transcended reality. He seemed to be floating above himself, watching his body press Linda against the floor. Watching himself use his arms to lever off the woman, grab her wrist, and loop it with clumsy knots. Elaine rolled Linda onto her stomach, and tied both hands behind her back.

Linda roused with renewed strength and fury. She flopped like a fish, yelling incoherent threats. He hurt too much to prevent her from struggling to her feet.

Elaine grabbed a coat tree and menaced the woman. "Hold still, damn you!"

"Tie her to the stove," Ric managed to choke out. Every breath left him cross-eyed with agony.

Elaine ran the long end of the rope around a leg of the cast iron, pot-bellied stove. She dragged Linda across the floor, away from Ric. Then she tied the woman off, snubbed short like a cow to a tree.

Elaine ran to Ric. A huge welt was darkening her eye.

"Find Jodi." He groaned. Pain was an old acquaintance, one he thought he knew well. This pain, however, had youthful vigor, fiery and sharp, as if demon hands wrenched and ripped at his spine. He imagined shards of broken vertebrae grinding, cutting, slashing against his spinal cord.

Elaine's boots thudded against the floor. "She's here!" she called.

Time distorted. He didn't know how long he lay, listening to Linda's ragged breathing and cinders popping in the stove. Then a long golden braid swung before his eyes. The elfin face he'd grown to love hovered anxiously over his. He couldn't muster the strength to touch her.

"Mommy, he's hurt," Jodi said. Her sweet face was tear-streaked. She ran anxious hands over his shoulders and cheeks. "Help him, Mommy, he's hurt!"

"I'll live," he rasped out, but wondered why. He couldn't move. As if he'd never be able to move again.

DAYS AND NIGHTS passed in a blur for Elaine. Ric was hospitalized in Durango with a sprained back. Fortunately, he was in such good overall physical condition that Linda's assault hadn't wrought permanent damage. Tom Greene wasn't so lucky. He was hospitalized up in Denver, in an intensive-care unit, having suffered a fractured skull, arm and ribs, and a punctured lung. Lillian had chartered a private plane to fly Gwen to Denver to be with her husband.

Despite exhaustion, whenever Elaine began to drift off to sleep, terror grabbed her. She'd startle and frantically search for her child. Jodi suffered her own nightmares. Mother and daughter slept in one bed, holding each other close. Jodi was unnaturally quiet. She spent a lot of time leafing through photo albums. She refused to leave the house alone.

Linda was locked up in jail. Claiming self-defense, she denied she ever intended to harm Jodi.

Finally, Elaine was able to bring Ric home from the hospital. A day of pure joy for her, but rather uncomfortable for him.

"Will you stop being such a big baby?" Elaine said. She steered her mother's Lincoln Town Car toward McClintock. Ripping noises made her grimace. Ric adjusted the Velcro fasteners on his back brace for about the ten-thousandth time since they'd left the hospital. "Quit playing with that thing."

"It itches," Ric complained. "It's pinching under my arms. Who designed it anyway? The Marquis de Sade?"

Elaine choked down laughter. He had to be feeling pretty good to act this grouchy. He had to wear the back brace for a while and take it easy for the next few weeks. He'd be back to normal in no time.

He fidgeted on the deep leather seat. "Any news about Linda?"

She slowed for a tractor on the road ahead. Even four days after the assault and kidnapping, she still couldn't believe what Linda had done. "She's still insisting that Tom attacked her first. I've known her all my life. She's not the nicest person, but she's never acted crazy. It just doesn't make sense."

"Maybe Cross made it worth her while," he said darkly.

She concentrated on the tractor, which was rumbling along at a sedate twenty miles an hour. The incident at Linda's house had taken on a surreal quality, as if she'd dreamed it or seen it at the movies. "We'll know more when Tom gets his memory back."

Tom didn't remember the attack at all. Jodi had little information to offer. After spending hours with Tom, driving from ranch to ranch, she'd fallen asleep in his truck. The next she knew, Tom was screaming while Linda beat him to the ground. A deputy had found a pry bar, sticky with Tom's blood, in the back of Linda's Wagoneer. When Jodi tried to help her grandfather, Linda had grabbed her. Linda had taken Jodi to her house and tied her up with the telephone cord. A sleeping bag and rope in the kitchen had not boded well for the girl. Linda claimed Jodi had been hysterical and tried to run off into the forest. Linda had tied her up for safety's sake.

Elaine forced images of what might have happened out of her mind.

"I want to talk to Linda."

"Like Uncle King will ever let that happen. He's in a royal state. Everyone in town is badgering him to investigate Bobby's murder. It's ugly."

"What about the phone call Herb overheard? Has Tate figured out who Tom called?"

Elaine blew a long breath. "He called the realty." Noticing his growing excitement, she shook her head. "But we don't know who he talked to. Linda swears she left the office at five. She swears she never talked to Tom. Axton has an alibi. He was showing properties to a client. Tate is checking out call-forwarding records."

"Linda is lying."

"I know."

The tractor finally turned off onto a field road. Elaine speeded up. Over a hill and around a bend, the town of McClintock came into view. From a distance it looked like a child's collection of toy buildings with its hodgepodge of architectural styles and the church spire pointing at the sky.

She drove to Walt Buchanan's house. Trucks and automobiles were parked up and down the street. A banner had been strung between two birch trees. In huge hand-painted letters, it proclaimed: Welcome Home, Ric! When the Town Car pulled into the driveway, people poured from the house. Elaine laughed in sheer delight.

Bardie Hoff the trashman marched to the head of the crowd. He had squeezed his stocky body into a blue uniform jacket and wore a blue garrison cap. The jacket buttons threatened to burst. He put a bugle to his lips and began to blow. Men pulled off baseball caps and cowboy hats. Several snapped to attention and saluted.

"He's playing the air force song!" Ric exclaimed. He stared open-mouthed at the gathering. Color climbed his cheeks and his ears reddened.

"Be nice. It's the only song he knows how to play." Elaine left the car. It appeared that half the valley had turned out to welcome Ric home.

Red-faced, he eased out of the car. Women, young and old, swarmed around him, vying for the honor of holding his arm. Leaning heavily on a cane, supported by laughing females, he hobbled to the front door. The house was decorated fit to beat Christmas with balloons and streamers. Flowers from well-wishers filled the tiny parlor with color and scent. The air was thick with the aroma of baked goods and roasting meats. Walt led his nephew, and his coterie of female fans, into a bedroom. Elaine glimpsed a "help me" look on Ric's face before he disappeared. He didn't need help; he needed to accept how much folks cared about him.

Elaine chatted with friends. Everyone was proud of their homegrown hero. Lillian arrived with Jodi.

"Is he okay, Mommy?" Jodi asked. She crouched to smooch Buster and ruffle his floppy ears.

Elaine smoothed stray hairs off her daughter's face. She prayed this mess ended soon. She didn't know how much more trauma Jodi could take before she cracked completely.

"Ric is right as rain," she said. "He'd love to see you."

With Buster at her heels, the girl rushed into the bedroom to welcome Ric home.

After a while, Walt convinced folks that Ric needed his rest. Elaine stood at the door to bid friends and neighbors farewell. She received so many kisses her cheeks chafed from whisker-burns.

She entered a small bedroom set up for convalescence. Ric lay propped on pillows. Several stuffed animals shared the bed with him. He appeared rather dazed.

"Comfy?" she asked.

"I don't know." He peered into a teddy bear's beady glass eyes. "I'm—I'm—"

"Grateful for so many good friends?" she offered. "Glad you're in a small town where everyone loves you, instead of a big, impersonal city where nobody knows your name? Proud of all you've done?"

He looked helplessly at her. His eyes were moist. She slid a hand over his cheek. "You're home, Ric. This is where you belong. I'm so very glad you're safe and sound."

Walt, Lillian and Jodi crowded into the bedroom. Lillian eased Elaine out of the way. She kissed Ric's cheeks. Then she turned to her granddaughter. "Jodi, take that poor little dog outside and find him a patch of grass to chew. I think some fool was feeding him cake."

"Okay, Grandma. Come on, Buster!"

The dog didn't look sick to Elaine. She glimpsed the hard smile her mother wore. Elaine tensed up inside. When Lillian wore that expression, it meant somebody was in trouble. Lillian's gaze drifted from Walt to Elaine and finally rested on Ric. He swallowed hard.

"All over town I've been hearing talk about guns and conspiracies and murder and official cover-ups. My brother has all but dug a moat to keep folks away. He's talking about firing Tate Raleigh for insubordination. I have a good idea that the three of you know the truth behind the rumors, gossip and innuendo." Lillian perched on a chair and lifted her chin. "Start talking. All of it, from the very beginning."

Chapter Thirteen

Worn out by confession, Elaine stood at a window and gazed at Walt's side yard. Lilac bushes were beginning to bud. A garden plot was dark and rich looking, ready for seedlings. Two of Jodi's school friends had found her. The girls were practicing cheerleading jumps and tumbles on a narrow strip of grassy ground.

Seated on a chair, her posture queenly, Lillian said, "So, let me see if I have this all straight. You found a note that threatened Bobby, but hid it because your father might have made the threat. Meanwhile, Tom Greene hired a private investigator who turned up insurance fraud in Axton's background. So you allowed Tate into the lodge where he discovered bullets that prove someone other than Del shot Bobby. Tom then went after Axton because he owns the right type of gun, only Linda somehow lured Tom up to Branch Road and near beat him to death in order to protect Axton. Is that all?"

Looking guilty, Ric said, "Plus the part about your brother, ma'am."

Lillian cocked an eyebrow, but made no comment.

"Uncle King didn't investigate the shooting properly, Mama. He gave Tate direct orders not to do anything. He's blocked us every step of the way and even hinted that if we didn't quit, he'd find a way to pin the murder on Ric. He might have been in cahoots with Axton about the riverfront property.''

"I know it sounds crazy when we tell it, ma'am," Ric said. "Talk to Tate. He can lay it out so it makes sense. He never thought the shooting was an accident."

"I've been a fool," Lillian said quietly. An edge of anger colored her voice. "Not long after…the shooting, I asked King flat out if Del had murdered Bobby. I never thought, never imagined Del was a killer, oh, but he had a temper. One foolish act, that's all it took. I wanted to know. *Needed* to know. King swore up and down it was an accident. Nothing more. He promised me that no one would ever say different." She pressed a hand over her eyes. Her shoulders rounded. "I wanted to believe."

"Oh, Mama, me too. I hated myself for even thinking Daddy could have hurt Bobby."

Lillian dragged in a long breath and patted her breast. "So, basically, this all started because Ric is Jodi's blood daddy."

Elaine's face warmed. She didn't want to feel shame or like a bad child, but she felt it nonetheless. That her mother accepted the information so casually made her feel worse somehow. "We think it started when Bobby hauled trash out of the realty. We still haven't figured what he saw. I'm sorry, Mama. I should have come to you earlier, but I didn't know…how you'd take the news about Jodi and Ric."

Lillian shared a mysterious, silent communication with Walt. He stood near the doorway, leaning a shoulder against the wall. "You can fool a lot of people, honey, but don't ever try fooling your mama. I've always known."

Elaine and Ric must have made a comical pair, because Lillian laughed aloud. "Oh for Pete's sake, child! I'm not stupid. I knew exactly what was going on between you and your daddy. How he pushed you straight into Ric's arms. Fact is, right after you told us you were expecting, Gwen says to me, that's Ric's baby. And I said, if Bobby don't give a never mind, then why should we? Way we saw it, if you were grown-up enough to get married, you were grown-up enough to handle your own private matters. We were just thankful you didn't run off to have an abortion or give the baby away."

Elaine clamped her arms over her bosom and huffed. "Did Daddy know?"

Lillian shook a finger at her. "Don't get all snippy with me. You're the one started this secret-keeping business in the first place. And of course he knew. Not that he'd ever admit it out loud. Too much pride in that man."

"Am I the only person in the whole world who didn't know I'm Jodi's father?" Ric asked.

"I didn't know," said a very small voice.

Walt startled and half-turned. Jodi stood in the doorway right behind him. Behind her, her school friends stood wide-eyed and silent, radiating communal embarrassment. Buster wriggled past the girls and sat beside the bed. He looked hopefully up at Ric.

Elaine stared at her daughter's white face and strained features. No telling how long the girl had been standing there, but it was evident that she'd heard more than enough.

Jodi's friends whispered. They sounded apologetic and uncomfortable. Jodi ignored them. She stood as still and pale as marble. The girls slinked away. The front door creaked open and then banged shut.

"Come in, baby," Elaine coaxed.

Walt reached for the girl. She shied away and gave him a look of pure disgust.

"Jodi, please," Ric said. "Let us explain."

"How will you do that? You're all a bunch of big fat liars." She thrust out a wiry arm, her pointing finger trembling. "Is it the truth, Mom? Is *he* my real father?"

"Biologically, yes."

Her young face contorted with fury. Hot spots flared over her cheekbones. "Then you're just one of those sperm donors, aren't you?"

"No!" Ric struggled as if to get out of bed.

"You never cared about me at all!" Jodi yelled. "You were just sucking up to me to score points with Mom!"

With sweat breaking on his brow, Ric got his feet off the bed. Grimacing, he reached for the girl. She burst into tears and ran away. Her pounding feet made the little house rock. The front door slammed.

Elaine and Lillian reached the bedroom door at the same time. Their shoulders knocked and wedged them between the jamb. Elaine broke free and ran after her child. At the door, she thrust out a hand to halt Lillian. "Let me handle this. Make sure Ric doesn't get out of bed."

RIC FELT LOWER than a worm's belly. He wished he'd never come back to McClintock. Wished Bobby had never told him the truth. He'd grown to love his daughter. Now she hated him.

"Walt," Lillian said, "I'd like a moment with Ric, if you don't mind."

Walt patted his nephew's shoulder. "It'll work out. Give the girl some time to get this all straight in her head." He left the two of them alone.

Ric decided if Lillian told him it would be best all the way around for him to pack up and hightail it out of town, he was going to do it. They couldn't force Jodi to accept him, and it would be cruel to try. His continued presence could only serve to embarrass her. He'd make arrangements for half his retirement pay to go to Elaine for child support. He'd start a fund for Jodi's college. He'd keep the lines of communication open so that if at some point in the future, Jodi wanted to establish contact—which he doubted she ever would—she could.

"Ric?"

He lifted sheepish eyes. One nice thing about misery. It made his back pain seem almost laughable in contrast. "Yes, ma'am?"

"I…" She tapped her chin with a manicured nail. No matter how rough the work on the ranch, she always had perfect nails and hair. "This is difficult. So I'll just say it. I apologize for my late husband."

He blinked stupidly. "It's not—"

"Don't interrupt me. This is something that should have been said a long time ago. Don't get me wrong, I loved Bobby dearly. He was a good son and a good husband. But this I know, if you and my daughter had married, it would have been good, too. None of this would have happened if Del had been more open-minded."

He couldn't believe his ears. Maybe he was trapped inside a drug-induced dream.

"I'm glad you and Elaine have worked out your differences. I'm satisfied you'll keep Jodi's best interests at the forefront."

"Yes, ma'am." He clenched his fingers into the softness of a teddy bear. "Do you think it's in her best interests if I leave town?"

Her mouth dropped open. Her big brown eyes blazed. She flicked him on the forehead with a finger.

"Ow!" He rubbed the stinging spot. "Why did you do that?"

"If you even think about deserting my granddaughter,

I will personally hunt you down and hamstring you. Do you understand?''

"Yes, ma'am.''

Her sharp gaze made him feel as if she were probing inside his skull. "Good. Now, about Del." Her smile turned rather sad. "You never saw his good side. He had a wonderful sense of humor and great generosity of spirit. And passion." She closed her eyes. "Oh, my, but he was a passionate man. Every day was an adventure for him. He had more big ideas than Carter's got liver pills."

"I know he had a good side," Ric said.

"Don't tell fibs." She laughed lightly, a musical sound. "He had a peculiar trait, an incompatibility that often made life more difficult then it needs be. He desperately wanted to be liked by everyone, and yet, at the same time, he needed very much to be right." She peered intently at him. "You don't suffer that affliction, do you?"

He thought about it, then shrugged. "I guess not."

"You are perhaps the most self-contained young man I've ever known. There is about you a certain confidence that never turns into arrogance. Self-assurance coupled with fine intelligence. Rare qualities in a man."

Now he was getting embarrassed. He fiddled with the Velcro fasteners on the brace.

"Del recognized it. Perhaps not consciously, but I'm sure he did all the same. You represented the man he wanted to be. Del had to work so very hard at being liked. He was so afraid of being wrong. Here you are, lacking the benefit of wealth and family name. Yet, you are naturally *more* than he could ever be."

Face hot, Ric struggled for words. She touched his hand, her slim fingers soothing.

"I don't mean to discombobulate you, hon. You were a good boy, despite Del's prejudice. You're a fine man. I know you and Jodi will work through this. Should you and Elaine decide to make a future together, you have my blessing.''

''Thank you,'' he muttered.

She carefully kissed his cheek. When he looked up, she winked at him. Then she shook a finger at his face. ''But if you knock up my daughter again, there better be a ring on her finger and your boots under her bed. Is that perfectly clear?''

He clutched the bear over his chest as if that might protect him. ''Yes, ma'am.''

''Don't ever forget that I'm a force to be reckoned with.'' She swept toward the door. ''I think it's time I had a chat with that brother of mine. God help him if he's involved in anything illegal.''

Warmth filled his chest and tightened his throat. It took several moments before he realized he was perilously close to tears. Leaving the hospital. The welcome home from the folk of McClintock. Jodi learning the truth in the worst possible way. Lillian's kind acceptance. The day had been too much.

By the time Elaine returned, Ric felt in control. It was ludicrous to expect that all was well with Jodi, but he searched her face for hopefulness anyway.

''How is she?'' he asked.

''Angry. Confused. We should have told her.'' A single tear slipped down her cheek and she dashed it away. ''I don't know how much more she can take.''

He clasped her hand, entwining their fingers. Heaviness in his chest made clear what he'd known subconsciously for a long time. He'd fallen in love with Elaine again. He wanted a life with her, a life with Jodi. Because of his own cowardice, because of old childhood fears and pride, he'd blown it.

"I need to go home," she said. "I'll call you."

She failed to kiss him goodbye.

In the now deathly quiet house, he peered into the face of the teddy bear. Its blank glass eyes seemed to mock his helplessness, his uselessness. Snorting in frustration, he flung the toy against the wall.

Buster fetched the plush bear and nosed it onto the bed.

Ric laughed dryly. "I don't deserve it, little buddy. Go be nice to someone else."

RIC HELD his breath while the telephone rang. Jodi's cheery greeting brought a wide smile to his face. "Hey, kiddo, it's me, Ric. How are you—"

Click.

Cursing, he punched in the number for Elaine's house again. Jodi answered, but suspicion marked her tone. "Please don't hang up, Jodi. I really need to talk to you."

"I don't wanna talk to you. Quit calling me!" *Click.*

He turned a baleful glare at the row of prescription bottles lined up on the bedside table. The pain in his back had settled in one spot, finally, but it was a doozy. No matter how he adjusted the brace and his position in bed, it felt as if a fist-sized knot pressed against his spinal cord. Prescribed pain killers dulled the pain, but also depressed his psyche. His mood was in a downward spiral, worsening by the hour. He could hear his uncle bustling around the kitchen, banging pot lids and cabinet doors.

Walt appeared in the doorway. "You want cornbread or sourdough?"

"I don't care."

"You barely touched lunch."

When Walt was at work, neighbor ladies dropped in to feed Ric and tidy the house. They also gave Walt full reports about what Ric did or did not do. "Wasn't hungry."

"This moping of yours is turning stale, boy. I'll do up a skillet of cornbread." Shaking his head, he turned away.

Ric called Elaine's house again. This time the answering machine picked up. He waited for the beep. He didn't know what to say or how to say it.

He knew what he wanted. He wanted Jodi to forgive him, to tell him she loved him in spite of everything. He wanted her happy. He hung up without leaving a message.

RIC PLACED the cane tip squarely on the floor, then took a step. His lower back ached, but his legs didn't protest. He took another step, then another. He concentrated on his footing. Once he reached the kitchen, he felt ridiculously proud of himself. He allowed himself to believe the doctors who claimed Linda's attack hadn't worsened his back.

He figured in two or three days, four at most, he'd be able to drive. He hung the cane on the back of a chair and set about making coffee.

The doorbell rang. He cursed. The neighbor ladies with their fussing and cooing made him feel silly. Plus, they wanted to stuff him like a turkey. He was going to end up with twenty pounds of flab around his gut.

"Ric?" Elaine called. "Are you decent?"

Pleasant tightness filled his chest. She'd been gone all weekend to attend her sister's college graduation. He hadn't even been able to talk to her on the telephone. On Monday he'd called her house dozens of times without success. He'd been waiting for a decent hour to call her this morning.

He raked his fingers through his hair and plucked at his T-shirt, hoping it wasn't as grimy as it felt. "Come on in," he called.

She stopped in the kitchen doorway and scowled at him.

He'd never realized how much he could miss a person. How much he'd missed her face, her bouncy walk, the heady scent that followed her in an alluring trail. He missed talking to her, listening to her, making her laugh. He missed Jodi.

Some lone wolf, he thought in disgust, moping like a whipped puppy when Elaine wasn't around.

"What are you doing out of bed?"

"I feel great. Boy, you look pretty."

"Don't try sweet talk."

"Real pretty." He stretched a hand toward her. Her expression dampened the urge to laugh.

Tate loomed behind Elaine. He seemed grim as well.

Ric took two, nonlimping, steps to the chair where he'd hung the cane. He gave the cane a jaunty twirl. "See, I'm fine. Want some coffee? It'll be ready in a few minutes."

It sank in that Tate was in full uniform. Ric had been under the impression that the sheriff had suspended Tate.

"Get back in bed."

"Not a chance." He pulled a chair from the table and sat. "I'm fine."

Eyeing him askance, she entered the kitchen. He pleaded silently for a kiss. If not for Tate, he'd pull her onto his lap and kiss her senseless.

"Sorry I haven't been by, ranger. Been busier than a one-legged man in a butt-kicking contest." Tate laughed while he pulled a chair from the table. "You won't believe what's going on."

"Has Linda given up Cross?"

Elaine blinked rapidly, as if not quite believing what she was about to say. She rearranged the salt and pepper shakers on the table, and straightened napkins in a wooden holder. Her fidgeting made Ric wary.

"The county commissioners and the town council held an emergency meeting last night. A closed-door session." She lowered her gaze to her hands. Her fingers twisted against each other. "Tate and I told them everything. Uncle King had to account for his actions."

"And?"

"They told him he had a choice. Either, he quietly accepts an undetermined suspension and cooperates with an investigation. Or, the commissioners will bring in the state police and Colorado Bureau of Investigation. They didn't say it out loud, but what they meant is that Uncle King would be the target of the investigation."

Ric breathed an incredulous curse. "Does your mother know?"

"Mama sits on the town council. She spearheaded the meeting." She passed a hand over her eyes. "Uncle King is furious. He's holed up in his house, won't talk to anybody. It was terrible, Ric. I thought he was going to break down and cry."

"So the council appointed the under-sheriff as the acting sheriff until this matter is resolved," Tate said. He fingered the badge on his khaki shirt. "I'm on full-time, with carte blanche to do whatever needs doing to solve Bobby's murder."

Ric was dumbfounded. Then, wondered why he should be. As Lillian had claimed, she was a force to be reckoned with. "So where do we stand on the investigation? Has Linda talked yet?"

Tate exchanged a look with Elaine. "Cross bailed her out of jail."

An unpleasant sensation slithered down Ric's spine and his gut jumped. "Then they are in on it together."

Tate shook his head. "Doesn't prove anything. She's essential to his business."

"What about the insurance? Cross's handgun?"

"The insurance angle is a bust. Turns out the warehouse fire in San Francisco started in an adjoining building. Arson was ruled out. As for the partner in Denver?" He shook his head. "Even with the insurance, Axton had to declare bankruptcy. No profit, no motive."

"The handgun?" Ric asked, but knew he was about to be disappointed.

"Without probable cause, can't get a search warrant. We have zippo on Cross."

"What about fingerprints?"

"His fingerprints are all over the plat map, but no hits off the lodge itself. I'm going back up there to see if I can lift some more. The district attorney says the map doesn't give us probable cause. I haven't found anybody who can testify Cross ever threatened Del. No witnesses can place him anywhere near the lodge. I've pulled phone records, but nothing looks promising. On top of that, his attorney has warned him not to speak to anyone official. Anything he says can be used against him if there is a civil lawsuit."

"Sounds hopeless."

"Not yet. The .44 slug had traces of blood on it. The lab is running DNA tests. If it matches Bobby, then I can get a warrant."

"Is there enough to run a test?"

"Keep your fingers crossed."

Ric passed a hand through his hair. Forced bed rest had given him plenty of time for thinking. His thoughts had returned time and again to Linda Pallo—a woman with solid standing in the community, steady employment, and no criminal record. Anyone, male or female, was capable of violence, given the right set of circumstances. Even so, he couldn't imagine the circumstances that would drive Linda to attack Tom Greene with a pry bar.

"What about Linda?" he asked. "There must be a way to convince her to turn Cross."

Tate displayed his empty palms. "She's sticking to her story that Tom forced her off the road, and she defended herself." His eyes narrowed. "Considering how much noise Tom's been making, a jury might buy it."

"Unbelievable," Ric muttered.

"Hate to say it," Elaine said, "but I sort of wonder if she isn't telling the truth." The men swung incredulous gazes at her and she sat straighter on the chair. "Well, Tom is obsessed. He's been making threats. Him going after her makes a lot more sense than her going after him. I don't excuse what she did, but if Tom assaulted her, he should have known she'd defend herself."

"She defends herself then kidnaps Jodi?" Ric swung his head in emphatic denial.

"She's always been prickly, not too trusting. Maybe she panicked. She doesn't have many friends. She could have thought no one would believe her side of the story."

"I don't believe it," Ric said. "Don't you have any leverage to break her story?"

"Actually," Tate said with a grin. "Elaine's already agreed to wear a wire."

"Isn't that entrapment?"

"We're not encouraging her to break the law."

Merely imagining Elaine being alone with Linda Pallo gave Ric the willies. "That woman is dangerous."

"I'm not afraid of her," Elaine said. She wouldn't look him in the eyes. "Not too much, anyway. Tate promises to stay less than a shout away."

Tate checked his watch. "I have to run Del's .38 to the lab. I'll give you guys a shout when I get back."

Elaine saw Tate out. When she returned, she poured coffee into two cups.

"I don't want you anywhere near Linda."

"It's a done deal," she said, giving him a wan smile. She pressed a finger against his lips, halting his protests. "I'll be perfectly safe. Change the subject."

Ric grumbled into his coffee cup, but she was unmoved. She met his glowers with bland patience. Stubborn. Brave. Irresistible.

He touched her hand, sliding his fingers over hers. "I've missed you. You really do look pretty this morning."

"Thanks."

He waited for her to say she'd missed him, too. Instead, she wore a distracted expression. He suspected something other than a murder investigation was going on. Sunshine streaming through the kitchen highlighted the weariness in her face.

"Jodi got into a fight at school," she said.

"What? Why?"

"Some boys were tormenting her. Calling her names. Teasing her about you. She bloodied a boy's nose."

He closed his eyes, haunted by memories of his own school days when he'd been the target of bullies. He'd been quick and strong. Necessity had made him handy with his fists. A few scraps in the schoolyard had earned him a reputation as a boy who didn't tolerate physical abuse. Words hurt, too—often times worse than punches or slaps.

"I've convinced the school not to suspend her for the last few weeks of the year. They do require she gets counseling. I tend to agree. I made an appointment with a therapist."

"It's me, isn't it?"

"Oh, Ric, don't blame yourself. Things are just too much for her right now. She keeps having nightmares about Tom and Linda. She had a crying fit the other day, saying it was her fault Tom got hurt.''

He ached for his daughter. He hated himself for being unable to help her.

"Getting away this weekend helped a lot. She just adores spending time with Marlee. But then this thing at school happened. I had a huge fight on my hands getting her on the bus this morning.'' She sipped from the coffee cup, her eyes downcast. "She even told me she wants to cancel her birthday party.''

He'd turned her into the butt of cruel jokes and malicious gossip. It wasn't only children who'd taunt her, either. Some adults never outgrew senseless impulses to pick on the vulnerable or the different.

He picked up Elaine's hand and kissed her knuckles, one by one. Then he pressed her soft palm against his cheek. "I wish she'd talk to me, but she won't. Can't say that I blame her.''

"If only I knew what to do for her.''

His throat felt thick. He had to clear it. "It's me.''

"It's not your fault. You didn't know.''

"It doesn't matter. Eventually she'll have to forgive you. She needs you too much. And she'll find some way to forgive Bobby, too. No matter what, he was her daddy. But me?'' He rolled his eyes. "I'm just the guy who wrecked her world.''

"You're underestimating her.''

"I've been playing this game all my life. There are never any winners.''

Chewing her lower lip, she studied his face. "I spoke to Walt. He said you're depressed.''

"I'm not depressed.''

"Then why does it sound like you're giving up on Jodi?''

"I'm being realistic. I embarrassed her in front of her friends. Hell, I humiliated her in front of the whole town! She isn't going to forgive that." He tried to hold on to her, but she pulled away. "I won't shirk my responsibilities. I'll pay child support. But we can't force her to accept me. She's suffered enough."

Cupping the mug in both hands, Elaine leaned back on the chair. "In a few days Jodi will be thirteen. The terrible teens. She's always been given to dramatics and high emotion. Toss in raging hormones, and, well, there goes the neighborhood."

"This is a lot more than hormones. This is the ultimate betrayal. It's better if I step out of the picture."

"How wonderfully noble of you." The dry sarcasm matched the arch of her brows.

Anger rose. He was being noble, damn it, putting his daughter first. "We can't be good together if Jodi is dead set against me being a part of her life."

She hung her head. Her shoulders shook with silent laughter. "You're such an idiot," she murmured. Her big, beautiful eyes snapped with heat. "We messed up, Ric. Now we have to deal with the consequences. We can't do that if you run away."

"Don't you think I know that?"

"I wonder. I really do."

"I love her! I want the best for her. If that means staying away from her, then that's what I have to do."

"Who are you really protecting?"

"Jodi! I'll do anything for her. I'd die for her."

She passed a hand over her face. "What about us?"

A stumper of a question. He tried a smile, knowing it was weak, even pitiful. "We'll work things out. Quietly. Keep a low profile. People will eventually find something else to talk about."

"Fourteen years ago we tried to hide from Daddy. We blew it big time. If I'd stood up to him, hadn't been such a coward, none of this would have happened. I'm going to carry those regrets the rest of my life. I don't intend to make the same mistake again."

"It's the only way. Every time Jodi looks at me, she's going to remember what I did to her. When people see us together, they'll be reminded."

"If our relationship has any chance at all, then you're going to have to face Jodi. Because I'm sure not going to sneak around behind her back."

"She won't talk to me!"

"Little known fact about parenthood, Ric. Sometimes your kids don't like you. Tough."

"I'm not talking about my feelings."

"Like hell you aren't!" She slammed the mug on the table. "You've been a good pal to her. But being a father means doing the hard stuff, too." She pointed a finger back and forth between them. "If you and I are going anywhere, it's going to have to be as parents. We don't have another option."

"But she hates me."

She threw her hands in the air. "Will you stop being so selfish!"

"I'm not—"

"Good Lord, that poor child has suffered more in thirteen short years than most suffer in a lifetime. She lost her father and her grandfather. Her other grandfather has practically lost his mind. She was kidnapped, for Pete's sake! Then she finds out that we've been lying to her. And you're whining because she *hates* you?"

Deeply offended, he crossed his arms. He was being both reasonable and realistic. She didn't need to go ballistic on him.

"You're the one who said we have to set a good example. Well, there's a whole lot more she has to learn than just how a man is supposed to treat a lady on a date. It's up to us to show her that, yeah, life can be unfair. We get hurt, get our hearts broken. But we still have to get up and go on. If you chicken out on her when she needs you most, what kind of example are you setting?"

"It's real hard to set an example when she won't even talk to me."

Slumped, she shook her head and sighed heavily. "Fine. We'll talk about this when you aren't so depressed."

"I am not depressed, damn it!"

"Then there's really no hope for us at all, is there?"

Chapter Fourteen

Elaine rested her arms on the fence rail. She watched Jodi work Savvy on a *longe* line. The fat Morgan was blowing and sweating from the workout, but he gamely went through his paces. Elaine wished Ric could see the girl being so diligent about caring for his horse. Sure, Jodi was confused and she was hurt, but deep down inside she loved Ric. She needed him. The way the girl was moping around lately said she missed him, too.

Lillian boosted herself higher on the fence and whistled to catch the girl's attention. When Jodi looked, Lillian called, ''Make him pick up his feet on the lead changes, honey!''

''Why the big sighs?'' Lillian asked Elaine.

''I'm tired.''

''Well, this is the first real breather you and I have had in a week.''

Between handling paperwork to satisfy EPA and Board of Health requirements, consulting with the ranch manager about cattle breeding and pasture use, and running supplies to various round-up camps, Lillian and Elaine had been putting in dawn to dusk days.

''It's not the work, it's…everything. I've made such a mess of my life.''

"Ah, honey, you're just feeling sorry for yourself. How about a nice cup of herb tea?"

Elaine followed her mother back to the big house. The temperature hovered around fifty. In the sunshine, it was warm enough to sit outside on the veranda. From there was a panoramic view of the barns, corrals and lower pastures. Mist from rapidly melting snow wreathed the mountain peaks.

Elaine watched a stock truck rumble and rattle on a dirt road. It headed for a high pasture corral where yearlings were being held for transport to market. A pang of grief tightened her diaphragm. This was the time of year for rounding up cattle in order to brand calves, castrate young bulls and doctor the herds. It had been Bobby's favorite time of year.

Lillian brought a pot of tea and a plate of oatmeal raisin cookies. "You're worried about Ric, aren't you?"

"That, too." She guessed what Ric's real problem was. He couldn't separate the boy he'd been from the girl Jodi was now.

"Are you in love with him?"

Elaine thought about it. "I think so. But Jodi really hurt his feelings, Mama. Even if he won't admit it." A cheeky scrub jay sailed to the edge of veranda and cocked a beady eye at her. She tossed it a bit of cookie. It snatched up the crumb and flew away. "McClintock hurt him bad. He's been running from that hurt all his life. He can't tell the difference between his situation and Jodi's."

"He's not talking about leaving, is he?"

"Not yet."

"I swear, sheep have more sense than men."

"I know one thing for certain. My days of sneaking around are over. I'm not going behind Jodi's back to see

Ric. Either he makes peace with her, or we don't stand a chance.''

The housekeeper brought the day's mail. Lillian sorted through the bundle of bills, advertisements and catalogs.

Sipping the lemon scented tea, Elaine watched her daughter. Standing tall, her golden hair shining, Jodi looked so much like Ric it made Elaine's heart hurt. Jodi worked the *longe* line with a deft touch, making it seem as if the Morgan read her mind.

Were Elaine young and dumb again, perhaps love would be enough. She knew better now. She and Jodi and Ric were a package deal. Either they worked out their problems together, or they fell apart.

"Oh, look," Lillian said. She handed over a thank-you card. "Pastor Rimes truly is a gracious soul.''

Elaine read the note written in the pastor's elegant, old-fashioned script. There had been enough donations to Del's memorial fund to repair and repave the church parking lot. The pastor intended to erect a plaque in Del's memory. He asked Lillian to prepare a few words for the unveiling.

"One thing I've always appreciated about the pastor. He knows when the time is right for a sweet gesture."

Donations. Elaine could almost smell dewy grass, feel the sharp cold of the October dawn. A hitch of old, instinctual fear over graveyard-ghost stories imprinted on her brain in childhood. *"What do I do with it then?" she asked Ric. "Buy me breakfast?" he replied.* As clearly as if she held it in front of her face, she saw the envelope: *I'm sorry.*

"Honey? What's the matter?"

"Did Daddy ever mention bad debts?"

"Hmm, not that I can recall. Why?"

"Last October I went early to visit Bobby and Daddy. I found an envelope stuffed with money leaning up against the mausoleum door. It was an odd amount, more than three thousand dollars. There were even some coins.''

''I'll be. Any idea who left it?''

Elaine pulled a facial shrug. ''Not a clue. I gave it to Pastor Rimes, and didn't think anything more about it. But whoever left it wrote *I'm sorry* on the envelope. Nothing else. No note or explanation.''

''Are you thinking Bobby's killer left it?''

''I do not know, Mama. Could you go through Daddy's paperwork? See if there were any debts that had to be written off as a loss. I'm going to give the pastor a call.'' She raised crossed fingers. ''Maybe he kept the envelope.''

Lillian gave her an admonishing look. ''Seems to me a lot of our recent problems are a direct result of certain people haring off on their own, and keeping information to themselves. Report this to Tate. Let him do all the questioning. But I can tell you right now, only one debt was written off.''

''Who was it for?''

''Your father loaned Dooley Nichols money to hold off foreclosure. But then Dooley up and died. Maria Nichols wanted to work out a payment plan, but I convinced her it was more advantageous tax-wise if it were written off as uncollectible. Do you honestly think our men died because of a bad debt?'' Lillian waggled a hand in a shooing gesture. ''Sounds to me like someone has a real guilty conscience. Call Tate.''

Elaine went indoors to do just that. She reached the acting sheriff. Before she could state her business, he said, ''You might want to go check on your uncle, Elaine.''

''Oh, Gil, what has he done this time?''

Gil made uncomfortable noises. At length he answered. ''He caused a row last night in Chuck's Feed Wagon when the bartender cut him off. They called me, but the sheriff was gone before I got there. He'd gone up to the Track Shack. Got into a fight with Tate.''

"He's drinking again? Oh no! Was anybody hurt?''

"Just a lot of yelling and blustering. Tate got the old man's keys away from him, then took him home. I ain't seen him drunk like that in twenty years.''

Elaine swallowed hard, her throat aching, remembering King's shattered expression when the town council demanded his suspension. Being sheriff was all he had; she'd been party to taking it away.

She asked Gil to have Tate call her whenever the deputy could spare a few minutes. Then she hurried outside to tell her mother about King.

ENOUGH WAS ENOUGH, Ric had decided. Television bored him to tears. He was sick of reading. Everyone he knew was working. Tate was too busy to give Ric updates on the murder investigation. Walt was knee-deep in a cabinet job he wanted finished by the end of June. Jodi still wouldn't take his phone calls. Elaine was helping her mother with ranch business, and he missed her so much even his hair ached. Ric felt as if he were in prison, in an isolation cell, forgotten by the world.

He strapped on the back brace. He kept the chest fasteners fairly loose and the waist fasteners tight, which made it as comfortable as a plastic corset could be. He buttoned a flannel shirt over the brace. A glimpse of himself in a mirror made him grin. He looked as if he wore body armor. ''Commando Buchanan reporting for duty,'' he said to his reflection.

Cane in hand, he made his careful way out of the house. Buster scampered ahead, his nose to the ground and his tail wagging. A shout caught Ric off guard. He'd been concentrating on his footing and hadn't noticed King McClintock swaggering up the street.

As the old man drew closer, Ric noted it wasn't a swagger, but a stagger. Buster growled. His hackles lifted while his tail tucked between his legs.

"I'm talking to you, boy!" King yelled.

Ric judged the distance to the front door. He'd never make it before King caught him.

King squelched all hope of escape when he pulled a weapon.

Buster took one look at the gun, yipped then darted for the house where he slithered out of sight beneath the porch. Ric stared into the bore of a blue-steel revolver pointed at his chest. Wishing he were wearing body armor, he forced his eyes off the gun and up to King's angry face. "Good afternoon, sir."

King's eyes were sunken and bloodshot. A miasma of boozy fumes surrounded him. His white shirt was wrinkled and grimy, with one tail hanging out. He swayed on his feet, but his gun hand was steady.

He was good and drunk. Mean and drunk. Ric's mouth went dry.

"Couldn't leave well enough alone, could you?" King's mustache was stiff and yellowish. His nose was bright red. When he talked he looked like a ventriloquist's dummy with his lower lip clacking up and down. "Shoulda followed my gut in the first place. Now I'll show 'em. I ain't over the hill. I ain't outgrown my usefulness. Uh-uh! Ain't no punk bastard gonna make a jackass outta me."

Ric kept his gaze steady on King. His ears strained for the sound of neighbors or an approaching car. He wished his dog was a hundred pounds of meanness rather than a gun-shy twenty-five.

"What exactly does your gut tell you, sir?"

"*You* killed Bobby and Del. They wrecked your big plans about worming your way into my family. Got your revenge on all of us, didn't you? Well, I'm onto you now. You're gonna confess. Gonna write it down." He wagged the gun at Walt's front door. "Get moving."

Ric suspected that if he entered the house, the only way he'd be leaving would be in a body bag. His only hope was to keep King talking until someone noticed them.

Ric pretended to chew over King's words. "My gut says *you* killed Bobby."

King reared back. His eyes were piggy, glowing red in the shadow beneath his hat. "What kinda nonsense is that?"

"Isn't that a .44 calibre revolver?"

King scowled at the gun as if he'd never noticed it before. "That's right."

"Bobby wasn't shot with Del's .38. It was a .44 round that killed him. Probably a revolver, too, since there weren't any ejected shell casings."

"I'd no more shoot that boy than I'd shoot my own foot. Get in that house. You got a confession—"

"And there's your motive to consider."

"What motive?"

"Greed. Big money from selling your riverfront property. You were conspiring with Axton behind Del's back. Hiding it from Lillian, too. You stood to make a lot of money if Axton developed that land. Bobby caught you."

King used the gun to scratch his cheek. "That's just plumb stupid. Damned Axton's been bugging me about that land ever since he showed up. Got to be a regular joke, 'cause he's knows for damn sure I ain't selling off nothing with the McClintock brand on it. Is this Raleigh's big investigation? Trying to prove I killed Bobby? Good

God almighty, he's an idiot! Town should know better than to trust some slick talking yahoo from back East.''

"If you didn't do it, then who did?"

"You!"

"Aren't you forgetting something, sir?"

"What's that?"

"At the time I'd just been released from the hospital. Remember, sir? I was on crutches. I couldn't drive. And I don't own a handgun."

"Huh." King chewed a corner of his mustache. "Mebbe you had help?"

"An accomplice." Ric nodded as if it made sense. "You have a point there. But who? Bobby was the only real friend I had in town. He wouldn't help me kill himself."

"What about your uncle?"

Ric wagged his head back and forth. "Come on. Walt's a pacifist. He doesn't hold with fighting. Doesn't have much use for firearms either. We have to come up with a better suspect."

King was relaxing, looking less belligerent and more interested. Ric took what comfort he could from Elaine's assurances that beneath all the bluster, her uncle had a good heart. He hoped that applied when King was drunk.

"Besides, sir, if I wanted revenge against your family, there are easier ways. A custody battle, for instance."

"I should have locked you up and thrown away the key when I caught you that time with Elaine. Why couldn't you leave that girl alone?"

"I loved her, sir."

"And I know exactly what part of her you loved."

"Hey, there!" came a high-pitched shout. "Is that you? It is you! What are you doing out of bed, Ric?"

King turned his head just enough to see Walt's next door

neighbor. In her eighties, she was a spry little bird of a woman. She strode purposefully down the walk. Sunlight glinted off her thick eyeglasses. Her health was excellent, but her eyesight even with glasses was as poor as a mole's. Her hearing wasn't good either.

"Sheriff? What you doing jaw-jacking with this boy when he's supposed to be in bed? I told Walt I'd keep an eye out for him. What's he do as soon as I turn my back? Sneaks right outside. Ric, you should be ashamed of yourself." Her nostrils flared and her nose wrinkled. "Hoowee! What's that stink?" She leaned close to King and sniffed. "It's you! Smell like a pot of bad whiskey, young man. What are you doing drinking? Ain't you learned nothing at all?"

"Go on back in your house," King said. "This is official police business." He gestured with the revolver, but she either didn't notice it or ignored it.

"Don't you be official police business-ing with me, King McClintock. I know darned good and well you're on suspension. You're drunk, too. Ought to be ashamed."

If not for the gun, Ric would have burst out laughing. "Ma'am, this really is police business."

"Son, you got to the count of three to get your butt back inside or I'm calling Walt. One, two, three! Fine!" She spun about and marched back to her house. She muttered about foolish children and drunken hooligans.

"Old biddy's blind as a bat," King said.

Ric pulled at his lower lip to keep from laughing. "I know. But she makes the best apple crisp I've ever tasted. And her pork roast is something else."

"*Mmm-mm.* You ain't tasted heaven until you've tried her Christmas cake. Uses enough rum to float a ship. Darned things should be illegal." King was grinning, his eyes gone mellow. He made motions as if to shove his revolver into a holster, except he wasn't wearing a holster. He crammed it into the front of his pants.

Ric half-expected the old man to shoot himself. When the weapon didn't do worse than make King's trousers sag, Ric breathed a sigh of relief.

"Where was we, boy?"

"Figuring out who killed Bobby, sir." He wanted to make a dash for the house, but dashing was out of the question.

"Oh, yeah." He cocked back his hat and squinted into the sun. "If it weren't you, and it weren't me, then who did it? You sure about the .44 bullet?"

"I saw it myself. Tate is having it tested for Bobby's blood. Del discharged his weapon that night, but all he hit was the wall. Are you sure you and Axton weren't scheming to develop the riverfront?"

King snorted in derision. The force of it made him rock and thrust out his arms to maintain his balance. Ric wondered how long and how much he'd been drinking. He vaguely recalled someone saying that King was an alcoholic. Pity mixed with disgust.

"Let's walk on over to the Track Shack. I'll buy you a cup of coffee and we can discuss this."

"I don't like you, boy."

"I know, sir."

"Been hard on you for a good reason. Boy like you, growing up without no proper daddy, a no-good mama, you're wrecked before you leave the chute."

Ric clenched his jaw against an angry rebuttal. King was calm, and Ric wanted him to stay that way.

"Reason you turned out good as you did was 'cause I kept a hard eye on you. Yessir. Hard eye and discipline, that's what keeps a boy straight. Oughtta thank me."

When the sun turned to ice.

"Don't know what 'Laine sees in you."

"No accounting for taste, sir."

King laughed, his belly jiggling against the revolver's grip. The laughter faded into a hiccough. "Always the smart mouth. Ah well, my mama always said, can't be nice, at least be polite. Reckon since you're Jodi's daddy, damn it all, I can be polite across the table from you."

"I am more than happy to return the courtesy, sir."

King shook a grimy finger. "But I still don't like you."

"The feeling is entirely mutual."

King began scowling again, his gaze gone distant. "Hold on just a minute! Did you say a .44?"

Ric's scalp prickled with impending trouble. "Tate knows all the particulars. Let's give him a call. He needs all the help he can get with his investigation. With your exper—"

With speed and grace that was astonishing in light of his drunkenness, King whipped the revolver out of his waistband. He waved it wildly in the air. "That old fool Tom wasn't just blowing smoke! He knew all along Axton did it!" He set off in a shambling run.

Ric shouted at King to stop. His heart sank. Just what this town needed, a hostage situation on Main Street.

The neighbor came outside again. "I called Walt. He says you best get back in bed pronto or he's coming home."

"Call the sheriff!" he shouted.

"What?" the old lady asked and cupped a hand around an ear. "Call who?"

"Call the sheriff!"

"He was just here."

Ric ground his teeth in frustration. "Please call the sheriff! Tell them there's an emergency at Crowder Realty!"

He set off as fast as he could. His jaw clenched against

pain flaring through his back. He made it to the corner of Second and Main. From what looked like a distance of a thousand miles uphill, he could see the realty sign. He didn't see King, or anyone else. Usually the sidewalks bustled with foot traffic, but there was no one out at the moment. There weren't any vehicles driving on Main either. Ski season was over. The summer tourist season hadn't begun. Locals were taking care of cattle or planting hay or tending peach orchards.

"If not for bad luck," Ric muttered, hobbling onward.

He prayed Axton Cross could get King talking and keep him talking. This town didn't need another tragic shooting.

ELAINE PROWLED the back streets of McClintock. She'd been to her uncle's house, his favorite fishing spot on the river, and even to the sheriff's station. She glanced at the cell phone on the passenger seat. Mama was supposed to call if she found King. Her uncle couldn't have gotten too far. His truck was still parked behind Chuck's Feed Wagon. All four of his horses were in the corral behind his house. She prayed he wasn't lying in a ditch, drowning on snow melt.

She turned onto Main and spotted a familiar figure limping up the hill. Her mouth fell open. Had every man in the valley gone loco? She pulled up beside Ric and honked the horn.

She was ready to blast him for his foolishness. He yanked open the passenger door. "King has gone gunning for Axton!"

Incredulous, she searched his face for any sign he was making a joke. He was flushed and sweating. His eyes were wild.

"First he came after me. Drunker than Clooney Brown. Looks like he hasn't slept in days. But I got him to talk.

Got him calmed down. Then he latched onto Axton for the killer.'' He paused to drag in a long breath. ''I'm sure he's at the realty. Call the sheriff or Tate or somebody.''

She had no time for fear or thinking. She ordered Ric into the Jeep. He hadn't even closed the door before she punched the accelerator. He used her cell phone to call the sheriff's station. Elaine steered into the realty parking lot. Axton's car was there, and so was Linda Pallo's. The only other car had Pennsylvania plates.

A man and woman, strangers to Elaine, burst out of the building. Both were wide-eyed and white-faced. The man waved both arms in the air. ''Help! Help! Call the police!'' He pointed at the door. ''There's a crazy old cowboy in there with a gun!''

The woman sniffed and smoothed her blazer jacket with both hands. ''We came out West to get away from crime. I can tell you right now, we're not buying a house in this town!''

Elaine turned to Ric. ''I've got to put a stop to this. Call my mother.''

He began punching numbers into the phone. ''You aren't going in there. King is nuts.''

''He won't hurt me.''

''He's going to hurt somebody,'' the tourist said. ''He's holding two people hostage. He has a *huge* gun.''

''What he wants,'' Ric said, ''is a confession. I got him calmed down before. Maybe I can do it— Lillian? Here's Elaine.'' He thrust the telephone at her and headed for the door.

Glaring at him, she said into the phone, ''Mama? Get into town right now. King has a gun. He's inside the realty with Axton. The sheriff is on his way.''

''I'll kill him,'' Lillian said, menacing and low. ''Tell Gil not to shoot King— I'm gonna do it!''

Elaine ran after Ric. He stood just inside the door. He put a finger over his lips in a shushing gesture, then tapped his ear. He wanted her to be quiet and listen.

They stood in a short hallway. On the left was a deep niche where the office workers could prepare coffee and keep snacks in a small refrigerator. On the right was a storeroom. The door was slightly ajar. Bagged trash and a stack of boxes awaited pick-up.

"Keep typing, boy," King said, his voice graveled and raw. "Every detail. Don't be leaving out no words."

Elaine exchanged a look with Ric.

"Confession," Ric mouthed.

Elaine could see Linda Pallo's desk. A free-standing cubicle wall gave the office manager a semblance of privacy when viewed from the Main Street entrance. Elaine could see Linda's computer monitor. There was an accounting program on the screen. She couldn't see King or Axton. She had no idea where Linda might be.

Ric touched her shoulder. He whispered in her ear. "Talk to your uncle. Let him know we're here."

"Woman, sit your butt down," King said. He sounded peeved. "Ain't you in enough trouble? Ought to shoot you for what you did to poor old Tom and Jodi."

"This is crazy!" Axton said. "You can't force me to confess to murder! I didn't do it!"

"I said, keep typing, boy. And while you're at it, explain the real reason you bailed this blockheaded old heifer outta jail. Are you two conspiring? Is that it?"

Elaine peeked around the corner. Axton Cross sat before the receptionist's computer. Mouth scrunched into a thin line and arms crossed, Linda sat on a chair. King had his pistol pressed against the back of Axton's head. King's appearance dismayed Elaine even more so than the gun. His complexion was mottled, his expression was grim. The

mustache of which he was so proud was dirty and un-
kempt, and his cheeks bore several days of stubble.

"Cavalry is here," Ric whispered.

She knew it already. Emergency lights flashed on Main
Street. A deputy was peeking through the window. The
door squeaked open behind them. Ric waved at the acting
sheriff, indicating silence. Gil Vance's smooth brown face
twisted in a scowl. He used emphatic hand movements in
an attempt to make Elaine and Ric leave the building.

Ignoring Gil, Elaine shifted her stare to Linda's cubicle.
She looked at the storage room and back to the computer
screen glowing on the desktop. Memories of another desk,
another place coalesced in her mind. Dusty bank receipts.
A ledger sheet. Bobby's blood staining the floor.

"Ric," she whispered. "If Bobby walked in that door,
to pick up trash out of that room, what kind of shabby
stuff could he see?"

"I want you two out right now!" Gil whispered harshly.
"That's an order."

"Remember the money at the graveyard?" she asked.
"'I'm sorry,' it said. Remember? And the lodge? Those
receipts you asked about? I didn't think much of them, but
I should have. Those were from rental properties. Linda
has always managed Daddy's rental properties. He never
bothered with it."

Comprehension dawned and his eyebrows raised. "Do
you think she was embezzling from your father?"

"Bobby could have witnessed her tampering with the
accounts or found evidence in the trash. Oh my God, she
didn't attack Tom to keep him away from Axton. She did
it to stop a lawsuit. She managed to hide what she did
from the probate audit, but they weren't looking for irreg-
ularities."

"If Tom brought suit," Ric said, "his attorney would be looking specifically for evidence of theft."

"Hold on a minute," Gil said. "Linda killed Bobby?"

"Who's that over there?" King roared.

"It's me, Uncle King. Elaine. Ric and Gil are with me."

"I'm working, girl. Go on home."

"Not until you leave Axton alone."

"I know the law, young lady. I been the law almost longer than you been alive. Let me do my job. And it is my job, damn it! Had no right to go snooping around behind my back. Filling your mama's head up with lies and nonsense. Turning her against me. Betraying our family for some no-account boy. Git! And you, killer, keep typing."

"But what about the gun?" Ric asked Elaine. "Tate went over every inch of Linda's property and didn't even find a shell. He can't find evidence she ever owned a handgun."

That stymied her for a moment. "What if she borrowed Axton's?" Only one way to find out. She stepped into the office.

"Girl," King said. "I told you to git."

Quite a crowd had gathered on Main Street. Deputies were having a hard time keeping rubberneckers away from the realty's plate glass windows.

"I have to ask Axton a really important question," she said.

"I'm doing the questioning around here."

"You are a mess, Uncle King. When is the last time you got any sleep? Oh, never mind. I'll let Mama deal with you. She's on the way right now." She looked Linda up and down. Anger rose, tightening her muscles and filling her chest with a shaky sensation. Del Crowder had respected Linda, trusted her, admired her. "Axton, you own a revolver, don't you?"

"Has everyone in this town gone nuts?" he cried. His tie was askew and his eyes were wild, pleading for rescue.

"Just answer the question, please."

"Yes! Your father talked me into buying it. You can't honestly think I shot your husband. I've never even fired that gun. Or taken it out of its case, for that matter."

"Where is it?"

Axton rolled his eyes toward King and his shoulders hunched as if in anticipation of a blow. "In my desk drawer. Go on, look at it. I think the price tag is still on it. I only bought it to get Del off my back. I'm begging you, Elaine, don't let him shoot me!"

Elaine watched Linda. She was as furiously rigid as she'd been the night she attacked Tom. "One more question. Does this office have a manual typewriter? An old electric?"

Color had drained from Linda's face. Her complexion was as gray as her hair.

"I—I—I think so." Axton gulped. "Back room, I think. Had it for envelopes until we got a new printer. Why? What is going on?"

"Axton didn't shoot Bobby," Elaine said. "It was you, wasn't it, Linda? He caught you stealing from Daddy. That's why you lured Tom up to Branch Road. You were trying to hide what you did. You meant to kill Tom. If Jodi hadn't been there, you would have, wouldn't you?"

King cocked his head as if he were trying to make out words in a foreign language.

"Bobby came by after hours to pick up trash from the office. You were here. Either you didn't hear him come in or you were away from your desk. He saw what you were doing." Elaine walked across the office. Emotion choked her throat. "He told you to confess to Daddy. Only you threatened him. If he blabbed, you'd blab about Jodi to Ric. Bobby didn't want to embarrass you, Linda. He wanted to keep it quiet. He didn't even tell me what you'd done. That's why he went to the lodge. It's the one place where there was complete privacy. But Bobby wasn't expecting you to be there."

King looked past Elaine. She sensed Ric and Gil behind her.

"Do you know what's really pathetic?" Elaine swiped a tear from her eye. "Daddy thought the world of you. He used to boast about how you held your head high even when life got you down. He would have worked it out with you."

"It wasn't really stealing," Linda said quietly. Her face looked carved from wax. "I paid it back to him. Every penny." She looked from face to face as if seeking support.

King lowered the revolver. Axton stared at Linda as if she'd sprouted another head.

"None of you know what it's like to want. To be so far in debt there aren't enough lifetimes to dig myself out. To see a no-account man spend every penny I earn for his drinking and gambling. To finally get my feet under me, then get dragged under again and again. Bobby didn't understand. Del *could* not understand. I wasn't stealing."

Linda lifted her chin in defiance. "If Bobby had kept his nose out of my business, none of this would have happened. It wasn't my fault. The gun went off by accident."

King shoved the revolver into the front of his trousers. He shoved Axton's shoulder. "Get out of here, damned fool," he grumbled. He slapped at his pockets. "Anybody around here got handcuffs?"

Elaine turned away, unable to listen to Linda's excuses

or watch her uncle make a drunken fool of himself. Ric was there to hold her against his broad chest.

Acting Sheriff Vance strode forward. Linda stood in stony silence while she was handcuffed and read her rights.

Chapter Fifteen

"You're a dangerous man, ranger," Tate said. "Guy with your powers of persuasion could rule the world." Chuckling, he set a bottle of very old, very expensive cognac on the table.

Ric and Elaine shared a table in the Track Shack. Tate had closed the place for this day of special celebration. She smoothed hair off her face, still not quite able to believe it was all over. She still couldn't believe what Ric had done.

He'd somehow convinced Axton not to press charges against King. Then, with Lillian and Gil Vance's help, he'd convinced the town that King and Axton had been part of a sting operation to get Linda Pallo to confess. King received credit for solving Bobby's murder. His suspension was made out to be part of the ruse. Now everyone believed King had been investigating the murder all along. In exchange, he retired from office, with honors; Lillian convinced him he needed twice weekly AA meetings instead of just going once a month. Business was returning to normal at the realty. Folks were treating Axton like a hero, applauding his courage.

When Elaine asked Ric why he was being so magnanimous toward her uncle, he'd said, "Our little town has been through enough. Time to get back to normal."

Our little town. She liked the sound of it.

Tate poured cognac into three delicate crystal snifters.

"Is it really over?" Elaine asked. "Is Linda really going to plead guilty? No trial?"

"Her prints were all over Axton's gun. We got a match on the threatening note and the typewriter from the realty. Auditors ferreted out her embezzlement. With that much evidence, she doesn't stand a chance at trial. The plea bargain should be signed and sealed by now." His broad shoulders rose and fell. "Depending on what Tom Greene wants to do, she still might have to stand trial for attempted murder. Meanwhile, she's going away for a long, long time." Tate raised his snifter. "To Bobby. A stand up guy. Rest in peace."

"To Bobby," Elaine said and clinked her glass against Tate's.

Ric echoed the toast, then added, "To Del. Unsung hero. A good old boy in spite of himself."

"To Daddy." She tossed back the cognac. It burned a smooth trail of fire down her throat. Tears filled her eyes. Let them think it was because of the liquor.

ELAINE DROVE Ric to Walt's house. "You're hardly limping today. Are you about ready to go home?"

Ric tapped his lower lip. He stared at the house where he'd grown up. "No place will feel like home without you in it, Laney." He touched a knuckle to her cheek. "I love you. Always did. Always will."

"Oh, Ric…"

"You're my soul mate. I want us to be together. Forever. I want to marry you."

She kept her eyes forward, showing him her profile. "What about Jodi?"

He considered the question. "Maybe I'm a symbol for everything that's wrong in her life. If I have to play the role of scapegoat for her, than that's what I have to do."

She looked at him then. "She needs you."

"She'll be eighteen in a few years. An adult."

"I'm supposed to wait patiently? Pretend you mean nothing to me? All because you're scared?"

"I'm not scared."

She cupped his face in her soft hands. He could smell her subtly vanilla scent and a hint of toothpaste, and grew dizzy on the sensations she roused. She whispered, "The thing about soul mates, Ric, lies are impossible between us. You have to be brave now and risk Jodi's rejection." She pressed her mouth to his in the sweetest of kisses.

He felt her love. He felt her determination, too. Until he faced his daughter, Elaine's love wasn't his to claim.

RIC DUCKED into the humid, earthy atmosphere of the main barn. He pulled off his hat and shook off rainwater. His back was aching from the weather, but it was nothing compared to the knots in his belly. Elaine was right. He was scared Jodi would prove as unforgiving as himself.

Lightbulbs beneath tin shades dispelled some of the gloom, and cast fantastic shadows inside the stalls and up in the hayloft. At the far end of the aisle, Jodi rubbed down Savvy. Ric could tell by her tense posture that she knew he was here. He listened for other people. Hearing nothing, he felt relieved. If he was about to be humiliated, he didn't want an audience.

"Hello," he called.

She dropped a brush in a bucket. It clanged. Then she picked up a steel comb and went to work on the Morgan's long, black tail. Ric walked down the aisle. Friendly horses stuck their heads over doors and snuffled at him.

The Morgan's red coat gleamed, stripped of coarse winter hair. He seemed to have lost some weight, too. "Savvy looks great. You're doing a good job with him."

Keeping her attention on her task, Jodi grunted.

"I brought you a birthday present." He fished a slim box from his jacket pocket and held it out to her. It was a gold necklace with a pendant engraved with her name and decorated with a tiny ruby. She glanced at the box but made no move to take it. He set it on a stool. "Sorry it's late, but I wanted to give it to you in person."

This was too hard. He raked a hand through his hair. "I loved your mother back then. I would have married her."

Jodi kept combing Savvy's tail.

"I know why you're mad at me."

She turned her head. Her expression was carved from ice.

"You have every right to be mad. I turned your whole life upside down. I deceived you." He loosed a long breath. He loved this girl, this child of his. Even if she did look at him as if he were a bug she debated whether or not to crush. "But here's the deal. I am *not* a sperm donor. No matter how you feel about me, I am your father."

"No you aren't."

"I haven't earned daddy status. Maybe I never will. That won't stop me from trying."

"Whatever," she said with snooty sarcasm that rasped his nerves like sandpaper.

Feeling put upon, he jammed his damp hat on his head. He wanted to leave, go somewhere private to lick his wounds. Even as his body started to turn away, his head and heart ordered him to stop. Maybe he hadn't been thinking about fatherhood and all it entailed when he cre-

ated this child, but here she was. There was no going back
to the way things were.

He thought of his uncle, who'd never complained about
having a nephew dumped in his lap. Walt had accepted
the responsibility because he was a real man. Ric thought
of his mother, who'd chosen booze over responsibility.
She'd been sick, but help had been available, and she
hadn't accepted it. Whatever Ric did right now would
prove if he were strong or weak.

"I'm going to learn how to be a father whether you like
it or not."

She peeked from the corner of her eye. Was that a hint
of a smile? "For starters, you're supposed to say, because
I'm the grown-up and I said so."

He arched his brows. "I thought kids hated hearing
that."

"We do." She shrugged to show it didn't matter. She
rested a skinny arm on Savvy's thick hindquarters. "Do
you know what they call me in school? Buke's Puke, the
bastard's bastard." Her glare held challenge, as if daring
him to comment on her coarse language.

Ancient hurts mingled with new ones. "Sorry about
that. I got the same crap when I was a kid."

"Did you get in fights?"

"Oh yeah."

"At least I'm finding out who my real friends are."

He considered the comment, and agreed.

"Are you going to marry my mom?"

Her question made him wary. He tried to guess what
answer she expected, then stopped himself. Jodi deserved
the truth, the whole truth and nothing but. "If she'll have
me, yes."

"And if she doesn't?"

"You're still stuck with me. Forever."

She dropped the comb in the bucket and picked up the gift-wrapped jewelry box. She stared at it as if it might bite her. "You grown-ups are so screwed up. You act like us kids are just toys. You should have told me. Everybody should have told me. I've got feelings, too, you know."

"You're right."

"Did Daddy even love me?"

He didn't know if his heart could take this. "You hung the moon and stars for him, kiddo. He wrote me a lot of letters. Mostly he talked about you. I kept them. Would you like to see them sometime?"

She tried to act nonchalant, but her eyes shone with hopefulness.

"I'll bring them over. You can decide if you want to read them or not." He loosed a heavy breath. "Your mom invited me to dinner. I accepted. Your uncle told me, if I can't be nice, at least be polite. Good advice. Can we be polite to each other?"

"Whatever."

"Good enough." Uncertain what he'd accomplished, he turned away. She called his name. "Yes?"

"I'm not going to call you Daddy."

"Ric will do fine."

"I'm not changing my name either. I'm Joanna Denise *Greene.*"

"It suits you."

Still uncertain, but feeling oddly lighter, he walked away. She called his name once more. He turned around. She jogged up the aisle. She skidded to a stop, sending up puffs of sawdust.

"When Linda had me, I was scared, but I didn't flip out. Not even a little bit. Know why?"

He shook his head.

"I knew you were coming. I knew you'd save me."

He touched her cheek. She didn't move. "Your dad used to say, once you figure out what you're willing to die for, you'll know what's worth living for." He chucked her chin. "You and your mom are it for me. See you at dinner, kiddo."

The rain had stopped. The clouds were thinning over the sun. He breathed deeply of the cool, wet mountain air. Scrub oaks and aspens were budding pale green against the darker pines. In the distance, mountain peaks still wore pale coats of snow. He'd run away from this valley once, but the pull of home had never left him.

Ah, Bobby, he thought. You stepped in for me, now I'll return the favor. With any luck, Jodi would survive despite them.

Elaine met him at the back door. He wiped mud off his boots. The savory aroma of roasting beef nearly bowled him over. She hung his hat and jacket on hooks in the laundry room.

"How did it go?" she asked.

"I think we established some ground rules." He followed her into the warm kitchen. Pots steamed on the stove. She'd set the table for three, with butter-yellow jonquils as the centerpiece. The optimism of the table setting touched him.

He gathered her into his arms. She had to tip her head back to see his face. Her smile entranced him.

"What number date is this, anyway?" he asked.

"I think it's proper for you to kiss me."

So he did. Deep and slow, tasting the full of her sweetness, feeling the depth of her love. Her hands worked through his hair. He imagined her heart beating as one with his.

When he came up for air, she whispered, "I love you, Ric."

"I love you." He smoothed soft hair off her forehead. "I have an idea for our next date. Let's go to Durango."

"Dinner and dancing?"

He grinned. "That, too, if you want. I'm thinking of a really nice jewelry store there. Custom pieces. Let's get you a ring made."

Her pretty mouth formed an *O*.

"We'll have one made for me, too."

"Are you asking me to marry you?"

"Your mom says I can't sleep with you unless we're married. And I really want to sleep with you." He kissed her again, reveling in the exquisite perfection of her lips. He trailed kisses over her cheek and ended by kissing her nose. "So what do you say?"

"As long you put it so romantically, how can I possibly say no?" She sealed her acceptance with a kiss.

* * * * *

Harlequin Intrigue delivers Sheryl Lynn's next McCLINTOCK COUNTRY *novel in April 2001—*

COLORADO'S FINEST.

HARLEQUIN®

INTRIGUE

opens the case files on:

TOP SECRET BABIES

Unwrap the mystery!

January 2001
#597 THE BODYGUARD'S BABY
Debra Webb

February 2001
#601 SAVING HIS SON
Rita Herron

March 2001
#605 THE HUNT FOR HAWKE'S DAUGHTER
Jean Barrett

April 2001
#609 UNDERCOVER BABY
Adrianne Lee

May 2001
#613 CONCEPTION COVER-UP
Karen Lawton Barrett

Follow the clues to your favorite retail outlet.

HARLEQUIN®

Makes any time special ™

HITSB

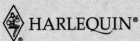

MAITLAND MATERNITY

Where the luckiest babies are born!

In April 2001, look for

HER BEST FRIEND'S BABY
by Vicki Lewis Thompson

A car accident leaves surrogate mother Mary-Jane Potter's baby-to-be without a mother—

and causes the father, Morgan Tate, to fuss over a very pregnant Mary-Jane like a mother hen. Suddenly, Mary-Jane is dreaming of keeping the baby…and the father!

Each book tells a different story about the world-renowned Maitland Maternity Clinic—where romances are born, secrets are revealed… and bundles of joy are delivered.

Silhouette®
Where love comes alive™

HARLEQUIN®
Makes any time special ™

Visit us at www.eHarlequin.com   MMCNM-8

Harlequin invites you to walk down the aisle...

To honor our year long celebration of weddings, we are offering an exciting opportunity for you to own the Harlequin Bride Doll. Handcrafted in fine bisque porcelain, the wedding doll is dressed for her wedding day in a cream satin gown accented by lace trim. She carries an exquisite traditional bridal bouquet and wears a cathedral-length dotted Swiss veil. Embroidered flowers cascade down her lace overskirt to the scalloped hemline; underneath all is a multi-layered crinoline.

Join us in our celebration of weddings by sending away for your own Harlequin Bride Doll. This doll regularly retails for $74.95 U.S./approx. $108.68 CDN. One doll per household. Requests must be received no later than June 30, 2001. Offer good while quantities of gifts last. Please allow 6-8 weeks for delivery. Offer good in the U.S. and Canada only. Become part of this exciting offer!

Simply complete the order form and mail to:
"A Walk Down the Aisle"

IN U.S.A	IN CANADA
P.O. Box 9057	P.O. Box 622
3010 Walden Ave.	Fort Erie, Ontario
Buffalo, NY 14240-9057	L2A 5X3

Enclosed are eight (8) proofs of purchase found on the last page of every specially marked Harlequin series book and $3.75 check or money order (for postage and handling). Please send my Harlequin Bride Doll to:

_____
Name (PLEASE PRINT)

_____
Address   Apt. #

_____
City   State/Prov.   Zip/Postal Code

_____
Account # (if applicable)   **098 KIK DAEW**

Visit us at www.eHarlequin.com

A Walk Down the Aisle
Free Bride Doll Offer
One Proof-of-Purchase

PHWDAPOP

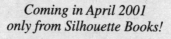

INDULGE IN A QUIET MOMENT
WITH HARLEQUIN

Get a FREE
Quiet Moments Bath Spa

with just two proofs of purchase from
any of our four special collector's editions in May.

Harlequin® is sure to make your time special this Mother's Day
with four special collector's editions featuring a short story
PLUS a complete novel packaged together in one volume!

Collection #1 Intrigue abounds in a collection featuring *New York Times*
bestselling author Barbara Delinsky and Kelsey Roberts.

Collection #2 Relationships? Weddings? Children? = *New York Times*
bestselling author Debbie Macomber and Tara Taylor Quinn
at their best!

Collection #3 Escape to the past with *New York Times* bestselling author
Heather Graham and Gayle Wilson.

Collection #4 Go West! With *New York Times* bestselling author
Joan Johnston and Vicki Lewis Thompson!

Plus Special Consumer Campaign!

Each of these four collector's editions will feature a
"FREE QUIET MOMENTS BATH SPA" offer.
See inside book in May for details.

Only from

HARLEQUIN®
Makes any time special ®

Don't miss out! Look for this exciting promotion on sale in May 2001,
at your favorite retail outlet.